"This Is a Night for Lovers, Season.

We shouldn't waste it."

He bent his head, his mustache tickling the side of her neck. She sighed as his mouth began to rob hers and he pulled her closer to him. She wound her arms around his neck and, remembering another time when he'd made the same offer, she smiled.

He lifted his head, his brows meeting when he saw her expression. "What are you smiling about at a time like this?"

"I was remembering the first time you asked me to share your bed. Your technique has improved."

"And you, Season? I hope your answer has changed. This time, please say yes."

ELAINE CAMP
dreamed of becoming a writer for many years. Once she tried it she quickly became successful, perhaps due to her reporter's eye, which gives her a special advantage in observing human relationships.

Dear Reader,

Silhouette Special Editions are an exciting new line of contemporary romances from Silhouette Books. Special Editions are written specifically for our readers who want a story with heightened romantic tension.

Special Editions have all the elements you've enjoyed in Silhouette Romances and *more*. These stories concentrate on romance in a longer, more realistic and sophisticated way, and they feature greater sensual detail.

I hope you enjoy this book and all the wonderful romances from Silhouette.

Karen Solem
Editor-in-Chief
Silhouette Books

ELAINE CAMP
In a Pirate's Arms

Silhouette Special Edition

Published by Silhouette Books·New York

America's Publisher of Contemporary Romance

Silhouette Books by Elaine Camp

To Have, To Hold (ROM #99)
Devil's Bargain (ROM #173)
For Love or Money (SE #113)
This Tender Truce (ROM #270)
In a Pirate's Arms (SE #159)

SILHOUETTE BOOKS, a Division of Simon & Schuster, Inc.
1230 Avenue of the Americas, New York, N.Y. 10020

ISBN: 0-671-53659-1

First Silhouette Books printing April, 1984

10 9 8 7 6 5 4 3 2 1

Map by Ray Lundgren

SILHOUETTE, SILHOUETTE SPECIAL EDITION and
colophon are registered trademarks of Simon & Schuster, Inc.

America's Publisher of Contemporary Romance

Printed in the U.S.A.

To Judy Eibeck, my treasured friend
Who, like all precious things, increases in her value.

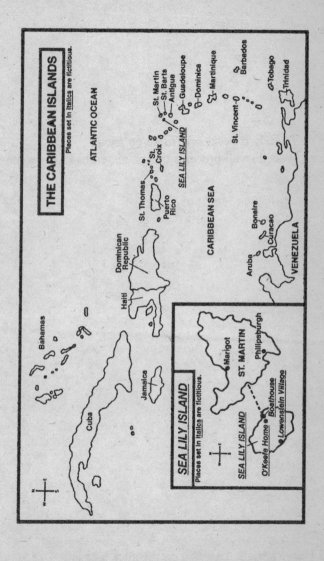

Chapter One

*T*he name intrigued her.

Season Templar stared at the crudely lettered sign swinging on rusty hinges above the tavern's entrance. Pirate's Arms. She smiled and glanced over her shoulder at the bustling dock. The Caribbean had seen its share of pirates, she thought. It was more civilized now, but signposts remained of those days when renegades anchored there. There was still an untamed streak that set the heart to pounding.

She looked at the tavern again, wondering how long it had stood near that dock on St. Martin island. It looked very old. Her green eyes took in the peeling white paint and the splintered wooden steps.

Drawing a deep breath, Season collected her nerve while chiding herself for feeling reluctant and . . . yes, a bit scared. She'd never been in a bar alone before, but there was always a first time, she told herself. The men on the dock had said that her escort to the island was inside this rustic tavern. So inside I must go, she thought. The sun at her back added a heated push, and she climbed the steps and entered the dark, gaping mouth of the tavern.

Blinking rapidly to adjust her eyes to the changing light, Season heard the deep rumble of masculine voices before a hush blanketed the room. The stench of tobacco, whiskey and sweat assaulted her, making her cough, and she longed for the crisp salty air outside. Her attention was drawn to the man behind the bar, and she caught sight of glinting gold teeth when he smiled. She moved toward the bar, agonizingly aware of the leering grins directed at her.

"Excuse me, but I was told I could find the owner of *The Touchstone* in here," she said, addressing the barkeep.

The man's eyes shifted sideways, and he nodded toward a cluster of men who were engaged in a game of darts. "Thar's the owner of *The Touchstone,* missy. Want a drink?"

"No, thank you." Season left the bar, taking a few hesitant steps toward the men at the dart board. For some reason that she couldn't fathom, her eyes were immediately drawn to the tallest of the men. His back was to her and he was aiming a dart at a much-pocked bull's-eye. She could see the flex of muscles along his shoulders, pulling against the white cotton of his T-shirt as he pitched the needle-sharp missile for a perfect bull's-eye. A grizzled old man let out a whoop and slapped the player on the back.

"Looks like your lucky day, Champion," the old sailor said with a chuckle as he plucked the dart from the board. He glanced at Season with faded blue eyes. "You've won another game and you get to take this pretty little thing back to the island with you. Old Morley knows how to pick 'em, eh?''

Her discomfort momentarily forgotten, Season held her breath, waiting for her escort to turn and face her. He made a slow pivot, and Season felt a current of excitement sizzle through her.

"Mr. O'Keefe," she said, extending her hand. "It's a pleasure to meet you. I'm Season Templar from *Treasure Trove* magazine. I had no idea that you'd be the one to . . ." Her voice drifted away when she realized he was looking at her proffered hand, making no attempt to shake it. His rebuff rattled her, and she let her arm drop to her side. "As I was saying—"

"Where's your luggage?"

Season counted to ten and forced a smile to her lips. She'd been told he was impossible, but she hadn't expected downright rudeness! "I left it on the dock near your yacht."

"That was stupid. It's probably been stolen by now." He held out his hand to the old man. "Pay the piper, Corky."

The old seafarer chuckled and reached into his pocket, withdrawing a ten-dollar bill which he gave to Champion O'Keefe. "Thar you go, you rascal. You ought to be ashamed . . . taking advantage of an old man."

"You're the one who insisted on another game, Corky." Champion glanced at Season before shouldering past her. "Come on, let's get going." He lifted a hand in farewell when some of the customers called to him. "See you soon, guys."

With as much grace as possible, Season followed him from the tavern and toward *The Touchstone*. In the sunlight, she noticed that his hair was a rich chestnut with a tendency to wave. Windswept, it defied conventional styling, and the tips were a lighter shade of brown. He was dark-skinned, and she knew that the sun wasn't the sole reason for that. In the tavern, she'd noticed that his eyes were hazel and deep-set. When he'd smiled at Corky, half-moon laugh lines had creased under his eyes, and dimples had appeared in his lean cheeks.

The pictures she'd seen of him didn't do justice to his physique. Faded jeans hugged muscular thighs and narrow hips. His shoulders were wide, swaying with his supple stride. He had the look of a man who worked outdoors; a man accustomed to nature and the elements. As they neared the moored yacht with Season a good ten paces behind him, he shouted at someone. Season leaned sideways to look past his imposing form. Two native boys hovered around her luggage.

"That's got nothing to do with you. Get away from there! Go on!" His tone was no-nonsense, and the boys raced along the wooden dock, disappearing behind a mountain of cargo. He stood near her luggage with an I-told-you-so expression.

"I asked some men on that ship to keep an eye on my things," Season told him, answering his unspoken taunt. She pointed toward a small cargo ship moored beside *The Touchstone*.

"Around here people are expected to be responsible for themselves and their belongings," he drawled as he hoisted her luggage aboard the yacht.

"Please be careful with that one," Season cautioned, reaching for the case he held. "That's my typewriter."

He looked at the case, contempt lining his face for a moment before he placed it on board. He vaulted aboard effortlessly and began stowing her luggage.

Her apprehension mounted as Season eyed the vessel. No ladder or steps were in sight. While the yacht didn't sit too high in the water, it was high enough to pose problems for someone in a dress and high-heeled sandals.

"Climb aboard."

She looked up at him, shielding her eyes from the sun with one slim hand, and saw his full mustache twitch. Just as she'd expected. He was finding this very amusing.

"Mr. O'Keefe," she said in a voice that was rock steady. "One doesn't just climb aboard in a dress." She glanced down at her teal-blue sundress. "Don't you have a ladder or a . . . a . . . plank? I mean, a—"

"It's called a gangway," he said, pouncing on her misuse. "Planks are what mutineers walk."

"Yes, I know!" She tried to contain her anger. "Well, do you have one?"

"No." He held out one large hand to her.

Season glared at him for a few moments before slipping her hand into his strong grip. As his fingers wrapped around her wrist, she placed her foot against the side of the yacht and he pulled her up, steadying her as she stepped over the railing.

"I would think that a yacht this size would have a rope ladder or something like that," she said, smoothing her skirt when he had released her.

"It does, but I forgot to bring it along. I never use it." He spoke as he walked to the wheel, positioned behind the cabin. Having already released the mooring lines, he started the engine. "Take a seat." He motioned toward the padded benches along the sides of the cockpit.

Season settled on one of them, taking time to examine the yacht. Although she worked for a magazine that published articles about sailing crafts, her own knowledge was limited. Her department at the magazine dealt with people and places. Still, she could appreciate the elegant lines of *The Touchstone*. It was unlike other yachts she'd seen, and she wondered if it might be custom-made. She started to ask, but decided against small talk since Champion O'Keefe was absorbed in maneuvering them from the slip.

The Touchstone was a forty-three-footer of gleaming brass fittings that contrasted with the mossy-green outer shell. Her underbelly glinted gold beneath the waterline, and her name was scrawled in the same gold paint.

The sails lay packed, not to be used this trip. Season shaded her eyes and tried to see the color of them, but they were covered by a tarpaulin.

Rummaging through her purse, Season found her sunglasses and slipped them on. With her eyes disguised by the dark lenses, she managed surreptitiously to examine Champion O'Keefe. He was steering the yacht toward open sea, and his hazel gaze flitted over the vista as he checked their progress. A breeze combed through his chestnut hair, the sun catching in the lighter tips. His lower lip was full under a trimmed mustache that covered the top portion of his upper lip. Season remembered the flash of even white teeth when he'd smiled at Corky. He was scowling now, but the dimples still showed in his cheeks.

His sleeveless T-shirt exposed tanned, muscled arms. It stretched across his broad chest, and a curling mass of dark hair visible over the top added a stamp of masculinity. He stood over six feet, even in flat deck shoes.

Champion shifted his feet, and Season knew that

he was looking at her. She could feel his heavy-lidded gaze, and for a moment she wished she knew what he was thinking. She cleared her throat, forcing her gaze to his. His expression gave her no hint as to what was going on behind those green-gold eyes.

"As I was *trying* to say back at the tavern, I had no idea you were going to meet me, Mr. O'Keefe. May I call you Champion?"

He shrugged, folding his arms across his chest. "Ben Sweetsip was supposed to pick you up, but he's having a spot of trouble with his ketch, so I filled in."

"I see." She looked past him at the yacht's foaming wake. "How far is it to Sea Lily island?"

"Not far. We'll be there within half an hour."

"I'm looking forward to meeting your father and seeing your home. Alex Ketchum, my editor, was delighted when your father agreed to an interview. I'm sure our readers will be excited to—"

"I suppose you already know that I oppose this story you're going to do." He lifted one peaked brow.

She sighed, abandoning diplomacy. "Mr. Ketchum mentioned that you have issued strict orders that my articles must deal only with your father and not with you."

"That's right. I like my privacy. The last article that was done about me made my life a living hell from which I've only recently recovered."

"Yes, I read it." Season pushed her short dark hair from her forehead. "I think the problem with that article was the approach. Making you out to be the last of the modern-day pirates created a fantasy figure. Naturally, you appeal to the world's dreamers who long to meet a *real* pirate and join him in his adventures."

"The problem with that article, Miss Templar, was

that it was printed." His eyes challenged her to respond.

Season chose to sidestep any possible arguments. It was important that she maintain her professionalism. If she allowed him to draw her into an emotion-charged discussion, she'd lose her credibility.

"Perhaps you're right," she said, a smile accompanying her soothing words.

"I know I'm right," he snapped.

Season tried to appreciate the aqua waves of the Caribbean and the graceful swooping of gull and heron, but her thoughts kept wandering back to the captain of *The Touchstone*. She recalled the magazine article he'd referred to. It had been published in a national magazine that catered to would-be explorers and armchair sailors. Similar to the magazine she worked for, she admitted, except that *Treasure Trove* had a smaller circulation. The article had mentioned that Champion's wife had recently divorced him, prompting hundreds of women to write and offer themselves as replacements. Alex had said that Champion had been forced into the limelight, and as a result he'd become more reclusive.

The article had painted a romantic picture of Champion. It had described him as a throwback from pirating days—handsome, strong, arrogant, possessing a bawdy sense of humor. Champion scoured the seven seas in search of treasure and high adventure, according to the article. He was responsible for prestigious recoverings of shipwrecks, and for the discovery of treasure on islands in the South Pacific, the Seychelles and the Caribbean. Although the article had been published five years ago, repercussions were still being felt. When Champion was spotted on an island or at sea, people talked and government officials investigated, making sure that any uncovered treasures would be shared by ruling countries.

Season guessed that government intervention was the main reason Champion resented publicity. The letters and surprise visits from willing women might be irritating, but snooping government officials had to be deplorable to a man who valued his privacy and freedom.

Even though she'd been sent here to interview Morley O'Keefe, Champion's father, Season had been instructed to gain Champion's trust, in the hope that he'd consent to an interview. Glancing at his forbidding expression, Season decided her chances at such a journalistic coup were slim.

Fatigue inched into her muscles, and Season rolled her shoulders wearily. It had been a long trip from Baltimore, made even more trying by the weight of her assignment. She was still baffled by Alex's sudden decision to send her instead of a more experienced staffer. He'd assured her it wasn't nepotism, but Season had had her misgivings. Although she'd retained her maiden name at the magazine, she had never dreamt that she could conceal her identify from the magazine staffers; they had always known that she was the wife, then the widow, of Alex's son, Darren. She had worked her way up through the ranks at *Treasure Trove,* having started there as a circulation typist when she was nineteen years old. Six years ago she had been promoted to a copy reader. Alex had encouraged her to take a few college courses in creative writing and try her hand at some human interest articles.

A tender smile curved her mouth as she recalled Alex's subtle proddings. Knowing that she was the breadwinner for herself and Darren, Alex had encouraged her to improve her skills and her salary.

He'd called her "stubborn and prideful" when she had declined a raise while she was still just a typist. It had been a handout, not a merit raise. She had already allowed Alex and Marilyn to pay for their son's therapy, and Season had felt that was enough sympathy money. Darren had been receiving every month from the government a disability check that he would squander on liquor, fast cars and selfish whims. He could have paid for his own psychiatric therapy, if it had meant anything to him. He'd gone to the psychiatrist only to appease his parents and Season, not because he wanted help.

Guilt welled within her, and Season shoved aside the painful memories. When she dwelled on her life with Darren, she always felt guilty. Thoughts of Darren bred hundreds of "what if" scenes. What if she'd been more understanding? What if she'd been more patient? What if she hadn't fought with him that night? Would he be alive now, and perhaps recovering from the mental anguish he'd suffered because of his tour in Vietnam?

"That's Sea Lily island on the horizon," Champion announced, halting her mental merry-go-round.

Season scanned the waters, her gaze following the flight of pelicans as they stretched their wings above the Caribbean. Their long necks were bundled against their chests, giving their bodies a streamlined grace. Her heart bumped against her rib cage when her gaze collided with the outline of an island. Sea Lily! One of the loveliest privately owned islands in the world, and one few people had been allowed to explore.

Unlike the other Caribbean islands, Sea Lily was relatively flat except at the northern end where a series of low hills broke toward the sky. They were approaching from the northeast, and Season couldn't see any beaches. Moss-backed rock and rough limestone rimmed this side, and Season tensed as *The Touchstone* sped closer, showing no reduction in speed.

When they were close enough for Season to see several rusty cannons pointing menacingly toward open sea, the sound of the engine lessened, and the yacht slowed. Season stood up, searching for someplace where the vessel could be docked or moored, but she couldn't find a likely spot. Then she saw the slit.

A few feet wider than the yacht, the canal cut through the limestone, giving entrance to . . . what? A lagoon? Suddenly, the engine revved, and *The Touchstone* lurched forward. Season gasped, sinking onto the bench again as the yacht raced toward the narrow slit.

She expected to be crushed against the limestone walls, but the yacht zipped through the opening. Silence wrapped around them as the engine died abruptly and the vessel glided atop calm waters.

Feeling as if she'd entered never-never land, Season held her breath, her surroundings thrilling her senses. They were floating toward a red-tiled boat house, and the sound of rustling palm fronds and lapping surf greeted her. Exotic birds called a welcome as *The Touchstone* neared the pier where the forty-seven-foot, famed *Pirate's Pleasure* was moored.

She'd heard about this ship since joining the magazine. It was as famous as Cousteau's *Calypso*, but for different reasons. While oceanographers begged to be part of the *Calypso* crew, adventurers with a lust for buried treasure pleaded for passage on *Pirate's Pleasure*. This vessel didn't have the sleek sophistication of *The Touchstone*. *Pirate's Pleasure* was strictly business. Ropes and pulleys hung from her, and her white, patched sails were serviceable, but not the least bit pretty. She was painted white with black trim, and her name was written in small letters at her bow and stern.

This lady wasn't meant to take your breath away, Season thought with a smile, but the legends surrounding her did just that.

A small cabin cruiser was anchored near the boat house, and as *The Touchstone* edged toward the pier, a dark-skinned man appeared on her deck and waved.

"Did you get her running, Sweetsip?" Champion called to the man.

"No, but I've located the trouble."

"I'll deliver our guest and come back to give you a hand. Catch these, will you?" Champion moved with liquid grace to the coiled mooring lines.

Season looked down into the crystalline water. She could see the sandy bottom, strewn with coral and shells. *The Touchstone* pitched forward slightly, then settled to a bobbing halt like some great, expensive cork. At the squeak of rubber-soled shoes, Season turned to watch Champion pitch the ropes with practiced ease toward the steel cleats on the pier.

"How do, ma'am." The dark-skinned native tipped his cloth hat. "The name is Ben Sweetsip, jack-of-all-trades and master of none."

Season smiled at him. "I'm Season Templar from *Treasure Trove* magazine."

"Yes, I know." He bent to tighten the lines around the cleats.

"Sweetsip, can you find that stepladder for the lady? I think it might be in the boat house." Champion leaned against the railing, an impatient scowl on his face. "I'll see to your luggage while he looks for the ladder."

"Thank you," Season said, trying to sound pleasant, but feeling something akin to hatred. She despised the way Champion O'Keefe made her feel inadequate. Instead of being a gentleman and making her feel welcome, he was doing his utmost to make her feel like an imposition.

He removed her luggage from the yacht, placing it on the pier. As Season watched him leap to the pier with impeccable athletic poise, she acknowledged a grudging envy.

"I found it!" Ben Sweetsip leaned one end of the ladder against the yacht and held up a hand to assist her. "Be careful, ma'am."

With as much grace as possible, Season lifted her skirt an inch or two and stepped over the railing. She took her time, making sure her feet were firmly planted on the top rung, before descending with Sweetsip's help. She breathed a sigh of relief when she was finally standing on the pier.

"Thank you, Mr. Sweetsip," she said with a smile.

"You're welcome, and the name's Ben." He glanced at her luggage. "Need help with those, Champion?"

"No, I can get them." Champion shouldered her luggage and nodded in the direction of a path. "It's this way. Just follow me. I'll be back in a few minutes, Sweetsip."

"Aye, aye, sir." Ben doffed his hat again before walking back to the cruiser.

Season followed Champion along the beaten path. Palms created a cathedral-ceiling effect, allowing spears of sunlight to lance through to give dancing illumination. Wild flowers grew along the path, adding splotches of carefully cultivated color.

The incline leveled off, and Season craned her neck to look past Champion's broad shoulders.

An arbor covered with bougainvillea marked the entrance to the house. Bordered by spider lilies and hibiscus, the path gave way to stone steps and an airy porch where bamboo furniture invited scenes of sunsets and tall glasses of lemonade. An archway, scrolled and decorative, shadowed a massive door of polished oak with iron fittings and a huge ring pull. Above the door, etched in a block of limestone, was a snatch of verse: *We are islands connected by a sea of love that binds, but does not imprison us.*

The words wove a spell around her, and she stood in the shadows as sentimental tears pricked her eyes.

"Are you coming? I'm not going to hold this door open for you all day."

Champion's gruff voice broke the spell, and Season threw him a killing glare before she marched past him into the cool interior of the house. The large room had whitewashed walls of stone and a gleaming hardwood floor. The furniture was oversized, carved from glistening teak and mahogany. Windows, shaped like portholes, lined one wall, and a sunroof spilled light into the room. Signs of a nautical life—seashells, starfish, ship models and driftwood—were displayed in cabinets and on tables, but it was the portrait above the fireplace that drew the eye.

Season stepped closer to read the inscription on the brass plate, but she didn't need the identification. This, undoubtably, was Lily O'Keefe. Olive-skinned, her complexion was flawless. Her eyes were dark brown, and her long dark hair was gathered in a sleek chignon. She wore a white lacy gown, and a milky pearl was suspended by a thin gold chain around her swanlike neck. The pearl rested in the hollow at the base of her throat, translucent and creamy.

"This is your mother?" Season asked, sensing Champion's nearness.

"Yes, and my father is waiting for you on the back terrace."

His voice was close to her, making her jump slightly. When she turned, he stepped back and looked pointedly at the doorway to his left. "Through there."

She glanced at the striking portrait again, intrigued by the full pouting lips and the dimples Lily had passed on to her only child. Season moved toward the indicated door, passing through a dining room that was dominated by a table large enough to seat twelve, and a kitchen gleaming with chrome. A dutch door opened to a terrace where grass grew with stubborn persistence amid the cracks in the cobblestones. Palm trees added a sun-screening border, and a flower garden stretched beyond, each plot carefully landscaped according to color and size of bloom.

Morley O'Keefe sat at a white wrought-iron table, his gnarled hands resting on its top where sheets of paper were scattered. Nut-brown eyes peered at her with keen interest, and a charming smile bathed his face. He stood up, stretching his wiry body to its fullest height and puffing out his barreled chest. He doffed his Greek fisherman's hat, revealing white hair that grew full and thick. Matching brows wiggled as his lined face emanated good will and a dash of mischief.

"Welcome to Sea Lily island, Miss Templar. I'm Morley O'Keefe."

He had an Irish brogue and his voice was deep, not unlike his son's. As Season shook his hand and murmured a response to his welcome, she could see more family resemblance in the stubborn set of jaw, the pugnacious nose, the proud carriage and the blatant virility in his firm handshake and appraising eyes.

"I guess you've locked horns with my acid-tongued son, eh?" He pretended chagrin; then amusement sparkled in his eyes. "He doesn't cotton to a reporter being on the island."

"Yes, he made that perfectly clear." She tilted her chin at a challenging angle, sensing immediately that Morley was on her side.

"Sit down, girl." He held out one of the chairs for her, then reseated himself when she was settled. "Champion, why don't you take her luggage to Lily's room?"

"*Lily's* room?" Champion didn't try to hide his surprise. "Why Lily's room?"

"Why not?" Morley squinted one eye. "Go on with you."

Champion frowned but left to do his father's bidding. Season faced Morley with an apologetic smile.

"He doesn't seem too pleased with your choice of rooms," she said. A bird shrieked, and Season glanced around again. "This is a beautiful place, Mr. O'Keefe. There aren't many places like this left in the world."

"Aye, that's so. Why don't you call me Morley and I'll call you Season." He winked at her. "Don't let Champion worry you, girl. He's put out with me for letting a reporter set foot on this island."

"I can understand his distrust of journalists. I read the last article that was done on him. It made him seem bigger than life."

Morley nodded as he lit his pipe. "At times he is.

He values his privacy, but I'm starved for attention!"

Season joined in his laughter, feeling more at ease now that she'd met Morley and been accorded his welcome. "Do you and your son live alone here?"

"No, Ben Sweetsip and his family live here, and then there's Mrs. Lowenstein."

"Mrs. Lowenstein?" Season asked, her mind sharpening as she lapsed into a question/answer routine.

"Aye, she's our chief cook and bottle washer. A dear widow who fusses over Champion and me as if we were helpless. You'll meet her later." His brown eyes flickered over her. "So, you're Alex's daughter-in-law?"

"I . . . yes, but I'm a widow." Season hurried to bypass any discussion of her marriage. "Alex sends his regards. I think he hero-worships you."

Morley chuckled. "Poor fella's chained to a desk, so he envies anyone who's led a free life. He's a good man. I never had the pleasure of meeting his son . . . Darren?"

"Yes, Darren." Season swung her purse into her lap, needing something to occupy her hands. "What will our schedule be, Morley?"

He gave her a speculative look, then shrugged. "I ring the bell every morning at seven, and Mrs. Lowenstein serves breakfast at eight."

"The bell?" Season asked.

"A ship's bell in front of the house. You entered through the back. The front of this house faces the ocean. Anyway, I ring that bell to get everybody up and moving."

"Oh, that's fine with me. After breakfast . . . is that when you'll be free to—"

"I'm always free to do anything I have a mind to,"

Morley interrupted with a wicked grin. "But I think it will work out fine if we talk after breakfast. That will leave our afternoons open and I usually nose around then." He wiggled his white brows. "I like to keep on top of things, even though I'm sort of retired."

Season nodded as she estimated the time she'd need to complete her interviews. Two weeks? A month? Surely, no more than a month. . . .

"You can spend your afternoons exploring Sea Lily island and getting some color on you. By the time you leave here you'll be as brown as a gingerbread man."

"I don't know about that," Season murmured. "I have a lot of work to do. I'll probably spend my afternoons compiling my notes and writing."

"What?" Morley asked in surprise. "I thought you liked the island."

"I do!" Season leaned forward, her eyes mirroring her sincerity. "It's lovely, but—"

"You'll need to know this island, girl. Sea Lily is as much a part of me as . . . as my right arm." He looked past her, his gaze lifting. "Ah, Champion. Get everything squared away, did you?"

Season turned in her chair, tipping back her head to look into Champion's green-gold eyes. His expression was guarded, and Season sensed that he had posted a "No Trespassing" sign on himself years ago. If only she could convince him to stow away that sign and consent to an interview, it would add so much to the series of articles.

"Thank you for taking my luggage to my room, Champion." She noticed the lift of his brows when she used his first name.

"You're welcome." He flicked his hand in a choppy wave, and went back into the house.

"I've got a good-looking son, don't I, Season?"

Season whirled to face Morley, and the twinkle in his eyes made her blush. "Yes," she whispered, clutching the chair arms as if for dear life. "Could you tell me how to get to my room? I'd like to freshen up before dinner."

"Sure." He rose from his chair. "I'll do better than that, I'll give you a tour of the house. Don't worry. You've got plenty of time. Dinner isn't served until nine." He smiled at her gasp of surprise. "We partake of a big lunch and a light dinner here on Sea Lily island. It's better for the digestive system."

She nodded, feeling pangs of hunger in response to his announcement. With an inner grimace, she fell into step with Morley.

The house was a one-story bungalow with large rooms and French doors that opened to wide, airy porches. Ceiling fans stirred the tropical air. Bamboo mats were strewn across the parquet floors. The entire house smelled of lemons, hibiscus and Morley's aromatic pipe tobacco.

During the tour, Morley told Season that he had built the house with the aid of twenty St. Martin natives in 1945. Paths had been cut through the dense jungle, and flower beds had been planted to add patches of red, yellow, blue and lavender to the overall green landscape. A guest cottage had been built, along with the boat house, pier, bathing pavilion, servants' quarters, tennis court and a house for Mrs. Lowenstein on the other end of the island. Season was relieved to hear that eight cisterns had been dug underground, connected to gutters on the roofs to catch rainwater. The cisterns held at least 25,000 gallons of fresh water for bathing and cooking.

"So you can use that shower and tub in your room, girl," Morley said as he escorted her along the corridor leading to the bedrooms. "Mrs. Lowenstein brings around basins of water every morning for each of us—mainly for shaving purposes." He chuckled and shook his head. "She's used to catering to bachelors, you see."

Season laughed. "I hope she doesn't mind my trespassing in this male society."

"Oh, she's all excited about your visit, girl." Morley opened a door. "Here's your room. I hope you like it."

Oyster-colored walls and white wicker furniture lent the room a spaciousness. Season entered, feeling right at home. The ceiling-fan blades were rococo-carved, and the draperies and throw rugs were shell-pink, matching the satin spread on the double bed. A lacy mosquito net provided a dreamy canopy, and a hammock was suspended in one corner of the room.

"This was your wife's bedroom?" Season asked as she sat on the bed, testing the firm mattress.

"Aye, and my daughter-in-law's. Champion's divorced, you know."

"Yes, I read about that." She chided herself for feeling as if she were invading sacred grounds. "It's lovely, Morley. It's the most beautiful room I've ever stayed in."

"I'm glad you like it. You get settled in and I'll see you around dinnertime, okay?" He winked, then backed from the room. The door closed softly behind him.

"I'm here!" The whispered words escaped, followed by a delighted giggle as Season clasped her hands and tucked them under her chin. How her co-workers would envy her if they could see her now! Humming an appropriate Broadway song, Season went to the French doors and pushed them open.

Through a grove of palms, she could see the ocean in all its vast glory. The ship's bell Morley had spoken of stood a few yards from her window, suspended between two thick poles. It was a greenish copper with a rope pull. Red spider lilies grew around each pole, and redwood benches were set in front of the bell's frame.

She spotted triangles of white and a cargo ship out in the ocean. A thrill raced through her when she thought of the privacy she had entered. She recalled the signs on either side of the narrow slit that gave access to the lagoon. "Private: Not Public" they warned in large black letters. Similar signs, no doubt, were posted along the island's coast. But she was one of the privileged few! How many adventurers and romantics would give their souls for a chance to explore this island and meet her owners? And to think she was a guest on Sea Lily with ready access to Champion and Morley O'Keefe.

A frown raced across her face. Well, she had access to Morley, at least. Champion was a different story.

She tipped her head to one side, wondering if Champion had any idea how much she wanted to gain his trust and cooperation. He wasn't a fool. He knew *exactly* how much she wanted those things. And Morley O'Keefe knew that Champion's participation was something she needed, too. She'd seen that twinkle in the old man's eyes when he'd asked her what she thought of his son.

Those hadn't been his exact words, she corrected

herself. Actually, Morley had asked her to confirm that he had a good-looking son. Could Morley O'Keefe be plotting a little matchmaking?

"Oh, no!" Season stepped back into the bedroom, her dark curls bobbing as she shook her head with conviction. There would be none of that! She'd just barely recovered from a marriage that had begun like a dream and ended like a nightmare. It would be a long, long time before she'd be willing to join her life with another's.

No matter how appealing Champion O'Keefe's hazel eyes might be or how attractive his muscled body might appear or how much promise his touch might bring, she wasn't in the mood for a dalliance with a man who oozed self-assurance and dominance! No way!

With brisk steps, Season went into the bathroom and began undressing. Her skin tingled appreciatively as she shed her clothes. Curling her toes against the cool tiles, she wrapped a thick towel about her head then turned on the shower. The spray washed away the last of Baltimore, leaving her open for the treasures of Sea Lily. The first thing she wanted to ask Morley was how he had happened on that name for his private paradise. She had heard it had something to do with another island in the Indian Ocean, but that was all hearsay. Morley, like his son, had been notoriously evasive when it came to interviews. His early days of exploring had been written up in various journals, but any private thoughts or adventures had been omitted. Alex had said that the past ten years had been idle ones for Morley, who had changed his mind about having his exploits written up for public consumption.

Yes, Morley's memories would make good copy, but it was Champion who possessed the stuff good readership was made of. Morley was history. Champion was contemporary. Champion's elusiveness had spawned a public curiosity that was raging. If only she could . . .

Season sighed, turning off the shower spray. There would be time to cajole Champion, she assured herself. First she had to crack that icy exterior, and *that* would take some doing.

"What I need is a blowtorch," she murmured with a smile. She toweled herself and wondered what sort of dress would be appropriate for dinner with two bachelors.

Chapter Two

The white silk gown felt like heaven against her skin. Season turned this way and that before the full-length mirror in her bedroom, a faint smile curving her lips. The gown was sleeveless, wrapping under her arms to fit tightly across her breasts. She'd almost decided not to wear it when she'd discovered that she'd failed to pack her strapless bra. Daring herself to wear it without a bra, she'd slipped into the raw silk and discovered that she liked the feel of it against her skin.

The hem whispered along the floor, and a slit on one side exposed her slender calf. Silver-strapped sandals with modest heels added an extra inch to her five-feet-six-inch frame. She fitted pearl studs in her earlobes, and wore a matching pearl ring on the third finger of her left hand. The gold band she'd worn up until a year ago was in a safe-deposit box in

Baltimore, and she still felt undressed without it. After all, she'd worn that band for nine years and she'd gotten used to it.

Idly, she adjusted the ebony curls at the nape of her neck, then fluffed the curling strands at her forehead. She pulled back the hair at her left temple, securing it with an ivory comb she'd purchased at an estate sale in Baltimore. Season traced the scrolled etchings with her fingertip and wondered how old it was. The comb had turned that warm, yellow color that comes with age and handling; Season had thought about having it appraised, but had decided against it. If it was antique and worth a fetching sum, she'd be reluctant to wear it, afraid it might get lost or stolen. It was better that she appreciate its beauty without knowing its worth.

Her gaze traveled from the comb to confront clear, emerald eyes with dark, spiky lashes. Her eyes were oblong-shaped, tilting up at the corners to emphasize her high cheekbones. For a few moments she was eighteen again and dancing with Darren Ketchum at a party given by mutual friends. He'd been a stranger then, but she'd enjoyed her evening in his company. When the last dance had ended, Darren had told her that she had the most beautiful eyes he'd ever seen, and that he expected to see them the rest of his life. His announcement had left her stunned, but captured. She had begun dating him, exclusively. They had dated for several months. Then, because Darren was going to be leaving for a year's duty in Viet Nam, they had decided to marry. A month after their marriage, following a carefree honeymoon in France, Season had stood sobbing at the airport in Baltimore as Darren had boarded a plane on the first leg of a journey to Indochina.

The year that followed had been one of wrenching loneliness for Season. She'd celebrated her nineteenth birthday without Darren, working at *Treasure Trove* and counting the days that seemed endless. Then, just two weeks before Darren had been scheduled to come home, a mortar blast had crippled him. He had been one of the last men wounded, coming home a broken man. His loss could have been much greater; he had not lost his entire leg— the prosthesis attached at his knee. He could walk well with it and even ride his motorcycle. But he had been unable to live with himself with his artificial leg, and he had been unable to live with anyone else, either, including his wife.

Season closed her eyes to the past, opening them again to face the present. She glanced at her watch, then went to the dining room.

Morley and Champion rose at her entrance, and she blushed when Morley held out a chair for her. When she was seated, Champion took his seat across the table from her, and Morley took his chair at the head of it.

"You add something very special to our meal, Season," Morley said, his brown eyes glinting as they took in her dark hair and smooth shoulders. "I feel as if I ought to be in one of those tuxedoes tonight."

"I think you look very handsome, Morley," Season said, running her gaze over his black trousers and white shirt.

Feeling as if she had no power to stop herself, Season looked at Champion and her breathing became strangely irregular. When he'd stood a moment before, she had noticed, in spite of herself, how the cream-colored trousers had emphasized the length of his legs. They were pleated in the front, and a thin, lizard-skin belt was buckled against his flat stomach. Now her eyes appreciated the pale green knit shirt. Four buttons had been left open to reveal a brown throat and an enticing vee of crisp chestnut hair. Something primordial surfaced when she looked at his tanned arms with their furring of dark brown.

She couldn't remember ever being so acutely aware of a man before, and she chalked it up to the fanciful article she'd read about him. Champion O'Keefe is just a man, she chanted to herself, dragging her gaze from him and focusing unseeing eyes on her plate. Just a man . . . just a man . . . a man who made her feverishly aware that she was a woman.

Silence jarred her from her revelation, and she hurried to fill it. "I think I'm overdressed. I didn't really know what to wear."

"Overdressed?" Champion's deep baritone wrapped around her, drawing her gaze to his again. "How can that be? There's very little to that dress, as far as I can see." He looked from her flushed face to where the white silk fluttered with the beating of her overtaxed heart.

Season was saved from a reply by a woman who could only have been Mrs. Lowenstein. She burst into the room, sending the swinging door flapping on its hinges. Her dark blond hair was pulled back severely into a bun, and her blue eyes darted from face to face as she placed a tureen before Morley.

"Hello, love," she said, her voice a deep alto. "I'm Belle Lowenstein. You're Miss Templar?"

"Yes, it's nice to meet you." Season smiled, grateful for the woman's timely entrance.

"My, my! You're younger than I expected. I

thought you'd be in your middle or late twenties!"
She uncovered the tureen, allowing curling steam to
spiral.

"Actually, I'm twenty-eight." Season's smile grew
when Belle Lowenstein's eyes widened.

"You're kidding me! No?" Belle placed her large
hands on her hips. "What's your secret, dearie?
Land sakes! You look like a teenager. Doesn't she,
Morley?"

Morley chuckled, sniffing the soup Belle ladled
into Season's bowl. She served Morley next, then
Champion.

"I hope you like clam chowder, dearie," Belle
said. She frowned at Champion. "What's wrong with
you? Why are you scowling? You like my chowder."

Champion looked up, his brows lifting when he
realized Belle was addressing him. "Yes, I do."

"Well, then, eat!" Belle shook a finger at him.
"I've got fresh bread to go with it and peach ice
cream, but you'll not be getting the cream unless you
eat that soup."

Champion grinned, shaking his head. "Belle, I'm
not a kid anymore. If I want ice cream, I'll have it,
with or without your permission."

Belle's eyes danced as she folded her arms across
her ample bosom. "You will, eh?" A deep laugh
rumbled in her throat, making her round frame
bounce. "You just eat that soup, Champion
O'Keefe. I made it special for you."

"I'm eating, I'm eating!" Champion bent his
head, blowing on the savory chowder before tasting
it. He winked, tipping his head to one side. "Delicious, Belle."

"Of course it is! I'll get the bread." She smiled at
Season before leaving.

Season spooned thick chowder into her mouth, and examined Champion through the veil of her lashes. The exchange between him and Belle had revealed a side that Season found most attractive. His eyes had twinkled mischievously, and his mouth had lifted at the corners to form a reckless grin that had deepened his dimples and twitched his mustache. Genuine fondness had been reflected in his voice, and Season felt a twinge of envy of Belle Lowenstein.

Belle entered again, this time placing a loaf of hot bread on the table and instructing Morley to slice it. She produced a tub of freshly churned butter and a jar of homemade berry preserves.

"Belle, I couldn't hardly stand that chowder," Champion announced, pushing aside his empty bowl. "I had to force it down."

"Ach! What a liar you are, Champion O'Keefe!" Belle clucked her tongue, then slapped playfully at a laughing Morley. "Champion, you're going to make yourself sick eating that fast. Look here at our guest. She's taking her time eating, like she ought to."

Champion's gaze moved from Season's full soup bowl to her crimson face, and one corner of his mouth lifted. "She's been too busy staring at me to pay any attention to her meal, Belle."

Season brought up her head with a snap, her eyes widening at Champion's assertion. She started to protest, caught the challenge in his eyes and demurred. He was right, blast him! She shrugged and continued her leisurely appreciation of Belle's creamy chowder. She had been examining him, and to deny it would only provoke stronger accusations.

"Will you listen to that conceited son of yours, Morley?" Belle whisked Champion's bowl from the

table. "He thinks every female lusts for him." Belle
smiled, her bright blue eyes shining as she moved
toward the kitchen. "If the truth be known, I'd
wager that it's Champion who can't keep his eyes off
our guest. How else would he know she's been
watching him?"

Season turned to see Belle disappear into the
kitchen, then swiveled to catch Champion's self-
mocking grin.

His lean fingers curled around the stem of his
wineglass, and he lifted it in a salute. "Touché,
Belle." His gaze touched Season's before he sipped
his wine and directed his attention to his father.
"The generator is shot on Sweetsip's ketch, Dad."

The conversation faded into the background. Season felt suspended in another time, another place,
where the meeting of eyes across a table was as
powerful as a lover's kiss, and where simple words
took on double meanings that were more potent
than whispered endearments. A threshold had been
crossed, but she wasn't certain of the territory. All
she was certain of was that Champion had an
uncanny ability to shake her senses, rip away her
social veneer, rattle her thought processes and expose her most basic femininity.

She had been sure he would deny Belle's observation, or at the very least become angry, but he had
acknowledged the wisdom, and in doing so had
acknowledged the attraction that had crackled
across the table.

The attraction was undeniable. Season was quiv-
eringly aware of him. His gaze seemed to sear her
flesh. The slightest hint of a smile set her pulse to
racing. It was frightening.

She felt like a child facing her first roller-coaster

ride; terrified of the journey, but eager to know each dip and turn. Self-reproach stirred as her heart resumed its normal pace. For heaven's sake! She was twenty-eight years old and she was regressing to the feelings of a teenager! She wasn't on this island to indulge in romantic overtures. She was here to do a job and must put aside these disturbing flights of imagination. Champion didn't approve of her being here. He'd stated as much. Any undercurrents were created by her overactive senses.

"Would you like that, Season?"

Season swung her gaze to Morley as she grappled for a foothold in the conversation. "I'm sorry, I had my mind on something else. What were you saying?"

Morley buttered a slice of bread and spread thick jam on it. "I was asking if you'd like to take a trip to St. Martin one afternoon."

"Yes. I didn't get to nose around today and I'm dying to see the island. It's fascinating that it's divided with one side Dutch and the other French."

Morley bit into the bread, his brown eyes flitting sideways. "See there, Champion? She doesn't mind your company."

"What?" Season's eyes widened. "I thought . . . Morley, I thought you meant—"

"Champion's heading that way next week for supplies and he can take you with him. You should see St. Martin. It's a friendly place, steeped in history. Do you like the study of history, girl?"

"Yes, but . . ." She took a deep breath, realizing she'd fallen into a trap. Her glance at Champion confirmed that he was enjoying her flustered state, and she drew herself up, placing a serene expression on her oval-shaped face. "If I can fit such a trip into my work schedule, I'd appreciate the opportunity to do some sight-seeing and shopping . . . on my own." Her gaze meandered toward Champion. "I wouldn't want you to feel as if you had to take responsibility for me, Champion."

"I've never been accused of feeling that way about any woman, Season." He spoke her name slowly as if experimenting with its sound.

His narrowed gaze burned into her, and Season wondered despairingly if he had a sharp retort for *every* comment.

"Then it's settled," Morley said, clapping his hands once. "I'll give you time off, girl, don't you worry. As I've said before, your afternoons are your own, and I'd hate to think you'd waste them with that infernal typewriter! That's cold company in such a warm climate." His grin was enchantingly wicked, and Season responded with a smile. Morley pushed himself from the table with a flourish. "We generally have brandy and dessert out on the front porch, Season. Won't you join us?"

He didn't wait for her answer, but took the matter in hand by helping her from her chair. He tucked her hand in the crook of his arm, gently pulling her with him toward the front of the house.

Feeling manipulated but strangely content, Season allowed Morley to escort her outside to the wide porch furnished with swings, chairs, tables and plants. She laughed when Morley liberally sprayed her exposed arms and neck with insect repellent before leading her toward one of the cushioned redwood chairs.

"Sit here, girl, and enjoy the view. Those pesky mosquitoes won't bother you now."

Season sighed, relaxing in the chair and directing

her gaze to the sky and the glistening darkness of the Atlantic Ocean. The sound of the surf created a rocking rhythm, and Season's eyelids drooped to partially obscure the scene.

"Here we are!" Belle balanced a bamboo tray that contained dishes of ice cream, snifters and a decanter of brandy. "I've brewed coffee, if you'd rather have that, Miss Templar."

"Brandy is fine, thanks, and please call me Season, Belle." She straightened, accepting a bowl of peach ice cream from the woman.

"Okay, Season." Belle smiled and nodded her sleek head. "It *is* friendlier-sounding, isn't it? Here you go, Morley, Champion. I'll let you pour the brandy, Morley. If you won't be needing me again, I think I'll go home now."

"Sure, and be careful how you go, Mrs. Lowenstein," Morley said with a wave.

Season glanced at the older man, wondering why he called his housekeeper "Mrs. Lowenstein" when everyone else seemed comfortable with "Belle." She decided it was a throwback from his more courtly days. Morley still had the manners he'd been taught as a boy in Ireland. Finding this characteristic endearing, Season made a mental note to include it in her articles.

She took the glass of brandy Morley offered and set it on the table beside her. Cradling the cold bowl in one hand, Season dipped her spoon into the peachy ice cream, and slid it between her lips. It was delicious, cooling her throat and sending a shiver down her spine. She touched the tip of her tongue to the corner of her mouth where a drop of the cream rested. Inexplicably, her skin heated. Her gaze lifted to collide with hazel eyes ablaze with golden fire.

Frozen, she dared not move a muscle as a high-pitched awareness enveloped her again. Champion seemed to bore into her, reading her mind. He looked at her mouth before meeting her eyes, and Season summoned an iron will, tearing her gaze from his. Frantic to break the tension he had created, she turned beseeching eyes on Morley. The old man glanced at her, then his white brows shot up at the pleading expression on her face. Looking from her to Champion, Morley smiled.

"She's enchanting tonight, Champion," Morley said softly.

"Hmmm?" Champion blinked, turning his head to look at his father. "Who?"

Season's shoulders slumped. She'd looked to Morley for a release from Champion's mysterious hold, and now he was commenting on—

"The ocean, boy!" Morley's brows lowered. "What did you think I was talking about?"

"Oh!" Champion cleared his throat, straightening from his lounging position against the waist-high wall that enclosed the porch. He presented his back to them, facing the ocean. "Yes, she is . . . enchanting."

Season relaxed, free of the spell. She smiled when Morley winked at her. The devil! He'd actually managed to unnerve Champion. No longer threatened by Champion's soul-shaking eyes, Season took in his broad back. Moonlight shimmered across the chestnut waves of his hair. A breeze fluttered the material of his shirt, bringing her hungry gaze to bear on his muscled back and narrow hips.

When the screened door opened, Season jumped as if she'd been shot. Belle threw her a curious glance as she fitted a bundle of clothes under one arm.

"I'll wash these tomorrow," she announced in her drill sergeant's voice. "I guess I'll be making my way home now. Good night, all."

"Hold up," Morley said, rising from his chair and stretching. "I need to unkink my legs. I think I'll walk with you, if you don't mind, Mrs. Lowenstein."

Belle lifted her shoulders in a shrug, her gaze lowering in a schoolgirl's ploy. "Fine with me, Morley. I'd enjoy the company."

Grinning, Morley fell into step with Belle. "I'll be back soon. You two finish your brandy and dessert."

Season smiled, enjoying the view of the tall, lanky man beside the plump, matronly woman as they strolled along the path. Moonlight spotlighted them for a moment before they melted into shadows. When Champion chuckled, pivoting to face her, Season tilted her head to one side, her expression questioning him.

"They go through that ritual every evening," he explained, his voice laced with laughter. "Belle says she's ready to go home, and Dad suggests that he might walk with her. She agrees, halfheartedly, and they set off for Lowenstein Village. Belle offers Morley a cup of tea which he accepts. And then he comes straight back home. I don't know why they keep it up."

"Are you saying that Morley and Belle . . ."

"Are sweet on each other?" Champion stroked his jaw, his eyes sparkling in the moonlight. "Yes, I'd say so, even though they've never done anything about it. I'd be willing to bet they've never even kissed! Belle's been here since I was twelve, and Dad has walked her home every night. He refuses to call her by her first name because he wants her to know that he respects her." Champion threw up his hands, tossing the subject into the air. "Who knows? I guess they enjoy their cat and mouse game."

Season smiled, wrapping her arms about herself. "I think it's sweet," she murmured, almost to herself.

"I think it's a bloody waste of time." His voice was a growl of impatience. "Personally, I like the direct approach."

It seemed as if every muscle in her body tensed. Season unwound her arms slowly, and made a show of grabbing her bowl of ice cream from the table. Her heart jumped into her throat when Champion pulled a chair close to hers and sat down. His brandy glass came into her line of vision, and she looked at the expectant expression on his face.

"A toast."

"A . . . a toast?" She fumbled for her brandy snifter, almost tipping it over. Champion moved with the speed of a cheetah, preventing its spill. His fingers closed over hers on the glass, steadying her trembling. Patiently he took the bowl from her other hand and set it on the table. His gaze never leaving her face, he removed his hand from hers, his fingertips trailing across the back of it. He dipped his head until there was but a breath of space between his lips and hers.

"A toast," he whispered, repeating his suggestion.

Zombielike, Season lifted her glass, touching his with a crystal clink.

"To the direct approach," he saluted in a husky voice that added to the cloudlike aura enveloping Season.

Barely registering his whispered words, Season drank the brandy. It burned a path down her throat, dispersing the clouds in her mind, and bringing

Champion's face into sharp focus. Instinctively she drew back, then gasped when his hand curled at the back of her neck to pull her toward him. His mouth sent a charge of white-hot passion through her, and Season closed her eyes. His lips moved against hers, creating a silky friction. She parted her lips on a sigh, and the tip of his tongue skimmed the soft inner flesh. His mustache added its own caress before his tongue surged into her mouth. Season opened her mouth wider, wanting him to delve deeper and discover her treasures. Breathing in his aroma of lemon-lime, she melted against him. He tasted as good as he smelled—he put to shame the tang of the brandy and the tartness of the peach ice cream.

The snifter slipped from her relaxed grip, crashing onto the porch and splintering Champion's seduction. He leaned back, examining the shards of glass.

"Oh, look what I've done!" Season's hands covered her warm cheeks as the import of her actions dawned. *Yes, look what you've done,* her inner voice chided. *You've allowed Champion to manipulate you.* She leaned forward, her hand groping for the shattered glass.

"Don't!" Champion barked, freezing her movement. "You'll cut yourself. I'll clean it up." He slid from the chair to his haunches, and took a white handkerchief from his back pocket. Carefully he picked up the broken glass, dropping the pieces into the handkerchief.

"I'm sorry. I'm not usually so clumsy." Season bit her lower lip, hating the way her voice wavered. With the intimacy gone, she felt foolish for giving in to his kiss so eagerly. It wasn't like her to fall into a man's arms like that.

"It's my fault," he said, standing. He dumped the

pieces of glass into a wastebasket, then pushed his handkerchief back into his pocket. "I know better than to kiss a woman when she's got her hands full."

Season stood quickly before she had time to calculate the move. She found herself very close to him, so close that she had to tip back her head to meet his eyes. She took a tiny step back, then resisted further retreat when she saw his mouth twitch into a grin.

"I'm tired," she said, moving to one side to pass him. "I'm going to bed."

His hand curled around her arm. "Nothing to get upset about, Season. It was just a kiss. You've been kissed before, haven't you? Your husband must have kissed you."

"I'm not upset about the kiss, Champion," she said between gritted teeth. "I'm upset that I broke the glass."

"The glass? Don't fret over that. It wasn't an antique. I'll walk you to your room."

"No." She pulled free of him and hurried toward the screened door. "I know the way."

"So do I."

She entered the main salon then turned to face him. Her narrowed eyes revealed her growing impatience. Amusement flitted over his face, curving his mouth into a boyish grin that was disarming coupled with the manly gleam in his eyes. She relaxed her fingers, which had been curled into tight fists, and adopted a casual pose, jutting one hip to the side and resting her slender hand there.

"I thought you didn't like cat and mouse games, Champion. Now you're resorting to Morley's old lines. Escorting a lady to her room . . ." She let the rest go unspoken, fixing a superior smile on her lips.

"You're right," he agreed as the amusement left his face, replaced by a jarring sobriety. "Why don't we sleep together tonight?"

Her breath whistled from her throat as if she'd been punched in the stomach. Stunned, Season could only stare at him for long moments, her mouth slack, her eyes wide with disbelief. His question buzzed in her mind until a bitter laugh tumbled from her.

"I don't believe you!" She shook her head when he cocked an eyebrow at her. "You're . . . you're crude! Yes, crude," she repeated when she saw the beginning of a smile. "I don't know where you learned your manners. . . . Yes, yes I do! Out there!" She flung a finger in the general direction of the ocean. "Out there among the primitives. Well, this might surprise you, Champion O'Keefe, but in the *civilized* world a man doesn't ask a woman he's just met to sleep with him!"

Placing his hands on his hips to mimic her stance, he gave her a mocking smile. "And what *civilized* world are you from, spitfire? It's not on this planet, I can tell you. I've been in my share of cities, and I know for a *fact* that men and women sleep together after knowing each other less than an hour!"

"Not *this* woman!" Season stabbed a thumb at her heaving breasts, which strained against her gown.

"Aha!" Champion smiled smugly. *"Now* we're hitting the nail on the head! Excuse me for assuming you were *that* type of woman, but you fooled me out there on the porch. From the way you kissed me, I thought you wanted more of the same."

"I believe it was *you* who admitted it was just a kiss, Champion." She smiled as she threw his words back into his face with panache. "Besides, I don't even know you, so I wouldn't think of sleeping with you."

He spread out his hands, palms up. "I'm offering you a chance to get to know me. There's no better way to know a person. . . ."

"Oh?" She tapped her temple, then threw him a pointed glare.

His grin was back in place, boyish and devilish. "You mean you want me to know you *intellectually* first?" He waited for her curt nod, then his rakish grin faded until his lips stretched in a firm line. "When I want to be intellectually stimulated, I'll go back to college." He strode toward her, brushing past as he headed for the bedroom wing. "And when I want sexual stimulation, I'll know better than to approach a woman with a girl's mentality—next time."

"What?" She whirled, her hands tightening into fists again.

"You heard me," he growled before disappearing around a corner.

She ached for something to throw at him, but her fingers clenched and unclenched nothing more substantial than air. She closed her eyes and counted to ten, then twenty, then thirty before opening them again. She couldn't remember having been this angry . . . not since that night when Darren . . . A moan moved up her throat as images appeared of red-faced fury and a striking hand that had seemed to come out of nowhere, sending her sprawling to the floor. She blocked out the memory and took stock of herself.

Inexplicably, she was relieved and tinglingly alive, having vented her pent-up fury on Champion. Maybe Alex was right, she mused as she walked slowly toward her bedroom. Maybe she'd been wrong to hold so much inside. Alex had always urged her to show her emotions. She recalled how he'd pleaded with her to cry after Darren's funeral, and she had stubbornly resisted while tears had scalded the backs of her eyes. Alex had even suggested that she see a counselor.

"You're carrying around a lot of guilt, anger and disappointment, and that's not good for you," he had said in a coaxing tone. "Marilyn and I understand that you've put up with a lot since Darren came back. It's normal for you to feel angry and guilty, but you have to let these feelings go. Get them out in the open and be done with them."

Yes, it was normal to feel those things, Season thought as she entered her bedroom and closed the door. But had it been normal to feel relieved? She leaned back against the door, staring at the restful room. Had it been normal for a woman to lose her husband in an accident and feel utter relief? Guilt washed over her again, and Season pushed herself from the door and began to undress. How could she have explained her feelings to Darren's parents? They could never have understood, and she wasn't quite sure she understood them herself. She hadn't wanted Darren to die. She'd wanted him to live . . . happily. She'd wanted him to adjust to his condition and learn to accept his handicap. She had wanted him to get a job and be productive again. Most of all, she'd wanted him to love her as he'd loved her before Vietnam. But wanting hadn't made it so.

With each passing day, she'd watched him climb into a bottle of whiskey and lose himself. She had watched a monster emerge; a man who had shouted vicious accusations, who had threatened her and who had finally made good his threats. She'd dreaded any confrontation with him, and on that last night he had severed the final, tenuous thread of affection she'd felt for him.

She hadn't hated him. She had just hated what he'd become, and she had despised the pale, timid, frightened woman he had made her.

When Alex and Marilyn had told her of Darren's motorcycle accident that had ended her nine-year-old marriage, she had slumped in blessed relief. She'd comforted his parents, hugging them close as they cried and feeling the first pangs of guilt. Darren was gone. The trap had been opened. She had been able to start over again.

She hadn't expected the guilt to last; but she couldn't shake it, though he had died almost a year ago. Over and over again, she relived moments with Darren, wondering what the outcome would have been if she'd tried this tactic or that approach. Had she attempted *everything* possible to reach him? Had she failed him? Was he dead because . . .

Season covered her face with her hands. She stood in the bathroom, her skin glowing under the electric light. By rote, she'd undressed as her mind had traveled this way and that in a torturous journey she knew all too well.

"Stop it! Stop, stop, stop!" The anguished words were muffled against the heels of her hands. Slowly she let her hands drop. Her image in the mirror above the sink undulated, then sharpened. Emerald eyes held a bruised, haunted expression. Her full-lipped mouth trembled. Her hair, in disarray, tumbled around her face in dusky profusion, and her hand shook when she reached up to pull the ivory comb from it.

How could she face a new life when the old one wouldn't relinquish its hold?

Champion O'Keefe threw himself across the double bed, yanking down the mosquito net with a vicious sweep of his arm.

Who did she think she was, anyway?

His anger began to subside, and his saving grace—an ability to mock himself—surfaced. The trouble with her was that she wouldn't throw herself on his bed, he thought with a smirk. He'd decided she was going to be a fairly easy conquest, and he'd been looking forward to the feel of her silky skin against him. After all, she had seemed desperate to sweet-talk him into an exclusive interview, hadn't she? Champion chuckled, pushing himself to a sitting position as he unbuttoned his shirt. He'd found out, on the porch, she wasn't *that* desperate.

All wasn't lost, he thought jovially as he stood to unbuckle his belt. When he'd kissed her there had been a promise on her soft mouth, and her body had fitted against his as if it had been custom-made.

Kicking off his leather shoes, he walked in his stocking feet to the bathroom. He finished undressing then turned on the shower. The cold bracing sting pelted his overheated body as the flash of jeweled eyes darted in and out of his mind. She was a beauty, but his instincts told him there was more there than met the eye. When he'd mentioned her marriage, for instance, what had shimmered in her eyes? Pain? Was she still mourning her husband?

Turning off the shower, Champion reached for his toweling robe. He pushed his arms into the roomy sleeves and belted it. Her kiss had told him that she was free, but her eyes had held a trapped expression when he'd spoken of her marriage. His brows met in a puzzled frown as he went into the bedroom. Stretching out on the bed, he cautioned himself not to become too involved with her. She was an interesting diversion, and he needed that right now since his work was at a standstill until he could get those ship's logs from the Bermudian government.

And there was that news of Trish's marrying a Texas oil millionaire. It wasn't that he still had any feelings left for Trish—with the exception of bitterness—but he envied her. It was infuriating how quickly she'd snapped back into circulation following a divorce that had left him devastated and feeling like a failure. She'd married a wealthy stockbroker only weeks after their divorce had become final, and then she'd divorced that man two years ago. Now she was married again. The pattern hadn't changed. Trish married for money, increasing her earnings with each marriage license. She'd started with Champion, and he'd played right into her hands. He'd denied her nothing until she'd suggested he sell Sea Lily and invest the money in her pleasure. When he'd issued a nonnegotiable "No," she had sued for divorce. The game had been over. Time to find a new doubles partner.

He still cringed when he heard himself described as divorced. He'd become part of a growing statistic, and he didn't like the company. Divorce. It was an ugly counterpart to marriage, but not for him. Not again, anyway. Champion flung an arm across his eyes, willing himself to relax.

The trick was to keep relationships simple and casual. No strings. No rings. Those emerald eyes entered his mind again, and a wistful smile tugged at his mouth.

Easy, Champ, he cautioned. The owner of those eyes was a very complicated woman. He'd have to proceed carefully. He had a feeling she was the type of woman who could spin a web around a man and make him peacefully thankful for the silken trap.

Chapter Three

Season listened to the faint whir of her tape recorder while Morley leaned back in his sling chair, lacing his fingers behind his head.

"I met Lily on Seaward Island," he said, puffing on his pipe.

"Where is that?" Season moved the recorder closer to him.

"It's part of the Seychelles chain. I was scouting in the Indian Ocean and ran up on a coral reef during a storm. I spent six months on Seaward Island." Morley smiled at his memories. "It took that long to talk Lily into marrying me. She didn't want to leave her island, but I promised to create a new Seaward Island for her. So I named this island after Lily."

"And she was the daughter of a missionary?" Season asked.

"Aye, her father was English and her mother

52

was . . . an islander." He glanced at her, his eyes searching for any sign of reproach.

Season nodded, silently urging him to continue. She'd expected Morley to feel her out on this subject, and she had decided not to make an issue of it. She had learned long ago not to judge another's choice in life. Morley seemed pleased by her placid expression and the interest that shone in her eyes. He sighed, gazing up at the azure sky as if collecting his thoughts. A bird twittered, and Season swung her gaze toward the singer. The yellow bird with black markings eyed her from his perch in a palm tree then took to the sky.

"She was never happy here on Sea Lily Island," Morley said, his mournful tone drawing Season's attention again. "She was lonely for the people she'd grown up with, and I didn't understand that until it was too late."

"Too late?" Season leaned forward to hear his quiet voice better.

"When Champion was ten, Lily went back to Seaward Island. I begged her to return, but she refused. She said she'd received a 'calling' and wanted to follow in her father's footsteps. She did missionary work throughout the Seychelles until she died."

"When was that?" Season asked, her voice softening.

"She passed away six years ago." Morley lapsed into a thoughtful silence, closing his eyes. "I corresponded with her, and she swore until her last days that she loved me and Champion, but her love for her work was stronger. We agreed that we would not divorce. We just gave each other the space to fulfill our lives. It's a shame we couldn't do that together."

Season remembered the prose carved in limestone above the Caribbean frontage. She touched Morley's arm, and he opened his eyes to reveal their reddened rims and mistiness.

"Is that why you have that verse above the back entrance to your home?"

He nodded, sniffed and began fussing with his pipe. "Aye. Lily liked those words. We lived by them, but we took them to extremes. I always felt connected to her, though. I still do."

His heartfelt words touched her very core, and Season lowered her gaze to the recorder. Tears built behind her eyes and she cleared her throat, trying to dislodge the lump of sentiment there. "Morley, how did Champion feel about his mother leaving him?"

"I wish I knew," Morley murmured, then strengthened his voice. "We never talked about it much. I tried to explain the circumstances, but Champion never had much to say about it. He's that way, you know. He keeps a lot to himself."

Season knew the symptoms all too well, and she offered a sympathetic smile. "I'm sure he's reconciled himself to it over the years."

"Aye." Morley tapped his pipe against a tree trunk and black ashes fell from the bowl. "He calls this island 'No Woman's Island.'" He lifted one white brow when she showed surprise. "He does. Lily didn't like it here and neither did Trish."

"Trish, his wife?"

"Ex-wife," Morley corrected. "She was a bad one, but he wouldn't listen to me. She damaged his pride and that's the worst thing that can happen to a man. Makes him bitter and self-contained."

The discussion was too familiar, and Season switched off the recorder. Morley could just as well be discussing Darren.

"Something wrong, girl?" Morley's shrewd eyes impaled her.

"No." Season fidgeted with the recorder. "I . . . I just wanted to play some of this back to make sure we're getting a good tone." She rewound the tape, then switched it on again. Morley's voice was strong, and his last words, playing a second time, twisted her heart.

"Sounds okay to me," Morley said, tamping fresh tobacco into his pipe.

"Yes, it's fine." Season shifted in the chair, crossing one slender leg over the other. "Let's go back to the very beginning, Morley. Where were you born? Tell me about your parents, and when you received *your* calling." She smiled when he chuckled at her reference to Lily's destiny. Picking up a notebook, she began jotting down key words and impressions on how she'd approach the stories Morley spinned. Having guided him to safer territory, Season relaxed. She wrote descriptions of Morley while he spilled his youth into the recorder.

When he paused to ask if she'd like some lemonade, Season glanced at her watch and the three cassettes stacked next to the recorder. She switched off the machine.

"I could use something to drink, and I'm sure you could. Let's call it a day, shall we?"

He nodded, pushing himself up from the canvas sling. "I'll go round up Mrs. Lowenstein, and be back with some fresh juice and a little snack."

"You'll do no such thing," Belle Lowenstein said. She stood in the doorway, her hands planted on her hips. "Lunch is ready, so you can snack on it."

"Is it that time already?" Morley lifted his black hat, his fingers inching underneath.

Season laughed and stood up. "Time flies when

you're having fun," she teased, linking her arm in Morley's and walking with him to the vine-covered arbor where lunch was served.

"I guess this is good for me," he said. "It's helping me put my life in perspective."

"Should I change for lunch?" Season asked, glancing down at her navy-blue shorts and white knit top.

"No, we're casual around here. Ummm, something smells good, Mrs. Lowenstein."

Season placed a cool smile on her lips when Champion half rose from his chair.

"It's about time," he drawled, addressing his father. "I'd almost given up on you."

"Time got away from us," Morley explained, sitting at the head of the table. "Ah, shrimp!" Morley clapped his hands, his gaze locked on the crystal bowl of shrimp cocktail. "Do you like shrimp, girl?"

Season darted a look at the pink shellfish, and her stomach turned over. "I . . . I never acquired a taste for them, I'm afraid."

"Neither have I," Champion said, folding a napkin across his lap. "If you're nice to me, I'll let you have some of my chicken croquettes."

Season ignored his conditional offer, although his smile was harder to ignore. "You don't like shrimp?"

"No." He took a drink of lemonade, his eyes meeting hers above the glass rim. "Why are you so surprised by that?"

"I thought sailors loved all varieties of seafood." She nodded when Belle offered her one of the croquettes, and couldn't resist flashing Champion a triumphant grin.

"Obviously you haven't met many sailors," Champion observed. "Enjoy your chicken. It might be your last, mate." He wielded his table knife, fixing a menacing sneer on his face.

Season smiled against her will, enchanted by his Long John Silver imitation. Forcing herself to enjoy her meal instead of Champion's expressive face, Season lunched on the croquettes, fruit salad, fried zucchini and bread. The shrimp was consumed by Morley, who lavished praise on Belle Lowenstein's culinary skills until she blushed with pride.

When the meal was finished and they were relaxing over cups of spiced tea, Season glanced down at the bowls of water under each table leg, curious as to their purpose. She looked up to ask Morley to solve the puzzle, but Champion's smile told her he'd read her mind again.

"It's saltwater," he said. "It keeps the ants away. They won't cross saltwater."

"Oh." Season rested her elbows on the table, propping her chin on her palms. "How clever."

"We didn't discover it, we just adopted the idea." Champion smiled rakishly, then turned to his father. "What are you going to do now? Relate more tales of your colorful past?"

"No." Morley tucked his thumbs into his canvas belt and leaned back. "I think I'll get on the ham radio and call a few of the boys."

"So?" Champion pinned Season with sharp eyes. "You're free for the afternoon?"

"Yes," Season said, drawing out the syllable. She presented a surface calm, although she was coiled like a spring. What was this leading to?

"There's a framed map of the island in the living room. You should look at it before you wander about the island. It helps when you know where you're going."

She hadn't been aware that she'd been holding her breath until it escaped in a long, quiet hiss. That sparkle in his eyes told her she'd played right into his hands, and she wanted to kick herself and then him. "I'll do that," she said, struggling to keep an outward calm. "The island isn't that large, is it?"

"No, not really." Morley levered himself from the chair and heaved a sigh. "She's about three miles long and . . . oh, about a mile wide. You won't get lost. Champion's just pulling your leg." He patted his stomach. "Excuse me, folks. I think I'll shake this food down a bit."

"I'm off, too." Season stood quickly, almost tipping over her chair. She righted it, sensing Champion's amusement at her hurried departure, and walked with Morley into the house.

"What will you do with yourself this afternoon?" Morley lowered his brows in a teasing scowl. "You're not going to sit in your room, I hope."

"No," Season assured him. "I'm going to take a look at that map, find a good place for a swim and dive right in. Satisfied?"

Morley chuckled and patted her shoulder. "I'm satisfied. There're plenty of places to swim here. Have fun!" He left her, going to the room next to the study where his ham radio was installed.

Season went to her room and shed her clothes. She dressed in a cranberry one-piece swimsuit, and threw a matching terry-cloth jacket over her shoulders. Telling herself that she should be spending the afternoon working, she tucked a pair of sunglasses and a tube of tanning lotion in her jacket pockets. She glanced at her portable typewriter, flipped her hand in a haughty gesture and stuck her bare feet into canvas slings. There would be time for work later, she decided as she made her way to the living room.

The map was easy to spot. It was gloriously detailed, with each cove, inlet and beach named. An aerial photograph was in the left corner, and Season studied the mandolin-shaped island. She looked back to two names that had captured her adventurous streak. Doubloon Cove and Champion's Inlet. The inlet was near Sand Dollar Beach, and the cove was near Lowenstein Village. She chose the cove, telling herself that the lure of doubloons was greater than that of Champion.

A study of the map helped her negotiate the journey, and she reached the cove within half an hour. Shedding her jacket and shoes, Season stood for long minutes, gazing at the beauty. The cove was serene, bordered by sea grapes and palm trees. Clear, greenish-blue water reflected towering trees and a patch of blue sky. Limestone walls created a basin that was deepest in the center, and a passage no more than four feet in width gave access to the sea. Without wasting another moment, she dove into the sparkling water. She swam for half an hour until her limbs felt weighted, then rolled onto her back and closed her eyes, content to let the water cradle her.

Her thoughts turned to fancy, and she daydreamed about pirates and swashbucklers. She wove an image of Champion dressed in scarlet knee britches, barefoot and bare-chested, with a nasty-looking patch covering one hazel eye. A dangerously wicked cutlass hung from his black belt, and a red bandana was tied around his head.

The image was so ridiculous that she sighed it away, turning onto her stomach to find that she'd floated toward the sea passage. A flash of silver caught her eye, and on closer inspection she found a small cave hidden by vegetation. Excitement surfaced, and she pushed herself closer to the cave opening. The sun caught at the silver object again, and she was tempted by dreams of treasure.

Doubloon Cove! Could it be that . . . Her mind spun pictures of treasure chests, gold goblets, pieces of eight and royal jewels. Season swept aside the overgrowth, peering into the darkness beyond. The flash of silver came again, begging her to grasp it. She thrust her hand inside, her fingers hovering over the spot as a trembling shook her.

"I wouldn't do that, if I were you, me beauty."

The booming voice broke her fever-pitched excitement, and Season jumped back from the cave as if she'd been bitten. Knowing the identity of her intruder before she turned in the water, she squinted against the sun at Champion standing on the bank. The sun played tricks, and for an instant she thought he was dressed as he had been in her daydream. She blinked, then almost laughed aloud when she realized her mistake.

He wore jeans, the legs rolled up to just below his knees, and he was bare-chested. His red T-shirt was rolled lengthwise and tied about his head in an impromptu cap. No cutlass swung from his belt, but a hammer and mallet hung there, making her wonder what he was up to.

Realizing that she was staring, Season looked back to the cave, searching for that elusive spark of silver.

"Champion, I saw something silver in that cave. It could be—"

"Almost anything," he finished for her.

"Yes, but—"

"And the moray eel that lives in that cave probably wants whatever it is to stay there, me beauty."

"What?" A vision of snapping jaws and needlesharp teeth sent Season back-pedaling, then swimming with all her might toward the shore's safety. When she'd scrambled to her feet to stand beside Champion, she realized he was laughing at her. Doubtful, she wondered why she'd taken his word.

"There isn't an eel in there, right? You're pulling my leg again."

His laughter dwindled to a low chuckle as he swept his shirt from his head. "As far as I know, he's still there. I spotted him when I was ten, and again when I was sixteen." He gave an expansive shrug. "I don't know if he's dead or not, and I'm not interested enough to find out."

Season looked toward the cave, now concealed by the vegetation. "I saw silver, Champion! It could be part of a pirate's treasure!"

He mopped his face with his shirt before pinning her with his expressive eyes. "Silver? A pirate's treasure? Are you forgetting what I do for a living? Do you honestly think I would spend thirty-six years on this island and not search the place with a fine-toothed comb for any hint of treasure?"

"No," she admitted, momentarily agreeing with his reasoning; but then the lure of treasure was too great and she couldn't keep silent. "I *did* see something in there. Isn't there some way to . . . well, bypass the eel and have a look?"

"Bypass the eel?" His rich laughter circled the cove, and Season reveled in the picture he made, standing there with his head thrown back and the expanse of his chest glistening with a fine film of perspiration. "Go ahead, Season. I'll watch your progress . . . or lack of it."

"Oh, Champion!" She sank to the ground, wrapping her arms around her bent knees and resting her chin there. "It *could* be silver coins or something like that. Sand shifts, and suddenly there's a piece of silver!"

"You don't have to tell me how treasure hunting works, Season," he reminded her in a droll tone. Several seconds ticked by before he heaved a sigh of defeat. "All right, all right! I'll investigate."

Season looked up at him with a delighted smile. "I'll show you where it is."

"You stay here. You shouldn't be swimming near that cave. In fact, this cove is off limits."

"Off limits? But it's beautiful here."

"Yes, and there's Mister Moray Eel to contend with, plus some nasty coral over there near that opening to the sea. Doubloon Cove isn't for inexperienced sailors from Baltimore."

She wrinkled her nose at his exaggerated East Coast accent. "I don't say it like that," she objected. "Bal-ti-moah, indeed!" She pointed to the cove. "It's just inside and to the right."

He unbuckled his tool belt and laid it on the grassy knoll. "Normally I'd skinny-dip over there, but I don't want to affend your good, little-girl morality . . . so here goes!"

His body blurred past her into the water. A splash sent droplets into the air, and for a moment sun rays caught at them, changing them into rainbow circlets. His body undulated under the water as he crossed the short distance to the cave, his strong arms propelling him through the liquid showcase. He surfaced, pushing back the foliage before turning to her. Dark brown curls fell across his forehead, and droplets sparkled on his lashes.

"To the right?"

"Yes, and be careful!"

"Now you're concerned," he teased before peering into the cave. The muscles tightened in his shoulders as he thrust his arm in the cave, and Season pressed her knuckles to her lips and closed her eyes. She waited, holding her breath, while silence drove her to the brink of a scream.

"Champion? Champion, answer me!"

She jumped when she heard the *slosh* of water, and her eyes flew open to find Champion standing over her, water running in rivulets down his brown arms. He clutched something in his right hand, and Season stood, her heart fluttering.

"Chicken," Champion accused. "I bet you shut your eyes during scary parts in movies."

"What is it?" She grabbed his wrist, her anxiousness blocking out his comment. He turned his hand over, the fingers opening slowly.

"Here's your treasure. The treasure I risked my right hand for, I might add. And, by the way, I rather like my right hand. It goes so well with my left hand. I'd hate to lose it . . . especially for the likes of this."

His biting sarcasm added insult to injury. Season stared at the wadded gum wrapper, its aluminum foil shining in the sunlight. Crushing disappointment made her shoulders sag, and she batted the wrapper from his hand.

"Oh, pooh!"

"Pooh?" His brows rose. "Is that all you can say after goading me into risking my—"

"What are you doing here, anyway?" she shrilled, powerless to ward off her mounting frustration. She kicked at the hammer and mallet. "And what are you doing with these? Hitting trespassers in the head? I was minding my own business and having a lovely afternoon until you showed up to spoil everything!" She bit her lower lip, realizing she'd allowed her emotions to get the best of her.

"If I remember correctly, you begged me to search out your treasure."

"I didn't beg you, I asked you."

He picked up his belt, buckling it around his waist. "In answer to your question, I was working on Sweetsip's ketch. *And* I happen to live on this island, so I feel free to go wherever I like. I was on my way to Lowenstein Village for my laundry when I heard you splashing about. I decided it might be a good idea to warn you about our resident eel."

"Oh." It was an inadequate comment, but the best she could come up with at the moment. Season reached for her jacket, the charm of the afternoon paling.

"Would you like to come with me and see where Belle lives?" He pulled the red shirt over his head.

His softly spoken question drew her eyes to him, and her heart flipped over when she saw his hopeful expression.

"Yes, I'd like that." She pushed her arms into the sleeves of her jacket, and belted it.

"What a shame," Champion murmured, his gaze wandering over her body and pausing at her slim legs. "I like that suit. It's too bad you've covered it up."

"I'm chilly," she lied, pushing her feet into her shoes.

He shook his head. "You must freeze during the Baltimore winters. Come on, Lowenstein Village is this way."

His fingers curled about her elbow, and Season resisted the urge to pull away. That would only draw sarcastic comments from him, and she had discovered it was difficult to best him at that game. He shortened his long strides to match hers, and Season smiled, admitting that she liked the touch of his fingers and the scrape of his body against hers when the path narrowed. He didn't apologize when his body bumped gently into hers, and she liked that, too. The path followed a gradual incline, and Lowenstein Village sprawled on top of a gentle rise. A hand-lettered sign proclaimed: Lowenstein Village. Population 1.

"Whose idea was that?" she asked with a laugh.

Champion followed her gaze and shrugged. "Dad's. He likes to name things on the island. It makes him feel like a monarch, I suppose."

"A monarch? Then that makes you heir to the throne," Season observed.

"Well, not exactly." He paused, rubbing his palm against his jaw. "Dad turned over the island's deed to me as a wedding present."

The regret in his voice made her hasten to lighten his mood again. "That makes you the ruling monarch, and Morley the king father."

His smile was a sweet reward, and Season took pleasure in it. Those attractive half-moon lines appeared under his eyes, dipping down to dimples that many women would kill for. His teeth glinted under his mustache.

"King father?" His laugh delighted her. It had a ring of youth, a bubbling sound that lifted her spirit. "Don't you dare tell Dad that, Season. His ego is inflated enough as it is."

"And what about yours?" She feigned interest in

Belle's house with its white picket fence and hand-crafted birdbaths.

"Mine?" There was a sharpness in his voice. "It's been bruised, but it's recovering."

She sensed that he'd admitted something he rarely spoke of to others. Though his self-description conflicted with her image of him, she smothered any retort. She went to the gate, pushing it open.

"Who made these birdbaths?" she asked, running her fingers across one.

"Belle. She collects rocks, shells and bits of glass, and then sticks them all together with mortar. At the back of the house she has some benches and a table she made in the same way."

"It's unusual." Season examined the center of the birdbath where a starfish was displayed. "How lovely. Can we see the others?"

"Sure, come on." He took her hand. "I don't know if she's home. She might be out collecting shells. That's her favorite hobby. She knows a man on St. Martin who buys some of her shells to sell to tourists." He glanced in one of the windows they passed. "I don't think she's here." They walked around to the back of the house.

"Oh, how cute!" Season pulled her hand from his, eager to examine the four chairs and table. They were rough to the touch, but the chair seats had been smoothed for comfort. The table was large enough for a picnic, and a starburst of multicolored shells rested in its center.

"I used to come here when I was younger to have cookies and milk with Belle," Champion said, strolling toward the cluster of furniture. "Belle used to make up stories about leprechauns and elves, and I swear I heard their footsteps and laughter." He shook his head, his fingertips trailing across the back of one chair. "Where does all that magic go, I wonder?"

His melancholy mood prompted her to touch his hand in a tentative gesture that sent his gaze to her face. When she started to draw back, he turned his hand over, catching hers.

"Who are you, Season Templar?" His whisper, filled with wonder, was more potent than his fingers curling around hers.

She was speechless, as time ground in its heels to a jarring halt. For long, silky seconds, she was content to stare into his eyes, letting her own trace the complicated gold pattern against the greenish-brown background.

"Well, well! Visitors to Lowenstein Village! To what do I owe this honor?" Belle's gruff voice preceded her. She stepped from the shadows at the back of her property, her arms cradling a large canvas bag.

Champion tore his gaze from Season's. "Just as I thought. You've been out looking for shells, haven't you?"

"Sure have, and I've found a few." She dumped the contents of the bag onto the table. A variety of shells spilled forth, five in all. "I think Pete might buy this one," she said, picking up a large conch. "I'll use the others for my planters."

"Are you making planters, too?" Season sat in one of the chairs; both the table and the chairs were built on a small scale, as though part of a miniature world for children. Season thought how perfect they would be for a child with an active imagination. There was something about the place that wove fantasies of fairy lands, elf rulers and sleeping beauties.

"Yes," Belle said, smiling. "I've already made a

couple, and I'm going to plant flowers in them soon."

"I think your creations are beautiful, Belle. You're very talented. It must take a lot of patience to make these." Season stroked the table's surface.

"Sure, but there's no hurry on this island, dearie. Haven't you learned Sea Lily's motto? No?" She placed her fists on her hips. "There's no better time than tomorrow."

Season laughed, looking up at Champion, who was grinning. "I *had* noticed that no one around here seems to wear a watch," she said, "and there aren't any clocks at the main house."

Champion lowered himself onto the chair next to Season. "Time is one thing we don't worry about here. Dad says there's plenty of time to do the things you want to do, and those you don't want to do will take more time than you've got to spend." He shrugged, his hand closing on a shell. "He's right."

"How do you keep appointments?"

"We're men of the sea. We can tell time by the position of the sun, the moon or the stars. It's about three now." He glanced up. "Make that three-thirty."

Season reached into her jacket for her watch. "You're right! It's three thirty-two!"

Champion snapped his fingers, placing a superior expression on his face.

"Okay, Mr. Show-Off, enough of that," Belle grumbled as she plucked the shell from his hand and dropped it back into the bag. She collected the others, then tucked the bag under her arm. "Are you just nosing around or did you want something?"

"I wanted my laundry, if it's done, and a glass of juice, if it's made." Champion leaned back, stretching his legs before him and lacing his fingers across his shirtfront.

"Your laundry is done and I've already taken it to the main house," Belle said with a swift nod. "As for the juice, it's made. You wait here and I'll bring it out. I've got some sponge cake, too. That'll add zip to your lazy bones, Champion O'Keefe." She went to the house and through the back door.

Season wasn't sure she would be hungry enough for cake, until she remembered that dinner was served late, and that a snack would tide her over until then. She stared at the back door, wondering if Belle had ever been married. Where was she from?

"What's puzzling you?" Champion asked, smiling. "You were frowning."

"I was just wondering about Belle. I can't quite place her accent."

"She's Scotch, and she married a German when she was sixteen. He was ill through most of their married life and left her a widow when she was thirty. They couldn't have children, and Belle missed that part of life, so she started hiring on as governess and maid in Scotland, and later in England. Dad placed an advertisement in a London newspaper for a live-in maid, and she answered it." Champion unlaced his fingers, flicking one hand in a finishing flourish. "And the rest is history."

"I suppose she helped fill the void when your mother left the island." Season voiced the question with a degree of hesitancy.

A muscle tightened in his jaw, relaxing when he took a deep breath. "Yes, she helped. I don't think anyone can really take the place of a mother, though."

"Morley talked about Lily today," Season ven-

tured, searching for any sign of displeasure from
Champion. "He said you never seemed ready to
discuss her or why she left."

"Is he bothered by that?" Champion asked, worry
edging into his voice.

"Well, I think he's concerned. He doesn't want
you to hate her. He loved her so very much."

Champion leaned forward, crossing his arms on
the table. He stared straight ahead. "I don't hate
her. I just feel . . . well, cheated. I don't remember
very much about her except that she was gentle and
she had a soft, musical voice. Most of what I know
about her comes from stories Dad told me, and
those stories made me ache to know her better." He
blinked as if coming out of a trance. "A child can be
scarred by things he doesn't understand. For a long
time I avoided women because I was afraid they'd
leave me. Belle helped me over that hurdle."

"Why didn't you ever go to Seaward Island and
visit her?"

He looked at Season, and her heart contracted
from the pain in his eyes. For a few moments she
could see him as a boy, and she wondered how any
mother could leave such a wide-eyed, vulnerable
child.

"Stubborn pride, Season. That's why I didn't visit
her. I decided that she had rejected me and I would
die first before I'd seek her out." He shook his head.
"When I thought about going to see her, this voice
inside of me asked: Why doesn't she come to you? I
wish I hadn't listened to that voice. Of course, I'd do
a lot of things differently, if I were given the
chance."

"What other things would you change?"

A wistful smile curved his mouth. "I wouldn't

have married Trish, for one thing, and I wouldn't have been so stingy with my affection and feelings." He traced the outline of a shell in the table. "I wish I'd learned earlier to give. My tour in Viet Nam reinforced my survival instincts. I took and took and took. After Viet Nam, it was a long time before I realized the battles were over and I could trust people again. I'm not sure I've completely recovered. . . ." His voice trailed into silence.

Season shook herself, realizing that she'd stiffened and that the blood had drained from her face, leaving her pale and shaken. She gasped softly when Champion's hand covered hers.

"What's wrong? Did I say something?" His eyes bored into her, trying to ferret out her feelings.

"You were in Viet Nam?" She cleared her throat, trying to rid her voice of its huskiness.

"Yes, I was there."

She removed her hand from his. "So was my husband."

"So were a lot of other men, Season."

She nodded, unable to explain why the very mention of Viet Nam sent her tumbling back to a life that offered its own battlefield. Belle joined them again, setting a tray on the table, and Season slumped in relief.

"Here we go." Belle served them, and Season didn't miss the curiosity in the woman's eyes.

It was no wonder, Season thought as she sipped the cool orange juice. She knew that her emotions showed on her face. Uneasy, Season shook off the clinging shroud of her past.

"This cake is great," she said with a smile. "You'll have to give me the recipe."

"Do you like to cook, dearie?"

"Yes, I like cooking almost as much as I like eating."

"I'll be glad to give you the recipe. It's simple to make." Belle's eyes flickered to Champion. "Are you showing Season the island?"

"Actually, I just bumped into her at Doubloon Cove and I offered to show her the highlight of the island." He made a sweeping gesture. "Lowenstein Village."

Belle threw back her head and laughed. "Go on, you! This place isn't nearly as grand as the main house."

"But the main house doesn't have the charming Belle Lowenstein in residence." Champion reached across the table and tweaked Belle's flushed cheek.

Belle batted his hand, then fussed with the collar of her pink gingham dress. "Stop that!" She smothered a smile. "I'm glad you two are getting along. He swore he was going to make your life miserable, dearie."

Season turned wide eyes on Champion. He grimaced and ducked his head. "Why, Champion?" she asked.

"Because he doesn't want you on this island and he doesn't want you to print anything about him," Belle answered, narrowing her eyes when Champion threw her a warning glance.

"Well, now he knows that I don't intend to print anything about anyone without prior approval," Season said, her gaze leveled on Champion. Then she addressed him. "As for making my life miserable, I hope you've changed your mind."

"I have." The directness of his gaze convinced her. "Besides, I didn't expect someone like you."

"Oh? What did you expect?"

"I don't know exactly, but I didn't expect eyes as

green as emeralds, and hair as black and soft as a summer night."

The compliment came from left field, and Season could only stare at him as his words slowly registered. Her color heightened, and she looked away. Belle's chuckle added to Season's discomfort. She knew that Champion and Belle were exchanging glances as she attacked the cake as if it were her last meal, but she kept her gaze averted from them. A part of her blossomed to life at Champion's softly spoken observation. Suddenly she remembered the intensity of his kiss, and she shoved the memory aside as she set her fork on her empty plate.

"Would you like another piece, dearie?" Belle asked.

"No, thank you."

"I guess I'd better get going, Belle." Champion stood up, draining his glass before setting it on the table. "Sweetsip is probably wondering what's keeping me." He glanced down at Season. "Can I walk you back to the main house or are you going to swim some more?"

Season pushed herself from the chair. "I'm going back to the house, but you don't have to—"

"It's on my way," he interrupted, placing the flat of his hand between her shoulder blades. "Thanks for the siesta, Belle. See you later."

Belle waved them on, a smile wreathing her face. When they'd walked along the path some distance, Season could no longer stand the silence. She looked up from her careful study of the path and saw that Champion was lost in thought.

"Do you ever see your ex-wife?"

Surprise arched his brows. "How did you know I was thinking of Trish?"

"I didn't." She shrugged. "Maybe it's telepathy."

"Maybe." He shoved his hands into his pockets. "No, I don't see her. I heard the other day that she's taken her third husband."

"Third?" Season whistled. "She's a busy lady." She brought her gaze to him. "Did you love her?"

"That's a strange question." He stopped and leaned against a tree. "Of course I loved her. I married her, didn't I?"

Season dug the toe of her shoe into the red earth. "Do you *still* love her?"

His bitter laugh made her look at him.

"No, I don't love her anymore. Unlike my father, I'm not one to carry a torch for a woman who obviously doesn't want me around." His expression softened as he looked up at the canopy of tree branches. "Of course, I never loved Trish with the devotion that my father had for my mother. A love like that comes once in a lifetime, if you're lucky, and I've never had that kind of luck." He watched the flight of a bird before lowering his gaze to hers. "When I think back on it, I can see that what I really loved about Trish was what I thought she saw in me." Pushing himself from the tree, he began strolling along the path again. He checked his progress, letting Season fall into step with him. "I met her after I returned from 'Nam, and I was living on automatic pilot. Do you understand what I mean by that?"

She nodded, knowing all too well his meaning. She'd discovered that "just going through the motions" way of life, and it had saved her during those years with Darren when each day had been too painful to face.

"Trish breezed into my life and made me feel human again," he went on. "In her eyes I saw the man I used to be before all the horror of the war descended on me. I was ripe. I *needed* someone. Unfortunately, Trish views marriage as a means of financial security."

"She married you for your money?" Season stopped, and Champion turned to confront her.

"Yes." His laugh was self-derisive. "If I'd had all my faculties about me, I would have known that. I think Dad knew it all along, but I was blinded by Trish's apparent devotion to me. I gave her everything she wanted until she asked me to sell the island. That's when I awoke from my walking dream."

"She wanted you to sell Sea Lily?" Season looked around her at the beauty. She could hear the rush of the ocean, the rustle of leaves, the lilting songs of birds. "What for?"

"For money, of course. That's all that interests Trish." His face contorted for a moment, and he looked away until he'd fixed a less telling expression on his face. "When I refused, she filed for divorce."

Season shook her head in a distracted gesture. "How in the world could anyone put a price on this?" She motioned toward the thick wall of trees on either side of the path. "It's unique and . . . well, it's *you.*"

Wonder spread over his face, and he removed his hands from his pockets, resting them lightly at his waist. "You mean that, don't you?"

Season smiled, vaguely amused by his awe. "Yes, I do. The O'Keefe personality is stamped all over this island. Sea Lily isn't just a place to live, it's part of your family."

A tender smile took his mouth as he stepped toward her, his hands curving on her shoulders. Bending at the waist, he kissed her; a light, impersonal kiss. Season smiled, her lashes fluttering up when he started to straighten. He froze, his fingers tightening on her shoulders. She sensed a change in him. His touch was no longer impersonal, and as he dipped his head again, he pulled her close until she was pressed against him.

His mouth crushed hers with renewed determination. He caressed her arms before circling her wrists, bringing her hands up to his neck. Season flattened her hands there as a deep ache arose in her. He nibbled at the corners of her mouth while his hands moved beneath her jacket to the exposed flesh of her thighs and back. She arched toward him, sensing his need for her, and he moaned. His kiss deepened as his tongue dipped inside to rub hotly against hers, melting any resistance she might have reserved.

Champion drew away slowly, pressing the side of her face against his heaving chest. His fingers slipped through her hair, and Season breathed in the spicy aroma that was part of him. Closing her eyes, she listened to the thump of his heart, wondering if he was aware of her own erratic heartbeat. He drew a deep breath then held her at arm's length.

"Did *you* love *him?*"

His question sent her stumbling backward. When his brows met in a puzzled frown, Season knew that he'd seen the anguish on her face and the guilt darkening her eyes. Desperate to conceal her other feelings, she lowered her head and fidgeted with her loosened belt.

"You mean my husband?"

"You know that's who I mean."

"Yes, I married him, didn't I?"

He sighed softly, and Season regretted throwing his line back in his face.

"I get the feeling you're not over him yet. Am I right?"

She wanted to tell him the truth, but the words escaped her. How could she tell him of her failings . . . her guilt . . . her lost love for a man she'd vowed to love for her whole life? Her silence narrowed his eyes, and she felt his frustration at her refusal to say more. He ran a hand through his hair, turning sideways.

"Can you find your way to the main house from here? Just follow this path." He was moving off the path as he spoke. "I'm going to take a shortcut through here. Sweetsip is waiting for me."

Season watched him stalk from her, his arms thrashing at the bushes and underbrush blocking his way. When she couldn't see him, and when the sounds of his angry departure had vanished into the distance, she buried her face in her hands. Tears wouldn't come, and for the first time she wished she could cry. She wished Champion was holding her, nestling her face against his fragrant skin. Then she could cry. She could let all of it out, and he'd be strong enough to take it. He would tell her that he understood. . . .

How could he understand? She lifted her face, staring at the place where he'd left the path. How could she expect him to understand? He'd been there. He'd seen the tragedy of war. He'd come back and taken a wife who hadn't been able to give him what he needed, just as she hadn't been able to give Darren the strength he had required.

Season began walking back to the house, still feeling the searing passion of Champion. She couldn't let that happen again, she told herself. She knew her weaknesses, and Champion was one of them. She couldn't lead him into another disillusioning relationship, not when he'd been so hurt. Then self-preservation reared inside of her, causing her to lengthen her strides and tip up her chin. She couldn't cope with another man's war wounds, either. She'd failed at that before, and she had no intention of failing again.

Morley was standing on the steps leading to the arbor, and she waved at him as she resolved to devote the rest of her afternoons to her work. She wanted to prove to herself and her superiors that she could handle the assignment, and that was going to be her sole objective on Sea Lily island.

And the sooner she accomplished her mission here, she thought, the better . . . for everyone concerned.

Chapter Four

The night crowded into Season's bedroom, filling the corners with inky pools and shadowing the doorways with curtains of gray. Season pinched the bridge of her nose and squeezed her eyes shut, blocking out her typewriter and the wads of white paper littering the floor like discarded dreams.

Her work was going slowly, the words refusing to dislodge from her mind. Just when she thought she'd finally found the right way to begin her first article on Morley O'Keefe, visions of his son shattered her plans. She kept reliving Champion's kiss, the security she'd found in his arms, the barely checked passion in his eyes. She wanted to scream at the injustice of it all.

Everyone had warned her that Champion was a difficult customer. She had prepared herself for his distrust, his resistance to her invasion; but she hadn't been prepared for the pleasure of his company and the earth-shaking desire yawning within her.

Recalling her excitement when she'd researched him, she realized she'd been far more interested in Champion than in Morley. The photos of Champion had fascinated her. The strength she had seen in his lean body, and the intelligence she'd detected in the angular lines of his face had intrigued her. She smiled, remembering how the mischievous gleam in his eyes had touched a sensitive chord in her. She hadn't needed the article's flamboyant prose to know that this man shouted at the devil and defied conformity. He was a bulwark of strength disguising a soft heart.

Yes, she'd been prepared for his cool rebuff, but not for the seduction of his embrace. Season could feel herself falling in love with him, and it surprised her. She wasn't given to impulses. People described her as pragmatic and cautious. Her heart never interfered with her cool logic. How could she become entangled so quickly with Champion? What had happened to the deep well of reason that coated her life with icy precaution? How was it possible for that man to storm her defenses so effortlessly, leaving her sighing at the moon and reaching for the stars?

Confused, Season stood and went to the French doors, closed against the velvety night. She crossed her arms, running her hands along the white satin of her dressing gown. Her heart ached for Champion. He'd left four days before on a business trip to the Bahamas and she hadn't been herself since. It couldn't have come at a worse time in her life, she thought. She was still sifting through the debris of a marriage that had crashed on top of her. She was scavenging for some clue as to why she hadn't been strong enough to help the man she'd vowed to love for better or for worse. Was she just a sunshine girl, crumbling at the first sign of rainy weather?

Wrapping her hands around the gold handles, Season pushed open the doors. A balmy breeze feathered across her face, and she closed her eyes and breathed in the scent of the sea. Maybe she was being too hard on herself. When Darren had returned from Viet Nam, she'd tried desperately to make him happy. It hadn't been until the last two years that she'd given up, deciding just to exist with him. One could only take so much rejection, and she'd suffered more than her share. Time and time again she'd tried to comfort Darren, and make him believe that she still loved him. Gradually, he'd killed that love. His insults, drunken fits and cruelty had been too much to take.

Against her will, she recalled the last evening she'd spent with him. He'd been drinking again, and her patience had snapped. Seeing him sprawled on the couch, his eyes bleary from alcohol, had sickened her and loosened her tongue. . . .

"Darren, I've had it!"

"Oh?" His lips flexed into a smile. "Good. Why don't you pack up and get out? I don't need your sympathy."

"I'm not leaving. I've paid for this house. If someone leaves, it will be you." Season glared at him, refusing to back down this time. "If you want to wallow in the gutter, fine, but I'm not stooping to your level. You won't drag me down, Darren. I've tried to help you. I've been patient and—"

"I don't want your help." He levered himself from the couch and swayed before her. "I can take care of myself."

Her gaze traveled from his unkept hair to his grimy tennis shoes. "You can take care of yourself," she repeated, mockingly. "Is this how you take care of yourself? You're filthy! When was the last time you were sober? Can you remember? I can't. When are you going to stop this self-pity? You should count your blessings, Darren. Some men returned in wheelchairs. They'd gladly trade places with you."

"Don't lecture me!" He looked down at his right leg, his upper lip lifting in a snarl. "You don't have to wear this . . . this thing!" He lifted his jeans leg to reveal the prosthesis that attached to his knee. "I drink so that I can tolerate this!"

"How many times do I have to tell you that it doesn't bother me?" She put her hand on his arm. "Darren, I married you because I love you. I'm thankful that you came back to me. I want us to be like we were before Viet Nam. I want children and—"

"Children? You're out of your mind!" He jerked his arm from her, his face contorting into an ugly mask of hatred. "Why don't you find yourself a man and leave me alone! I don't want you."

"You don't mean that." Season fought the tears that burned her eyes.

"I do mean it. I can't stand to look at you, much less be touched by you. You remind me of what I used to be . . . of what's been taken away from me." He started past her.

"Darren, don't walk away from me!" She grasped his arm, sensing that this was a final confrontation. "Fight for us, please! We used to love each other, and we can love each other again if you'll only—"

His hand arched, striking her across the face and sending her falling to the floor. Stunned, she smothered a sob and stared up at the stranger she'd married years ago. Automatically, her hand covered the cheek that would be bruised tomorrow.

"Get out of my life, Season. I'm sick of your whining. I'm sick of you!"

"Darren, don't—" The door slammed behind him, and moments later she heard his motorcycle's engine and the scream of tires. She rose to her feet slowly and went to the bedroom. In the mirror she saw a dry-eyed woman who bore a red mark of hatred on her cheek. . . .

A shudder coursed through her, and Season blinked away the ugly memory. Darren hadn't meant those things, had he? Had he really despised her? What had she done to make him want to hurt her?

The memory of Champion's kiss seared her again. Why couldn't she have met Champion years ago? He was unearthing emotions within her that made her wonder if she'd ever truly loved Darren Ketchum. A touch from Champion aroused her more than her most intimate times with Darren ever had. No wonder she had failed Darren when he had needed her! She hadn't loved him deeply! Had Darren known all along that her love was a shallow thing?

"I did love him, in a way," she murmured, stepping out on the balcony. "I just didn't love him enough."

Season rested her hands against the wrought-iron railing circling the balcony. Her head dropped forward in a defeated slump as her thoughts returned unfailingly to Champion O'Keefe. She couldn't avoid Champion when she wanted so desperately to be near him. The thought of leaving the island and Champion filled her with a painful urgency to grab everything she could get. If she missed him now, how could she exist in Baltimore?

A tune floated into her mind, and she hummed softly as she lifted her face to the stars and crescent moon. A snatch of verse drifted from some far recess in her memory, and her heart twisted as the lyrics crystallized.

> *When I'm alone*
> *With just my memories to see me through,*
> *What'll I do?*

She closed her eyes on a soft moan. What an evil trick for her mind to play on her. That song had been haunting her for days, relentlessly floating in and out of her mind, reminding her that she'd soon be living without the sweet promise of Champion's proximity. Eventually she might find a man she could love, but no one would ever erase the memory of Champion. He had changed her. He had made her aware of the frailties lurking within her and of the searing passion she was capable of when touched by the right man . . . the only man.

"Are you an alluring apparition or flesh and blood, me lovely?"

She jumped backward as if she'd been struck, her eyes flying open at the sound of the voice she'd been playing in her mind like some old dearly loved record album. Her hand went to her throat in a protective gesture as she squinted into the darkness. She was imagining things, of course . . . he wasn't here . . . another cruel joke on herself. Then she saw movement on the balcony next to hers. Champion unfolded himself from a chair tucked in the shadows.

"It *is* you!" Exalted with joy, Season planted her teeth into her lower lip to keep from exposing her feelings. Calm down, she warned. Don't let him see what a fool you are . . . how the mere sight of him excites you.

"I'm sorry if I frightened you." He stepped into a pool of moon glow. "I was having a nightcap." He raised a glass as proof. "Would you care for one?"

She shook her head. "When did you get back?"

"A few hours ago." He eyed the railings and the few feet of open space separating them. "It's been a while since I've negotiated these balconies, but . . ."

"Is your room next to mine?" The realization that a mere wall was the only barrier keeping them apart at night sent a weakness through her, and she clutched at the railing again. It should have occurred to her. This had been Lily's room, then Trish's. Naturally Champion's room would be adjacent to his wife's.

"Yes," he answered. "You know what that means, don't you?" A wicked smile bathed his face. "It means we've been sleeping right next to each other."

Suddenly she was hot all over, and she knew that her face was a bright pink. His eyes told her that her heightened color pleased him. He examined the space between them again before lifting a leg over the railing and wedging his foot along the narrow ledge. Season gasped. He wasn't going to—

"Champion, please don't! You'll fall." She reached out, her body giving the lie to her warning.

He ignored her, devoting his attention to his task. Gripping the rail at his back, he stood teetering on the ledge; then, in a fluid leap, he was balancing on her balcony ledge. Climbing over the railing, he stood before her. He drew a short breath as if to say something, but he froze, his gaze sweeping her from head to foot and back up again. Baffled, Season followed his gaze. Her gown crisscrossed at the bodice, exposing her graceful neck and the tops of her breasts. A belt cinched her waist, gathering white satin into folds that draped over the curve of her hips. Season looked at him again, seeing the quick shudder course through him before his hands gripped her waist. He hauled her to him, crushing her breasts against his chest.

"My God! You're so beautiful, Season, and I want you so much." His voice was strained, his lips warm against the side of her neck. "I missed you. Couldn't keep my mind on my work."

"I know the feeling." She reveled in his embrace for a few moments before easing from him. With an iron will that astounded her, she turned her back to him and prayed he wouldn't pursue. "I've been thinking about you, too. We're heading for choppy waters, and I'm not up to the trip."

He sighed then cursed softly. "I left my drink over there and I could use it right now."

She pivoted slowly. He was dressed in dark trousers and a navy-blue shirt that had been pulled from his waistband. It was unbuttoned, the shirttails wrinkled.

"Did you complete your business in Nassau?" she asked, not really interested in his answer.

"I was throwing up a smoke screen, and I think it worked." He stepped closer, and his teeth flashed with his quick smile. "I shouldn't be revealing the tricks of my trade to a journalist."

"True," she agreed. "We haven't been kind to you in the past." She was throwing out meaningless dialogue while every part of her trembled. The scent of lemon-lime filled her, and she was enthralled with the way the muscles in his forearm tensed and relaxed as he stroked the railing. Dark hair furred the skin on his arm and the back of his hand. She looked at her own hand, small and smooth. The contrast was oddly alluring.

"After that last article I was swamped with the

most outrageous offers!" He shook his head, and a chuckle vibrated in his throat. "Women from sixteen to sixty wrote me and offered their . . . services." His eyes slid sideways to catch her expression. "I guess they thought I needed a good woman after mine flew the coop."

"There are a lot of lonely people out there." Season gazed up at the canopy of stars, feeling her own loneliness. "Don't be too hard on those women. They were just reaching out. They didn't mean any harm."

"I know." He ran a hand through his hair in a distracted gesture. "Boys and men came out of the woodwork, begging to join my crew. I hated throwing their dreams back in their faces. I guess that's why I was so upset over that article. It put me in a . . . well, an awkward position. It made me out to be some kind of devil-may-care pirate who broke the chains of boredom."

"Aren't you?" When confusion pulled his brows together, Season hurried to explain. "I mean, aren't you a devil-may-care pirate? You thumb your nose at the nine-to-five world and live your life as you please."

A sad smile twisted his lips. "I thought you were beginning to know me." He stared out at the vast ocean. "Everyone pays dues. Even so-called pirates, which, by the way, I'm not. Pirates take things that don't belong to them. I take things that are there for the taking." His hand covered hers on the railing. "Like you."

Her brows arched, and she forced out a shaky laugh. "Like me? I think *I* have something to say about that."

"Say it now, or forever hold your peace."

He wasn't jesting, and his eyes told her so. Season

would have backed from him, but her hand was still his captive.

"Champion, I'm not here to have an . . . an affair." She winced. It seemed sacrilegious placing such a tag on what she felt for him. "I'm not ready for you." She lowered her chin until her jaw touched her collarbone. There, she'd said it! His force was too strong for the defenses of her feeble walls, and now he knew it.

His fingertips eased under her chin, lifting her face to his. "Get ready, Season."

"Oh, Champion . . ." It was a weak whimper that was silenced by his mouth on hers. His thumb nestled against the pulse under her ear, and his fingers spread across her neck. He took her lips gently, pulling at them with his own, tickling them with his mustache. Lifting his mouth from hers, he smoothed fret lines from her face while he seemed to memorize every curve, every hollow, every skin tone. He pressed the side of his face against hers, rubbing cheek against cheek, his words whispering into her ear.

"I know something's bothering you. I'm not so hardheaded that I didn't notice I'd stepped on forbidden territory when I mentioned your husband."

"You don't understand. . . ." Season closed her eyes.

"I understand. There are certain things I don't like to talk about, too. You can't let your past destroy your future, Season. I won't let you do that."

"It's not your problem. I don't want to involve anyone else. . . ."

"I'm already involved. I'll help you. Trust me."

"You're not listening to me!" She wrenched from

him, putting space between her trembling body and his enticing one. "I don't want your help. I . . . I have to sort this out on my own."

His face seemed to crumple before he bowed his head, his hands still held out to her, tentatively. "Season, don't do this to me. It's been a long time since I've reached out to someone. Don't reject me."

The ragged edge of his voice propelled her back into his arms.

"I'm not rejecting you. I should, but I can't."

"We'll take it one day at a time. I'll try not to push you, but my lack of endurance is shameful where you're concerned." There was a smile in his voice, and the warmth of his hands on her back bled through the material.

Season listened to the tapping of his heart. There was nothing she could say. She didn't want to entangle him in her emotional turmoil, but she was too weak-willed to push herself from his arms.

"I'm sailing to St. Martin tomorrow and I want you to come with me. We'll make a day of it. Bring a change of clothes, and we'll have dinner with a friend of mine."

She nodded, rubbing her cheek against his hair-roughened chest.

"We'll leave right after breakfast." He laughed softly. "Are you going to say anything?"

Pushing herself from him, she gazed up into his face. "I can't promise anything. We'll probably end up—"

He touched a fingertip to her lips. "Did I ask for promises?" The tip of his finger parted her lips, skimming across the moist flesh. "Hush, and give me a good-night kiss."

Her mouth melted into his as that now-familiar

white-hot passion raged through her. His hands slipped between them to cup her breasts, and Season moaned softly when his thumbs teased the thrusting peaks. His hands moved, making the material of her gown slip up and down in an arousing way. His hair was crisp under her hands, his head tilting as he slanted his mouth across hers. His mouth closed more firmly around hers as he cupped her hips and urged her intimately closer. She felt his body with its need, and it fueled her desire.

"I'd like nothing better than to remove that . . . that gown from you," he murmured savagely.

She stood on tiptoe, her lips closing over his, the tip of her tongue parting them and darting inside. His tongue answered hers with long, hard strokes.

Oh, Champion . . . you're so good . . . too good.

Rocking back, she stood flat-footed again. His release was slow and halfhearted. Hazel eyes explored her upturned face for a few moments before he put her from him.

"If you don't mind, I think I'll exit through the door." He took a few steps then turned back to her. "Unless you've changed your mind? That bed is big enough for two."

Helplessly, she shook her head.

He shrugged, glanced longingly at the bed and left her. Still dazed from the aftermath of her emotions, Season stumbled into the room and closed the French doors. She winced at the bright light from the lamp and switched it off, throwing the room into gray shadows. With a ragged sigh, she flung herself on the bed.

He's only a room away . . . only a few steps down the hall. A moan eased up her throat, and she squeezed her eyes shut. Tomorrow . . . tomorrow . . . an entire day with him. How could she have agreed to that? It would be torture. It would be heaven. It would be so many things she couldn't cope with right now.

What'll I do . . . what'll I do? The song imposed again, presenting its bleak question, but offering no answers to save her from the abyss she had fallen into.

Chapter Five

Verdant peaks and strips of white beaches broke through the water, and Season trembled with excitement. Tearing her gaze from the sprawling beauty of St. Martin island, she looked up at Champion, who stood behind the wheel.

"There's something magical about approaching an island, isn't there?" she asked. She smiled, sensing Champion's understanding. "All of a sudden there it is, shooting up from the water like an oasis in a blue desert."

"I'll make a sailor of you yet." Champion tweaked her nose. "That's the sort of feeling that keeps one at sea. No matter that each island is inhabited and, for the most part, civilized. A sailor always feels like Columbus. Can you imagine what it must have been like for him? The delicious thrill of discovery he must have felt?"

Season pushed her hair from her forehead, lifting

her face to the warm sun. "I guess the closest thing we have to that now is our astronauts. They must experience those same feelings."

"I disagree." Champion adjusted the sails, catching the shifting wind. "When I come across the remains of a ship, and I see the glitter of gold or silver, it's very much like discovering a new world." He glanced up at the billowing sails. "I'm finding an old world . . . a lost world. That sort of thing gets the blood pumping. It's got to be a kissing cousin to pure ecstasy."

His expression was reverent, far surpassing what most people felt for their professions. He would explore the ocean floor even if there weren't a penny in it for him, Season thought. When he uncovered sunken treasure, did that curious boy lurking deep in his eyes spring forth?

He shifted his weight, his deck shoes squeaking on the boards. "We'll dock at Little Bay," he said, his voice booming above the sound of fluttering sails. "Great Bay is always so crowded. No cruise ships today, though. They're here during the week, not on weekends."

Wathey Pier was alive with tourists, sailboats, tankers and yachts. *The Touchstone* veered from the teeming pier, slipping through the waters for the more sedate Little Bay where the Pirate's Arms tavern was located. Season ran her hands down her legs, exposed by her white shorts. She tucked in her pink blouse and grabbed her oversized purse. They were approaching from the Dutch side—the Sint Maarten side; and Philipsburg, the capital, teemed with tourists. The other side of the island was French; its capital, Marigot. St. Martin/Sint Maarten was a study in harmony, Season thought with a smile. After centuries of battles, the people had divided the island. This decision had made St. Martin/Sint Maarten a natural for tourists.

Vacationers could step into a Creole French atmosphere in St. Martin, where shops catered to French lace, perfume and imported fashions from Paris. A short drive to the other side of the island resulted in an entirely different atmosphere. In Sint Maarten the flavor was definitely Dutch. Windmills, wooden shoes and delftware filled the shelves in these shops. The island, therefore, offered more than just one culture for tourists.

Champion secured the yacht. They strolled along Front Street in Philipsburg. The duty-free shopping enticed Season to buy several blouses and two bottles of perfume. Champion limited his purchases to a packet of tobacco for Morley. Season bought a few postcards, and Champion found a vacant table at a sidewalk café that offered a breathtaking view of the Caribbean. Season filled out two postcards, one to Alex and Marilyn, and one to her sister in Fayetteville, Arkansas. She sipped her mint tea, pausing in her message to her sister. How could she describe this place in a few words? White sand disappeared beneath foaming waves. Palm trees provided patches of cool shade.

"Are you hungry?"

Season frowned playfully at Champion. "How can you think about food at a time like this?"

"Like what?" His brows lifted as he surveyed the area. "You like this place, I take it."

"It's heaven!" She scribbled the description on the card before her as she spoke it. "It isn't as private as Sea Lily, but it has a certain bustling charm."

Champion grinned. "You really like my island, don't you?"

Season nodded, signing the card and pushing it

aside. "I think your island must be as close to paradise as you can get in this world. You're very lucky." She licked two stamps, placed them on the cards and glanced around for a mail depository.

"There's one on the way back to the yacht," Champion said, reading her mind. He hooked his thumbs into his waistband and leaned back. "Privacy can turn very quickly into loneliness."

She watched him finish his beer, wondering if he was admitting something to her. When he didn't offer anything else, she asked, "Are you lonely?"

He shrugged. "Sometimes, but I appreciate privacy. Most people can stomach it for only short periods of time."

"Not me. Privacy translates into peace of mind."

His smile was lopsided. He crushed his beer can with one hand then tossed it into a trash receptacle several feet away. "That's because you're running away."

Season jolted back as if he'd prodded an exposed nerve. "I'm not running from anything," she said with a shaky laugh. "I'm here on business. You know that."

Warm fingers curled around hers, and Season felt trapped by the gentle contact. Champion studied her hand, his thumb stroking the back of it.

"Business is your excuse. Right now you're drawing into yourself like a turtle into its shell. Is it so painful that you can't talk about it to anyone?"

She pulled her hand from his. "I don't want to discuss it now." She finished her drink, sensing Champion's keen regard. "Who is this friend of yours we're meeting for dinner?"

Champion's mouth twisted in disappointment. He turned his head to glare at the sparkling Caribbean. "I get the message," he ground out between clenched teeth. Drawing a deep breath, he answered in a calmer voice, "His name is Jake Winslow and he's my attorney. We've been friends for years."

"That's nice. I'm looking forward to meeting him." She wondered if the sun had really dimmed or if the chill were a result of Champion's gray mood. She wanted to confide in him, but such a confession would only elicit his sympathy, and she didn't want that. Time was her only salve. Someday she'd understand her failings and compensate for them. Champion seemed to have pieced his life together following his divorce, and she could do the same . . . given enough time.

"Let's grab a taxi and go over to the French side." Champion stood abruptly as if the café had lost its appeal.

After securing a taxi, Champion pointed out places of interest on the way to Marigot. They took the longer route, past the Low Lands where the French Quarter was located. They passed Juliana Airport, Mullet Pond and Simpson Bay. From the bay Season could see Saba, an island only a stone's throw from St. Martin. She breathed in the fragrance of frangipani, bougainvillea, hibiscus and dieffenbachia. Champion pointed out tamarinds, soursops and breadfruit.

Passing the Belle Creole, Champion told the driver to pull to the side of the road. Season stared at the partially completed complex. It looked like a ghost town.

"Will it ever be finished?" she asked.

"Who knows? Several million have already been spent on it. It was supposed to have been the jewel of the Caribbean . . . the finest hotel ever built. It's sad, isn't it."

"Yes." Season swallowed. The unfinished hotel

was just another reminder of what might have been, and she looked away quickly. "Let's go."

"Is something wrong?"

"No, I'm fine."

His scowl told her he wasn't convinced. "If you say so. . . ." He reached into his back pocket and withdrew his wallet. "Let's walk along Marigot's main streets and do some sight-seeing before we head back to the ship and change for dinner." He handed several bills to the driver, then reached across Season to open her door.

"We should have changed first," she protested. "Then we wouldn't have to make an extra trip back to Philipsburg."

Champion unfolded himself from the taxi to stand beside her. "This is the Caribbean." He smiled, his hand settling under her elbow as he guided her toward the busy shopping area. "Time is something we spend, not save."

She laughed, giving herself up to the moment. Time. It seemed so precious now that Champion had entered her life.

Jake Winslow never met a stranger. Blond and blue-eyed, he was shorter than Champion and small-boned. During dinner at a restaurant in the heart of the city, Season examined his lightweight tan suit and white knit shirt. He was handsome in a slick, sophisticated way and he had an easygoing, friendly personality.

Feasting on lobster and seasoned rice, Season listened as Champion and Jake discussed salvaging. She found their tales of treasure entertaining. Although Jake never joined Champion on his excursions, he knew quite a bit about the business, since he handled the sticky legal problems. Season noted how Jake spoke of the excitement of discovery, but omitted any locations, dates or figures. The sign of a good attorney, she thought. Never lose sight of the fact that you're talking to a reporter . . . an outsider.

"The headaches begin when gold is found," Jake said, finishing his swordfish. He poured another measure of wine into his glass. "No one pays much attention until gold is discovered, and then everyone wants a piece of the action."

"Right." Champion pushed aside his dinner plate and stroked his mustache with a linen napkin. "No one gives a damn about pottery or ship bells, but when you find gold or jewels—watch out! Last year I was salvaging a wreck and came upon a cache of jewels dating back to 1612. The word got out—it always does, somehow—and here comes Preston." He paused, then added for Season's benefit, "He's one of my competitors. Preston anchored his ship near mine, and when I filed a protest with the governing nation, Preston fired some shots at my crew."

"What?" Season's fork clattered to her plate. "He actually shot at you?"

"He sure did, and he paid for it dearly." Champion winked at Jake. "My friend here fired some shots of his own by obtaining an arrest warrant. Preston spent a few nights in jail and forked over a hefty fine."

Season shook her head, amazed that such pirating tactics still existed. "He didn't hurt anyone, did he?"

"No, he was just trying to scare us off. He should have known better." Champion poured more wine into Season's glass, then his own. "No one scares me off a job . . . especially when I've got first rights to it."

"Was that the discovery of the Santa Clara off the coast of Nassau?"

Champion and Jake both raised eyebrows at her question, and Jake chuckled.

"You've been doing your homework," Jake observed. "Or have you always been interested in salvaging?"

"I've become very interested in it," Season admitted, casting a quick look at a smiling Champion. "I had no idea how dangerous it could be. I mean, actually shooting at someone! That's insane."

Champion leaned closer to her, his breath fanning her cheek, his voice dipping to a gravelly purr, his speech tainted with days of old. "You should understand such things, me matey. Remember how obsessed you were when you thought you'd discovered silver in Doubloon Cove? Just think how you'd react to the sight of gold!"

"You discovered silver on Sea Lily?" Jake asked.

Season grimaced. "No, I discovered a gum wrapper."

Jake laughed, and Season exchanged a long look with Champion as they mentally recalled that afternoon . . . that kiss . . . that thrill. Champion shifted in his chair as if suddenly uncomfortable.

"It's getting late and—" he began.

"Before we call it an evening, I have an invitation to extend," Jake said, interrupting Champion. He smiled at Season, one hand moving across the table to touch hers briefly. "I want to invite you to my annual costume party. I've already invited Champion, and I hope you'll come as his date."

"A costume party?" Season glanced at Champion, wondering if he might have already asked another woman to accompany him. Was Jake putting his friend in an awkward position? "When is it?"

"Next- weekend. It's a short notice, I know, but please say you'll attend. It's at the Belle Princess Hotel. That's at Grand Case, Season. Have you been there?"

"I don't think so. . . ." Season looked at Champion, and he shook his head.

"We didn't travel that way today," he explained. "It's on up the coast from here at the French Cul de Sac. We'll be there, Jake," Champion added, giving Season a tender smile. "I wouldn't deprive Season of the pleasure."

"What sort of costumes are required?" Season asked, relieved that Champion was willing to escort her to Jake's party. "I'm afraid I didn't pack much in the way of party dresses."

"Don't worry about that," Champion reassured her. "Belle can whip us up something. She's a whiz on the sewing machine."

"Good. I'll be looking forward to seeing you both again—in costume." Jake dropped his napkin into his lap. "I've got my car, Champion. Can I drop you back at the ship?"

"Yes, thanks."

The drive to the pier was taken at a leisurely pace. Season insisted on sitting in the backseat so that Champion and Jake could talk business up front. Jake's Oldsmobile purred along the highway past Simpson Bay Lagoon, which sparkled darkly in the night. Season tuned out the rumble of masculine voices, her thoughts lingering on the hours she'd spent on St. Martin. A bittersweetness washed over her. The day was ending . . . it was so sad . . . but there would be another visit. The costume party would bring her back here with Champion.

The Touchstone loomed into view and Season

thought it was the most beautiful ship in the harbor. After bidding Jake good night, she and Champion boarded the yacht.

For a few minutes, they stood at the rail and gazed at the sparkling sky. A buttery slice of moon provided a hazy light that danced upon the water. A breeze fluttered the skirt of Season's jade-green wraparound dress and she smoothed a hand down her side to keep the culprit breeze from undressing her.

"We don't have to sail back tonight." Champion turned his head slowly, his eyes searching her face. "We could start back in the morning."

A shiver of anticipation rippled through Season. "Morley will wonder what happened to you. He'll be worried if . . ." Her words were silenced by the pressure of Champion's body next to hers. His thigh slid against hers, the heat of his skin searing through the fabric.

"I'm all grown up. Morley doesn't worry when I don't come home at night."

She swallowed hard as the vast seascape before her began to diminish. Suddenly she was aware only of the tangy scent of Champion's after shave, and the way the moonlight played over his cream trousers and striped knit shirt. He placed his hands on her shoulders, turning her toward him. The world slipped away as Season charted new worlds in his eyes.

"There's a double bed below, Season." He bent his head, his mustache tickling the side of her neck, his lips sipping her skin. "This is a night for lovers. We shouldn't waste it."

Season released a quivering sigh as his mouth continued to rob her senses. His hands glided down her back to her hips and he pulled her closer to him.

Season lifted her arms, winding them around his strong neck. Remembering another time when he'd made the same request, she smiled. He lifted his head, his brows meeting when he saw her expression.

"What are you smiling about at a time like this?"

Season laughed softly and framed his rugged face between her hands. "I was remembering the first time you asked me to share your bed. Your technique has improved."

"Do you think so?" He pressed his mouth to her palm. "It seems I have a one-track mind." The tip of his tongue tickled her skin before he rubbed his stubbled cheek against her hand. "I hope your answer has changed, Season."

The moment was upon her and Season stiffened. Champion's eyes moved to encompass her features and a frown furrowed his brow when he saw the trembling of her lips and the downward sweep of her lashes.

"What *is* it? I know you want me to make love to you. Why are you backing away from me?"

She stopped, surprised to discover that she had retreated a few steps from him. "I'm scared, Champion."

"Scared of what? Surely you're not frightened of me."

"No." She faced the rail again, her hands gripping it. "I failed at one relationship and I'm afraid of failing again. You can understand that, can't you?"

"You didn't fail, Season. Your husband died."

"It wasn't that simple. He . . . he needed me and I just wasn't there for him. It's hard to explain, because I don't understand all of it myself." She looked at him, forcing herself to hold his puzzled gaze. "I can't get involved with someone else until

I've sorted this out. I don't want to make the same mistakes."

"You won't. You'll make different mistakes," he said with quiet confidence. "It happens in every relationship. You've got to get on with your life." He leaned against the rail, his back facing the vista of water.

"I'm just not ready."

"Season, kiss me."

His command startled her and she half turned toward him, her lips parting in surprise. His mouth swooped, gliding over hers, his tongue slipping between her lips. He didn't move to take her in his arms, instead keeping his hands on the railing at his sides. When he started to draw away, Season lifted her hands quickly to his neck and pulled him back to her. For a few moments she cursed her weakness before surrendering to it.

The world tipped on its axis when his hands cradled her hips, moving the lower part of her body to him as his mouth ravaged hers. The kiss grew warmer, his mouth slanting across hers, his lips parting wider and wider with each caress until he was softly sucking hers in a way that seemed to tug at her heart and soul. Even while she warned herself that she was crazy to let this go on, her hands stroked through his hair, and her tongue curled around his. One of his legs inched between hers, his arms tightened at her back and his lips released hers. Tiny shudders shook her when his mouth grazed over her shoulder.

It feels so good to be held again like this, she thought; she was barely aware that his restless hands were gently cupping her breasts, his fingers expertly working their way inside her dress, his lips pressing swift kisses down . . . down . . . It has been so long, she thought. . . . A woman needs this. There are times when—

A low moan escaped her. His fingers had finally discovered her taut nipples. They raced over them, flicking them lightly, then working around them until fire shot through her veins.

"Champion . . . Champion . . ." Season's voice sounded strangely hoarse and sultry. "Oh, yes . . . yes!"

His lips covered one hard peak, kissing it gently before taking it into the warm, wet cavern. His tongue was rough velvet, stoking the fire he'd started. She pulled his shirt from his waistband, anxious to touch his vibrant skin. His back was smoothly muscled, alive beneath her searching hands.

Suddenly his mouth lifted, his eyes gleamed in the dusk and his lips formed her name. She was in his arms in one sweeping motion. Season buried her face against his neck. As he moved toward the cabin and down the stairs, she told herself to stop him now before it was too late.

"Champion, no. I . . ." Her voice came out weak, wavering.

"We're going to be good together, lady. So good . . . so good. . . ." He proceeded down with her to a wide bed, his hands untying her belt and parting the fabric to expose her lace-covered breasts. The fabric was a flimsy barrier. He did not bother to unfasten her bra but merely pushed it up until her breasts were released to his flicking tongue and massaging hands.

She wanted him. Season closed her eyes, struggling with her wild yearning and her growing fear of failure. It had to be perfect. He was so important to her. It had been so long since she'd given herself to a man. Doubt crowded into her mind, and she tensed slightly.

His hands caressed the insides of her thighs, his fingers exploring her. Season stiffened. Things were going too fast. She wasn't sure anymore. She couldn't *think* when his fingers were doing that! Her hands gripped his wrists, holding him still.

"Champion, I can't. Not until I get—" Season blinked, confused by the sudden flush on his face. For a few moments he glared at her, then his eyes narrowed and he cursed softly. He sat up on the edge of the bed and exhaled a sigh of frustration.

"Okay, okay!" He ran a hand through his hair, turning his face to her. "What do you want? I'm ready to deal." His tone was brusque with irritation. "You want an exclusive interview? You've got it!"

She stared at him, not wanting to believe her ears, yet knowing that she must. His expression was angrily expectant, and Season realized with a jolt that he was waiting for her answer. Did he really think she was holding out just because she wanted his cooperation? Did he believe that it meant so little to her?

"Well?" His voice was a chilling whisper. "Does the offer appeal to you?"

Slowly she sat up, gathering her dress around her again, straightening her bra and tying her belt with shaking fingers. She forced composure to her face, not wanting to crumble before him.

"What a magnanimous gesture, Champion," she said between gritted teeth. "I don't need an interview with you that badly." She looked at him. The dark flush was seeping from his face now. "But you've certainly put things in perspective for me."

His shoulders slumped and he half turned toward

her, one hand covering her knee. "Season, I don't know why I said that. I . . . it was stupid. I didn't mean it."

"It just slipped out?" she asked, moving her knee from his hand.

"Yes, sort of."

"But you must have been thinking along those lines." She laughed softly, feeling like a fool. Edging past him, she rose from the bed and smoothed her hair into place. "And here I was thinking how important this was. How this had to be just right . . . perfect. I was afraid that I would disappoint you." She met his gaze briefly. "It's been a long time for me and . . ." She shook her head. "No matter."

"It does matter." He stood up and gripped her elbows to prevent her from turning away from him. "I'm sorry. So sorry."

"I want to go back to the island . . . now." She stared at a button on his shirt.

"I want you, Season. I've come to the point where I'll do anything to get you, but I didn't really mean—"

"Did you hear me?" she interrupted, her voice sharp. She couldn't stand any more of this. It hadn't meant as much to him. He'd been willing to bribe her for her affections. Why didn't he just shut up and leave her alone? "I want to go back to Sea Lily. There's nothing more to say."

"Do you forgive me?"

She lifted her eyes to his. "No."

His eyes closed, his hands dropping from her arms. "Season, please. I didn't mean to hurt you."

Suddenly she was tired and her temples pounded. She sank to the bed and closed her eyes. "Champion, let's just leave it for now."

"Season?"

She opened her eyes to stare at Champion's silhouette in the doorway. "Yes?"

"I've ruined it, haven't I?"

She was moved by the sad line of his back, the tired hang of his head. "Oh, Champion, I don't know. I think we both let our emotions run away with us." She pulled her bottom lip between her teeth to keep herself from sobbing. "I told you I wasn't ready to become involved and . . . well, I just proved that tonight." Her anger was ebbing. It wasn't all his fault.

"Give me another chance." He bent his head for a moment before lifting his face to her again. "One more chance. You know I didn't mean to bribe you. I was . . . was thinking with another part of my body besides my brain." He grinned hesitantly, his teeth white in the dark room. "Don't hold it against me, Season. Please?"

He was telling the truth, Season knew. "Okay." She sighed wearily. "You've worn me down."

"I'll get us underway." He turned and bounded up the stairs.

Season stared at the empty space where he'd been. A slow smile captured her lips. He'd charmed her, damn him! She laughed softly. How could a woman resist a man like Champion? A man who begged for a second chance?

She'd give him the benefit of the doubt, she told herself. Mainly because she very much doubted if she had any choice.

Chapter Six

Stepping outside, Season breathed in the fresh air. She'd spent most of the past two days in her room. After several starts and stops, she'd finished her first article and Sweetsip had sailed to St. Martin yesterday and mailed it to Alex for her. Stretching her arms above her head, she enjoyed a sense of accomplishment. She scanned the vista before her, searching for Champion or Morley. Where were they?

Dusk was gathering on the island as Season strolled toward Sand Dollar Beach. The men were probably doing chores. They'd been busy with odd jobs for the past two days, making Season aware of the many hours spent on the upkeep of this paradise.

Funny, when she'd fantasized having her own island, she had never taken into account the work involved. During breaks from her writing, she'd taken walks and found Morley or Champion tending to island repairs. Sand was cleared from drains, furniture was mended, roofs were patched, lanterns were cleaned, debris was collected from the beaches and used as breakwaters. The list went on and on, boggling the mind. Paradise had its price.

She heard the rumble of their voices, and changed her direction to head for the lagoon. Giving in to the temptation to eavesdrop, she stopped just short of the thick foliage and watched, unnoticed, as Champion and Morley worked side by side. They were gathering palm fronds from around the boat house area, stacking them in a huge mound for a breakwater at some other place on the island. A smile shaped her mouth as she leaned against a nearby tree and listened to the father and son . . . so alike, and yet so different.

Morley emerged from the boat house carrying two old tires. He lumbered toward the pier. Shirtless, his wiry body gleamed with perspiration.

"Dad, what the hell do you think you're doing?" Champion barked, making fast tracks toward Morley. "I told you I'd do that."

"I can do it," Morley grumbled, plopping the tires onto the pier. "Been doing this since before you were born."

"You don't have any business exerting yourself like that. The doctor said for you to take it easy and—"

"That doctor can go straight to the devil. I know what my body can take and what it can't. I live with it, don't I?"

"I'm not going to argue with you." Champion dropped to his hands and knees at the edge of the pier and hauled one tire toward him. "You finish gathering that debris and I'll change these tires."

"You just quit treating me like I'm some feeble old woman!" Morley glared at his son's broad back for a few moments. "Mind that you tie those up tight so they don't come loose in choppy water."

"I know how to do it, Dad." Champion's tone was reserved, icy with strained patience.

Season grinned, squinting through the dusk to watch Champion secure the tire to the side of the pier with heavy rope. He was without a shirt, too, and his cutoffs were tight and faded. Stubbornly disobeying, Morley stood over Champion and supervised the process.

"That's not tight enough," he said when Champion reached for the other tire.

"It'll do."

"Do it right or let me at it."

"Oh, for pity's sake!" Champion swore viciously and yanked at the rópes. "There! Satisfied?"

Morley leaned forward, then nodded. "Aye, that's better. You're as sore as a broke-tailed cat these days. That girl must be getting to you."

Season sucked in her breath. That girl? Her fingers tightened on the tree trunk.

"I don't know what you're talking about," Champion muttered, his voice carrying easily to Season.

Morley chuckled and nudged Champion's shoulder with his knee. "Sure you don't. You think I haven't noticed how you two been keeping your distance since you got back from St. Martin? What happened that day? Did she say she could live without you?"

"Nothing happened." Champion jerked the other tire into position and began tying it to the pier.

"That's what I thought."

Champion turned his head, giving his father a sharp look. "I'm steamed because of you, not because of Season. I want you to follow doctor's orders. He told you not to lift anything heavy. He told you not to exert yourself. Are you taking those blood pressure pills?"

"Aye, every day."

"Good." Champion turned back to his work.

Season started to emerge from her camouflage, but Morley's next observation changed her mind.

"She's a good-looking specimen, that Season girl."

"Yes, I suppose so." Champion sighed heavily and sat back. He propped his elbows on bent knees and looked up at his father. "What's on your mind? Why all this talk about her?"

"Just thought you might want a little advice, that's all."

"Advice about what?"

Morley held out his hand to Champion and helped him spring to his feet. "I didn't like Trish, but I like this girl. She's got spunk, and she's nobody's fool. If I were you, I'd be after her like wind after a sail, I would."

"Dad, I appreciate the advice, but I'd just as soon you'd bow out and let me handle this. Besides, look who's talking. How many years have you made eyes at Belle? Have you even kissed her yet?"

Morley's mouth dropped open before he snapped his jaw shut. "Why, you rascal! I ought to belt you!" He doubled up a fist and thrust it near Champion's face. "Mrs. Lowenstein is a lady. I wouldn't think of . . . of . . ."

"Dad, Belle Lowenstein is a woman." Champion smiled as he swept his father's fist aside. "Just like Season Templar. You might not be thinking about it, but believe me, she is!"

"You upstart!" Morley's voice shook with merriment and he ducked his head for a moment. "You'd do well to mind your manners, son."

Champion chuckled and draped an arm around his father's shoulders. "Let's gather the rest of this junk and head back to the house. It's getting dark."

Morley looked at Champion, and Season strained her eyes against the gathering dusk to see his expression. Devotion was stamped on the man's face, and Season felt tears prick her eyes.

"I love you, Champ." Morley's voice was low and hoarse.

Champion smiled and hugged his father. "I love you, too, Dad."

Season swallowed a sob and stared at the grass. The sight of the two men and their deep affection for one another made her feel guilty for eavesdropping on such a tenderly private scene. She wanted to run to them and hug each one in turn. The impulse reinforced her awareness that she loved the O'Keefes. Her sessions with Morley were treasures, each one more priceless than the last. Through his stories, Season had surmised that the O'Keefe men were tragic. Both were leading exciting lives, but both had known great pain in their personal involvements. She had long ago sensed that, more than anything, Morley O'Keefe wanted his son to find a loving woman.

Had Morley decided she was that woman? Season brushed aside her tears and looked through the darkness. Morley was piling the last of the fronds onto the large mound, and Champion was stowing in the boat house the battered tires he'd replaced. He closed the boat house door and sauntered toward his father. Season cleared her throat and stepped from the security of the trees.

"Hello!"

They turned in unison. Morley lifted a hand, motioning her to join them.

"Good evening, girl! Did you finally decide to leave that room of yours?"

"Yes, I couldn't resist the lure of the island another second. It's a beautiful evening."

"That it is." Morley glanced at Champion and a sly smile raced across his weathered face. "I'll leave the rest to you, Champion. I want to wash up and rest for a while before dinner." When he passed Season, he touched her arm. "You enjoy the evening, girl."

"I will, thank you."

Season strolled toward the mound of debris. "Will you use these as a breakwater?"

"Yes." Champion kicked at the mound. "I'll carry them to the north shore tomorrow." He looked at her fully for the first time since she'd appeared, his gaze taking in her khaki shorts and yellow blouse that exposed her midriff. "I left some tools on Sand Dollar Beach. Would you like to walk over there with me to fetch them?"

"Sure, why not?" Shrugging, she fell into step with him. She tried to shake off her feeling of unease, telling herself that it was caused by the conversation she'd overheard. Was she imagining Champion's uneasiness? Glancing sideways, she noted the tense set of his jaw. Perhaps he was still thinking about his father's advice. Maybe he was still regretting the accusation he'd made on *The Touchstone* the other night.

"Now what's going on here?"

She looked at him again, saw his narrowed eyes and frowning demeanor, and followed his piercing gaze. A striped beach blanket was draped on the sand, and trash littered the area around it. A burst of laughter floated on the balmy breeze, pulling Season's attention to a couple splashing in the sea.

Before she could decipher the scene, Champion was striding toward the waterline.

"Hey! You out there! This is a *private* island!" His voice boomed across the water, stunning the bathers.

The man disengaged himself from the arms of the blond woman and faced Champion. "You don't own this sea!"

"No, I don't," Champion agreed. "But I own this!" He pointed to the sand at his feet, then swung his arm backward to indicate the towel and litter. "Is that your stuff?"

"Yeah, what of it?" The man was muscular. He threw out his chest with bravado.

"Clean this mess up, then haul your butt off my island. Can't you read?" He pointed to a conspicuous sign to his left, which proclaimed the area was private.

Season flinched, hoping he wouldn't provoke a fight. The other man's face flushed with bright color and she could see the veins in his neck stand out.

"I know who you are," the man bellowed, shaking off the woman's clinging fingers. "You're Champion O'Keefe! You don't scare me, buster! I know my rights. I can swim here if I want."

"I know my rights, too!" Champion whirled, his eyes blazing with anger. He stalked to the blanket and yanked it from the sand, then walked back to the waterline and hurled the blanket toward the couple. "There! Don't let me catch you on this island again or I'll have you arrested. You got that?"

"Why, you . . ." The man snatched the soggy blanket from the water and thrust it into the woman's arms. "I ought to take you down a notch or two!"

"Well, come on!" Champion stood his ground, his feet planted apart, his hands balled at his sides. "I'd like nothing better than to knock you into next week."

Season closed her eyes for a moment. *Oh, no! Not a fight . . . please, not that!* She opened her eyes, relieved to see the man backing away. The woman tugged at one of his arms, pleading with him to leave.

"Joey, come on, honey. Let's go back to St. Martin. Joey, baby. Please, sugar. Please! He's probably got a knife or something. He's a pirate, for crying out loud!" The woman's voice was high-pitched, scraping on Season's nerve endings.

Season's breath escaped in a long hiss when the man waved a dismissing hand at Champion.

"You ain't worth the trouble! Come on, baby." He jackknifed into the water, the woman following. They swam toward a small outboard anchored a few yards farther out to sea.

Champion waited until they'd climbed into the outboard, started the motor and raced away before he turned back to Season. His gaze swept the litter and he swore under his breath.

"Those leeches! Look at this mess."

"I'll help you clean it up." Season dropped to her knees and began picking up apple cores, paper plates and a half-eaten watermelon. "Does this happen often?"

"Too often. We have to guard the place night and day." Champion squashed a paper cup in one hand. "I don't like people using my property for a motel."

"A motel? You mean people sleep here on the beach?"

Champion gave her an engaging smile. "No, I

mean they do more than *sleep* here. What does a couple usually have in mind when they find themselves on a deserted tropical island?"

His devilish grin spoke volumes, and Season felt her cheeks flame as she averted her gaze. "Oh, I get your drift."

Champion chuckled. "What's the matter? Are you embarrassed?"

"No." Season swept up another paper plate. "We'd better get this cleaned up."

"Wait a minute. I'll go get a trash can." He rose lithely to his feet and ran toward the path that led to the pier, pausing for a moment to grab a hammer and saw he'd left earlier.

Season released a shaky breath and covered her flaming cheeks with her hands. She shook her head then smiled at herself. Good grief! Why should the merest mention of lovemaking make her so uncomfortable? Champion had her so totally aware of him that any reference to sex rattled her, reducing her to red-faced impotence. Knowing that lovers might have consummated their relationship here made this patch of beach strangely intimate. She shook off her misdirected embarrassment and piled the litter into a mound. By the time Champion returned, her composure was intact again.

"Here we go." He placed a can beside the debris. "I'll do it."

She sat on the sand and crossed her legs, letting him finish the job. A tropical breeze kicked up, blowing across her body in a delicious caress. Champion went to the water's edge and washed off his hands, then returned to her. The vision of Champion standing off that belligerent bully made her smile. That woman had called him a pirate. Had she expected him to produce a cutlass and make mincemeat out of her companion? Season closed her eyes, tipping back her head and letting the feathering breeze caress her face. There had been something thrilling about how Champion had been willing and ready to defend what was his. Would he do the same for his woman?

"Have you any idea how beautiful you are?" Champion said suddenly.

A pleased blush settled in her cheeks, and Season ducked her head. Champion stretched out on his side, his head propped on his hand.

Searching for a safer topic, Season seized on the trespassers again. "Can you really prosecute those people?"

"I don't want to talk about them. Let's talk about you."

She sighed. "Oh, Champion. Let's not and say we did."

"Season . . ." His hand reached across the space to cover her knee. "I'm a good listener. Trust me?"

She met his gaze, but it was hard to read in the dark. She looked up at a milky half-moon surrounded by a blanket of clouds. It seemed as if the moon were spotlighted, a halo of light circling it in the starless sky.

"How did he die?"

"A motorcycle accident almost a year ago," she answered before she could stop herself. Tensing slightly, she glanced at him. Motionless, he waited for her to continue. With a shrug of defeat, she added, "He was drunk and he crashed through a retaining wall and . . . into a ravine. He was killed instantly."

"Was he an alcoholic?"

"Yes, I think so." A sheet of soft rain spilled from the sky and she flinched.

"Do you want to run back to the house? The shower will be over in a few minutes."

"No." She raised her hot face to the soothing moisture. "It feels good."

He sat up, moving next to her and draping his arm across her shoulders. They faced the sea, watching whitecaps against a dark background.

"Was he injured in 'Nam?"

"Yes." She stared straight ahead. It felt as if each word were being wrenched from her. "A mortar blast. His left leg was amputated at the knee."

"It could have been much worse."

"I know, but he couldn't accept it." She drew her knees up, wrapping her arms around them. The rain pelted her back, making her blouse stick to her. "He started drinking and wouldn't stop. His parents paid for sessions with a psychiatrist, but they didn't help. He didn't want to get well, I guess."

"How long were you married?"

"Nine years."

"That long?"

She nodded. "It seemed like a lot longer."

His fingers curved around her shoulder, fitting her snugly to his side. "I think I'm getting the picture. Was he . . . well, violent?"

"Not really." Season closed her eyes tightly as the ugly scene whipped in and out of her mind. "He . . . he hit me once."

"What?" Champion straightened, craning his neck to look at her face.

"He didn't mean to." Season drew in a trembling breath. "I provoked him. We were arguing and . . . he just struck out. I really don't think he meant to hit me. Darren wasn't like that. He just punished himself." She opened her eyes to find that the rain had stopped. "After he slapped me, he left and . . . and he crashed his cycle a few hours later."

"Don't tell me you feel guilty?" Champion inched forward to see her face better. "It wasn't your fault."

"I don't . . . I . . ." She swallowed the lump in her throat. "I couldn't help him. I tried! I did try."

"Of course you did." His fingertips flicked damp curls from her forehead. "He brought a lot of nightmares home with him. I know. I brought a few home myself. But Season, you couldn't help him through those nightmares. He needed professional help."

"Did you?" She chanced a quick glance in his direction, relieved when he took her question in stride.

"No, but I wasn't wounded. Your husband had a lot more to deal with than I did." He looked toward the sea again. "It's impossible for civilians to understand what went down over there. It was ugly. Vile." He shook his head as if dislodging painful memories. "But if he didn't want your help, then you couldn't give it. You shouldn't feel guilty about that."

"It's not that . . . really." She felt his eyes on her, and she gathered a deep breath. "I was relieved when he died." Her gaze snapped to his to catch any sign of disapproval or shock. *"Relieved.* When his parents told me he was dead, I felt as if I'd been set free from some prison." Hot tears welled in her eyes, blurring Champion's face. "Don't you see? I couldn't have loved him. It was a sham! My husband was dead and I didn't shed one tear."

"Not one tear? I don't believe that."

"It's true." She stared straight into his eyes, forcing him to believe her. "His parents thought I was putting on a brave front, but I wasn't." She looked away, turning her head to stare at the line of casuarina trees permanently bent by the continual southeast trade winds.

"Look at me, Season." His fingers curled under her chin, bringing her face around to his. "Think back now. You never cried over Darren? Not even when it was apparent that he wasn't getting any better . . . when it seemed hopeless?"

"You mean when he was still alive?"

"Yes."

A frown settled on her face for a few moments. "Yes, I cried then, but—"

"Well, that's when you were crying over the death of your marriage, honey. Don't you see? You'd already mourned his loss." His hand dropped to the sand, but his gaze still held hers. "I remember when I grieved for the end of my marriage. It was long before we actually filed for divorce. After the divorce was final a few of my friends commented on how well I was taking it all." He laughed bitterly. "They didn't understand that I'd already gone through the disappointment, the failure, the pain of it all. By the time Trish filed for divorce, I was past the torture. You did the same thing. You grieved when you knew that Darren was lost to you. By the time he was physically taken from you, you were already resigned to it."

"But I was limp with relief!"

"Of course you were! You *had* been released from a sort of prison. That's a natural reaction."

"It is?" She shook her head even as she asked the question.

"Yes, it is." He framed her face with his hands, turning toward her to bring her closer. "I was relieved when I was granted a divorce from Trish. It was the end. A breaking of chains that bound me to a shallow relationship. I was given my freedom again, and I was thankful for it."

He was making sense, clearing her mind of ghosts. Suddenly she was tired and cold. She shivered and didn't resist when Champion pulled her into his arms.

The ship's bell tolled, its sound skipping on the cleansing breeze.

"Morley's ringing for us," Champion murmured, his lips brushing against her damp hair.

"Yes, we'd better go to the house."

"In a minute."

His lips were cool, but they warmed quickly against hers. He tasted of rain and sea spray, and Season licked the salt from his lips. The tip of his tongue touched hers, fired it, then drove like a searing flame inside as his mouth moved over hers. He fell back, taking her with him. His hands smoothed down the length of her, pressing her body to his. Season buried her hands into the moist sand on either side of his head, and let her passion for him spill forth in hungry, drugging kisses. She thought of that other couple . . . those trespassers who had made love on the beach where they didn't belong. But she belonged here with Champion, she thought. This patch of paradise was theirs at this moment.

"Oh, Season . . . Season, you take my breath away." Champion skimmed over her lips with his tongue, flicking at the corners. "Let go of the past. Let go for me."

"I want to." She kissed the dimples in his cheeks. "I want to so much, Champion." Unmindful of her sandy hands, she drove her fingers through his

chestnut hair, smoothing it back from his forehead.
Grains of sand caught in the damp curls. "I've never
felt like this before," she admitted. "It's scary. . . ."

"Don't be afraid. Don't. . . ." He took her mouth
again in a hot, wet kiss. His hands settled in the
small of her back, pressing her intimately to him and
making her fully aware of his desire.

The bell sounded again. Four pealing tolls floated
to them. Champion tore his mouth from hers and
smiled.

"He's a real pain sometimes."

Season laughed and rolled off him. "Yes, but he's
a lovable pain."

Suddenly the sky rumbled and released another
sheet of rain, this one wetting them to the bone in
seconds. Champion sprang to his feet, grasping
Season's hands and pulling her up. He stared into
her eyes as the rain plastered his hair into curls
against his scalp. His gaze moved slowly to her
breasts, the darker skin around her nipples showing
through her wet blouse. With infinite patience, he
untied the soaked knot of fabric just under her
breasts, and parted the material. Season groaned
with ecstasy as his mouth circled one hard peak,
tugging gently until her knees were weak. She held
onto his shoulders for support, her head tipped
back, her eyes closed against the pelting rain.

Again the bell tolled, and thunder answered it.
Lightning streaked across the black sky just as
Champion's mouth left her breast.

"We're coming!" he shouted over the next clap of
thunder.

Season laughed softly, opening her eyes to his
grim expression.

"Dammit, we're coming," he whispered for her

ears. He heaved a sigh as he knotted her blouse. "To be continued?" One winged brow lifted.

"To be continued." Season stood on tiptoe, placing a lingering kiss on his parted lips.

His arm curved around her bare waist as they turned and made their way toward the house. Inside they were spotted by Belle, who looked furious.

"Where have you been? Morley's been ringing that confounded . . ." She paused, her face screwing up into a frown. "You're both soaked to the skin!" She waved a hand toward the bedroom wing. "Best get out of those things and into hot showers. I'll hold dinner for another half hour. Go on with you!" She flapped her apron at them.

Season laughed and sprinted toward her room with Champion right behind her. She paused and looked at him before opening the door to her room.

"See you in a few minutes," he murmured as he closed his door behind him.

Champion leaned against the door for a minute, listening in wonder to the erratic thud of his heart. God! He wanted that woman!

He closed his eyes, enjoying such intense preoccupation with another individual. It had been a long time . . . a long time. A smile deepened his dimples as he pushed himself from the door and kicked off his soggy deck shoes. The soaked cutoffs and briefs followed before he strode to the bathroom. Stepping into the shower stall, he twisted on the water. Steam rose; the chill in his bones fled. Turning off the water, he grabbed a towel and roughly dried his hair with it. Wrapping it about his waist, he sauntered back into the bedroom and to his closet. He shook his head and laughed softly at himself when his hands trembled slightly.

"Grab hold of yourself," he cautioned, pulling a pair of khaki trousers from a hanger, then fetching a lightweight lavender sweater from his dresser.

The shower had erased from his body the chill, but not the wanting. Her face lingered in his mind, triggering a tingling reaction in the pit of his stomach. What a face! Had God ever created a more kissable mouth? A more beautiful pair of green eyes?

Dressing, he relived each sensation she'd stirred in him. Her body felt so delicate to his hands, her ebony hair so silky. He especially liked the way her hair framed her face, making him remember those pixies Belle had told him about when he was a child. He glanced in the mirror and scowled at his reflection. He needed a shave, but there wasn't time. Dad was probably livid by now. He hated to postpone dinner. For a man who defied timepieces, Morley O'Keefe certainly had a fixation about schedules. That comes with age, Champion thought. The older one gets, the more irritating change becomes. His dad was having difficulty accepting his advancing years. That's one reason why Champion hadn't kicked up much of a fuss when Morley had announced he was granting an interview with *Treasure Trove*. Champion had decided the interviews would keep Morley occupied and relieve the boredom of aging. It was hard for an active man like Morley O'Keefe to accept the fact that his body was wearing out.

Champion brushed his hair then splashed a cooling after shave across the darkened lower half of his face. He stared into his own eyes, seeing the spark of desire still there, but an inner voice cautioned him to go slowly.

She was vulnerable and confused. He'd gotten

through to her this evening . . . made her think about what she was doing to herself and to her life. But it would take a little time before she could accept what he'd said. He wanted to help her over the rough spots. He'd been there and he knew how excruciating it was to analyze a failed marriage.

He sank to the bed with a sigh. She'd been so beautiful out there in the rain with her hair clinging to her head and raindrops catching in the thick curtain of her lashes. Her body had been so lush and ripe straining against her wet clothing. . . .

Champion moaned softly, cursing himself for this act of self-torture. He recalled the incident at St. Martin and frowned. Why did he always say the wrong thing at the right time? When it didn't matter . . . when the woman was of no significance . . . smooth lines rose easily to his lips. But when the woman was important, when the timing was crucial, he invariably put his foot in his mouth.

Damn! He catapulted to his feet and toward the door. How in the hell was a man supposed to make his mouth work when he was consumed with desire? Women expected it. They expected lovely words, beautiful phrases, even poetry! But when he held Season Templar in his arms, when he felt her body arching into his, when her limpid green eyes roamed over his face, all he could think of was . . . I want, I want, I want.

Season sneezed once, twice, three times. She grabbed a tissue from its holder in the bathroom and dabbed at her nose. No—she couldn't have caught a cold out there!

She reached for a towel to dry herself. The hot shower hadn't helped to dispel the damp chill from her body; she was still shivering. After dusting herself with lilac-scented powder, she slipped into her underwear and white sundress. In the full-length mirror in her room, she was amazed to see that her tan had darkened, or was it just in contrast with the white dress? No, she had a deeper tan. She smiled as she plugged in her blow dryer and began fluffing her hair. The warm air felt good racing across her face, flinging her hair in all directions. Warm . . . like Champion's lips and hands. Shudders ran up her arms to her shoulders.

She switched off the blow dryer and ran her fingers through her hair, tweaking a few curls at the sides toward her cheekbones. She was dizzy-headed, and she didn't know if it was a result of Champion or the chill she'd contracted during the shower storm. She was certain of one thing. A weight had been lifted from her. The weight of her past. Champion had hoisted it when he'd talked of his own relief after his divorce and of his grief long before his marriage ended. Listening to him, she'd felt a profound alleviation.

She *had* grieved for Darren. How many nights had she cried herself to sleep? How many times had she fought the overpowering despair of knowing that her love for Darren was fading with each passing day?

Oh, Champion, Champion. You've come to mean so much to me.

Season closed her eyes for a moment as a wave of wanting washed over her. Yes, she wanted him. She wanted him to touch every inch of her. She wanted to feel him inside of her. She wanted to gather memories of him like souvenir shells from the beach. Because it couldn't last. Sea Lily wasn't her island, her life. It was his.

She looked over her shoulder at her typewriter;

her island, her life. It looked so bleak, so deserted, so lonely.

Season looked back into the mirror, placing a serene expression on her face. They were waiting for her . . . Champion and Morley. Poor Morley. Ringing that blasted bell while she and Champion tried vainly to ignore it. But sweet Morley was on her side. . . .

Her side? Season tipped her head to one side, studying her reflection. This wasn't a contest. Hmmm. Perhaps it was at that. A contest with no victors. A contest that would end—must end—in a draw.

Champion had regained his freedom. In her heart, she felt certain that he had no intention of relinquishing it again.

Chapter Seven

Season watched as Belle added finishing touches on the gypsy costume. Curiosity burned in her mind until she thought she might explode.

"Belle, please tell me what Champion's going to wear to the costume party," Season begged.

Belle set her lips in a stubborn line as her hands moved deftly along the three-tiered skirt of scarlet and black. "I told you that he wants to surprise you. My lips are sealed."

"Let me guess." Season lifted her eyes to the ceiling. "He's going as a . . . a gypsy, like me!" She looked down at Belle, who was fiddling with the skirt's hem. "That's why you insisted I wear a gypsy costume! I've guessed it, right?"

Belle shrugged. "I'm not saying, and there's no use in you pestering me. When I have a secret, the devil himself couldn't make me tell it."

"Oh, pooh!" Season sighed her defeat. Belle was as hardheaded as Champion!

Belle stood, stepping back with a discerning glance. "You look as pretty as a picture, you do. Look in that mirror behind you."

Season turned, loving the feel of the full skirt whirling around her. Her eyes widened at the transformation, and she laughed. "Is that me?"

"It is." Belle stood behind her, a proud smile on her face. "Poor Champion. One look and he'll be a goner for sure."

Rosy color pooled in Season's cheeks, but she couldn't help hoping that Belle was right. The gypsy costume certainly brought out her better points. The white, puffy-sleeved blouse had a scooped neckline, and the tight, wide, black leather belt paid close attention to her small waist. The tiered skirt fell to just below her knees, exposing her slender calves. Season made a note to wear her flat black shoes and dangling earrings to complete the outfit.

"Are you looking forward to the party?" Belle asked.

"Oh, yes." Season turned from the mirror to face the woman. "I'm in the mood for dancing and moonlight. Jake was so kind to invite me."

Belle smiled. "Oh, to be young again." She chuckled softly, and began helping Season from the skirt and blouse. "You're going to turn many a head, that's for sure."

Season returned her smile. Actually, there was just one head she was interested in turning, she thought. Champion had been so wrapped up in his business the past few days that he'd hardly spoken to her. Of course, she'd been waylaid by a slight head cold, giving her a chance to concentrate on her own work. She'd completed her interviews with Morley. All that was left was the writing, yet she found herself making excuses to continue her sessions with Morley. She loved his stories of the sea almost as much as she loved the storyteller.

"I'll make these final alterations, and the costume will be ready for its debut," Belle said, carefully folding the skirt and blouse and placing them near her sewing machine.

"Belle, I wish you'd let me pay you for your sewing," Season said as she slipped into her jeans and cotton blouse.

"No." Belle shook her head to emphasize her statement. "You bought the material from me. That's enough."

"Yes, but—"

"No, now off with you. I've got work to do. I'll have this finished by tomorrow."

"Tomorrow." Season's eyes widened. "Tomorrow's Saturday!"

"It always follows Friday," Belle said with a laugh. "You'll be sailing to St. Martin tomorrow afternoon, so you'd best take it easy and get some rest. What with you just getting over that cold, you don't need to be taking on too much."

"I'll do that. Thanks again, Belle." She started for the door.

"I'll deliver your costume after dinner, so you can pack it."

"Okay. Bye now." Season stepped from Belle's charming house into a pool of warm sunlight. She made her way toward the main house, taking a detour to the lagoon in hopes of running into Champion.

The Touchstone was in its slip, but the *Pirate's Pleasure* was gone. Where had it sailed to, Season wondered. Surely Champion hadn't left with it! Not when the costume party was tomorrow!

"Hello, Season."

She jumped slightly, then smiled at Ben Sweetsip, who was emerging from the boat house. "Hello, Ben. I was just wondering where the *Pirate's Pleasure* had gone."

"Oh, just on a little jaunt." Ben shrugged. "Nothing important."

"Did Champion go with it?"

"No, he's up at the house researching something or other."

"Researching?" Season looked toward the house as her reporter's instinct surfaced. That sounded as if Champion were immersed in another shipwreck. Which one? Where? She looked back at Ben, catching his uneasiness. He didn't want to talk about it, and she decided not to push him. "Well, I'll see you later, Ben." She waved, amused by his look of relief.

At the house, Season made her way cautiously toward Champion's office. The door was closed and no sounds came from the room. Season stood outside, debating on whether or not she should listen to her journalist's voice. She was rapping on the door before her mind registered the action.

"Yes?"

"Champion, it's Season."

"Oh, come in."

She opened the door and stepped into the airy room. Champion wasn't at his desk as she'd expected. He was sitting at a light table in the far corner of the room, hunched over a yellowed map, a magnifying glass in one hand, a compass in the other. The sight send a bolt of excitement through Season. He *was* planning some sort of scavenging operation! She clasped her hands behind her and sauntered toward him, her head tipped to one side, her gaze fixed on the aged map.

"What are you doing?"

"Working," he answered, but there was a lightness to his tone, as if he harbored a smile. "What are you up to?"

"Oh, I just had my final fitting for my costume, and I thought I'd find you and . . ." She offered up one of her most charming smiles. "What will you be going to the costume party as? A gypsy?"

He returned his attention to the magnifying glass. "You'll find out tomorrow night."

"Why the secrecy?"

He shrugged. "Just to get under your skin. It's working, isn't it?"

"Oh, you!" She abandoned the smile and studied the map. A frown creased her brow. "The Caribbean? Is that where you sent the *Pirate's Pleasure?*"

"Yes, to the Bahamas." He sighed and switched off the bright working lamp. "There's a possible salvage operation there."

She peered at the map again. "Then why do you have circles drawn off the coast of the Dominican Republic?"

He glanced at the map again, as if surprised. "I . . . oh, that." He grinned and began carefully rolling up the map. "I'm told there's very good fishing there. I thought I might cast a line next time I'm in the vicinity."

"Do you like to fish?" Somehow he didn't seem the type to sit for hours, waiting for a bobbing cork.

"No, but I love to eat." He stretched his arms over his head, lacing his fingers and yawning expansively. When he lowered his arms it was to lasso her. He smiled and pulled her toward him, his arms tightening at her waist. "I'm glad you're well again. Have you been working the past few days?"

"Yes. I . . . it's progressing." She pulled her bottom lip between her teeth. She'd almost told him that her interviews were completed, but something had stopped her. She didn't want to admit that there was no reason for her to stay on Sea Lily another day. She'd face that after the party—after the party she'd tell Morley and Champion that she would be leaving for Baltimore. "Why didn't you go with your crew to the Bahamas?"

"Because I have a date with a beautiful, green-eyed, raven-haired woman." He bent his head, his lips grazing the side of her neck.

"Champion, you should have gone. I don't like keeping you from your work." Season closed her eyes, her knees weakening under the assault of his sipping lips.

"I can join them later if anything important develops."

Telling herself that Alex would be ashamed of her for not seizing the opportunity and asking to join Champion on his next excursion, Season stiffened slightly. Champion lifted his warm lips from her neck and his hazel eyes twinkled. Season smiled, knowing that he was easily following her inner struggle.

"Have you ever been to the Bahamas?" he asked softly, one corner of his mustache twitching as he suppressed his own smile.

"No. I hear it's lovely." She fingered the collar of his white shirt.

"Very."

"Could this . . . this trip to the Bahamas turn into a major discovery?"

"There's always that possibility," he admitted.

Season wound her fingers into the curling hair at his collar. "Good luck. I hope it pans out for you."

His smile conquered him as he pressed a swift kiss to her mouth. "Where're those reporter instincts, Season?"

"I think I lost them in your arms," she said, surprised at her own boldness. For a moment she worried that such an admission might make him uneasy, but the doubt was swept aside by Champion's kiss. His mouth covered hers, lingering upon the soft fullness of her lips while his hands splayed across her back.

"I've been dreaming of you," he whispered against her mouth. "Dreaming of how I would have liked to make love to you on Sand Dollar Beach in the rain." He leaned back from her stroking hands until his gaze sought out hers. "You won't have to worry about Morley tomorrow night. When I attend parties on St. Martin I always spend the night there and sail home the next day."

"You do?" Her voice was breathy.

"I do."

"Alone?"

He grinned rakishly. "Not this time, I hope."

She smiled, admiring the way he'd skillfully side-stepped her more obvious meaning. Her smile faded as he gently pushed her from him and turned back to the light table. Switching on the light again, he heaved a regretful sigh.

"I'd love to continue this, but I do have some work to finish before we sail to St. Martin tomorrow evening." He glanced at her from the corner of his eye. "We'll set sail at six, okay?"

"Yes, that's fine." She released a shaky laugh. "I probably won't sleep a wink tonight."

"Nor will I." His eyes held a glint of raw masculinity that sent a shiver down her spine. "But I'm used to it by now. Since meeting you, I haven't been sleeping well."

An electric charge seemed to originate from him, jolting through Season's system and firing her with a white-hot longing. She took a few steps back, and was strangely relieved when he turned back to his map, unrolling it and pressing it flat against the worktable.

"Well, I'll see you later," she murmured, making her way to the door. She turned in the threshold, letting her hungry gaze take in his studied expression as he examined the map with the magnifying glass, then she closed the door behind her.

What *had* happened to her reporter instincts? she wondered. She should have pressed Champion about this new adventure in the Bahamas, but her feminine instincts had been stronger. She didn't want to spoil things now. After the party, she told herself. After the party she'd approach him about the Bahamian salvage.

Entering the living room, Season stopped in the threshold. Morley was standing in front of Lily's portrait, his back to Season. He seemed to be studying the woman's face as if seeing it for the first time, and this struck Season as odd. What had brought this on? she wondered. Why was he standing here, stock-still, staring at the woman he'd loved . . . still loved?

As if sensing her presence, Morley turned slowly, smiling when he saw her.

"Hello, girl. I was just thinking about taking down Lily's picture."

"Taking it down?" Shock registered in her voice and expression. "But why?"

"Oh, I thought I'd put it in the foyer. I might put a seascape up there instead." He nodded toward the portrait. "She wouldn't have minded."

"Yes, but . . ." Season moved into the room and sat in one of the chairs near Morley. "This is her island. Her portrait should be displayed in a prominent place."

"No, no." Morley shook his head and dropped to the couch. "It's never been her island. Sea Lily has always been my island . . . and Champion's." He stroked his white-stubbled chin. "I've been thinking lately that Champion might just be right. It's time I buried the past and all my shipwrecked dreams." His nut-brown eyes moved to glance at Lily's portrait. "Ever read that book by that Bronte woman . . . the one about a young girl falling in love with a man who had a bitter past?"

"Jane Eyre?"

"Yes, that's the one." He leaned back in the couch. "You think that sort of thing could happen in real life?"

"I imagine it happens all the time." Season smiled, easily following Morley's ambiguous conversation. He was talking about Belle. Belle, a young girl? The image didn't quite fit, but the sentiment was clear. Morley was contemplating his feelings for Belle and—

"Someday there will be a *real* mistress here," Morley said. "Then we'll place her picture there." He pointed toward the portrait. "In the meantime, I've got a nice seascape for that spot."

Season stared at the portrait, trying to imagine Belle's likeness there instead of the dreamy, exotic face of Lily. Somehow it was hard to accept.

"You think I'm wrong to move the portrait, girl?"

"What?" Season blinked, dislodging the strange

image of Belle's rather squarish face replacing the oval beauty of Lily's. "I think you should do what you think is best."

Morley grinned. "Well, I think it's time for some changes around this place. We've been stagnating here, and I'm in the mood for some alterations." His brown eyes twinkled. "Speaking of alterations, I hear from Mrs. Lowenstein that your costume for Jake's party is a real eye-popper."

Season laughed softly, then grasped the opportunity. "Have you seen Champion's costume?" Even as she spoke the question, she wondered why this secret was driving her to distraction. She chalked it up to her inborn curiosity. Her mother had told her once that the first word she had uttered as an infant was "why," and Season never doubted the farfetched anecdote.

"No, I don't know what he'll wear. He's not much for costumes. Last year he wore a business suit to the party."

"A suit?"

Morley chuckled. "Told Jake that he was costumed as a Wall Street broker."

"Oh." Disappointment made her spirits sag. Would Champion just wear a business suit, knowing she was decking herself out in a gypsy costume? Where was his sense of fun and adventure? And why keep such a mundane costume a secret?

"Sweetsip brought a letter in from Alex today."

"From Alex?" Season sat straighter, tensing at the news.

"Aye, to me." Morley waved a hand in dismissal. "Just blue-skying mostly, but he did mention that you'd have to return soon to complete your articles on me. He said your deadlines were approaching."

"Yes, they are." Season clasped her hands in her

lap, warding off the impending doom. "I have finished my interviews with you, Morley. I'm working on the second article now. I suppose . . . that is, I'll be leaving soon."

"We'll miss you."

Not half as much as I'll miss you, Season thought as a shaft of pain pierced her heart. Tears stung her eyes, and she averted her gaze from Morley's sad expression.

"I appreciate the time you've given me," she said, her voice sounding strained to her ears. "I'll always treasure my memories of you and Sea Lily."

"You'll keep in touch, won't you? There's no reason I can think of why you couldn't vacation here when you have time off from your work. The welcome mat will always be out for you, girl."

"Thank you, Morley." The threat of her departure was too much to bear, and Season stood suddenly and moved toward the archway. "I have some work to do. I'll see you at dinner."

It was an ungracious exit, she knew, but the best she could do under the circumstances. By the time she reached her room and the door was closed firmly behind her, tears were streaming down her cheeks. Season stood by the French doors, gazing out at the ocean and the part of the island she could see from her vantage point. She took the opportunity to gather her courage and resign herself to the cold facts of life. She would be leaving this paradise soon. It was time she faced that sad truth. She knew that she had faced more difficult things in her life, but for the moment, she couldn't remember confronting anything as painful. Leaving Sea Lily . . . leaving Morley . . . leaving Champion . . . Champion. Season closed her eyes, wrestling vainly with the sob that overtook her.

"What'll I do . . . what'll I do," she whispered to the island she'd grown to love almost as much as she loved its owner.

Love? The word brought her up short, opening her eyes and heart. Did she love Champion? She closed her eyes again as a sweetness invaded her.

Oh, yes. Yes . . . yes, I do.

"You can turn around now, me beauty."

Excitement lashed up her spine at hearing Champion's growling voice. Since he'd disappeared into the bathroom to change into his costume, leaving her in the cabin to slip into hers, Season had been breathless with anticipation. She only hoped he wouldn't be dressed in a business suit! Slowly Season turned to face him, and she felt her eyes widen as her hand covered her mouth for a moment. He stood in the doorway, his feet braced apart, his fists planted at his waist.

"A . . . a pirate!" Season laughed with delight. "I should have guessed that, but I didn't." She shook her head as her gaze encompassed his virile image. He was dressed as he had been in her daydream. Black knee britches, an open black leather vest, a wide belt where a cutlass swung, dark boots, a red-and-white bandana tied around his head and a sinister eye patch. A rakish grin lifted one corner of his mustache, and the one eye visible twinkled with devilry. Suddenly a subtle change overtook him, and he adopted an appraising expression. Season looked down at her own costume. "Do you think a gypsy and a pirate make a suitable couple?"

"Very suitable, me lovely. We're both free spirits, aren't we? Thumbing our noses at convention and throwing caution to the wind." As he spoke he approached her until he was standing close, so close that his breath fluttered the tendrils of hair on her forehead. "I should warn you . . . I won't take kindly to admirers at the party. I expect total loyalty."

"Jealous-natured, are you?" Season asked, a bit breathlessly.

"I have no right to be, but—"

Season placed her fingertips to his lips. "I'll make a deal with you. I'll be loyal to you tonight, if you're loyal to me."

He grasped her hand, pressing it to his cheek. "That will take no effort at all on my part. Tonight, I only have eyes for you." He grinned and touched his eye patch. "Or should I say, I only have an eye for you?"

Season tipped back her head and laughed, but her laughter died as Champion turned his head to place a soft kiss in her palm. Resisting the sweeping weakness that invaded her, Season gently pulled her hand from his.

"I—I think we should go to the party, don't you?"

His smile was knowing. "Yes, you're right. If we're going, we should make tracks now before it's too late." He stepped back, indicating that she should precede him.

On deck Season breathed in the perfume of the tropics and gazed at a latticework of stars overhead. Harbor lights twinkled, and Season smiled when she spotted the Pirate's Arms tavern. It seemed so long ago that she'd entered that establishment, filled with trepidation, and found herself face-to-face with the legendary Champion O'Keefe. He was no longer a legend to her, but a flesh-and-blood man who had captured her imagination along with her heart.

"Gypsy lady?"

She turned, smiling as she linked her arm with

Champion's. They made their way to the gangway, the sight of which sent another sweet memory to Season. She chided herself for placing such importance on the mere fact that Champion had dusted off the gangway for her use.

Champion spotted a taxi and hailed it. The driver gave them a toothy grin after they'd settled in the backseat, and Champion told him their destination.

"Seems like everybody on the island is going to that party tonight," the driver said. He was a native, and he spoke in a singsong voice. "I've taken six fares there already."

"Have you?"

"Yes sir, but you're the first pirate and gypsy, so far." His merry eyes sparkled in the dark interior. "Most folks are dressed up like royalty instead of riffraff."

Champion laughed, his gaze meeting Season's for a moment. "Riffraff suits us better, I suppose."

"You be Champion O'Keefe, yes?"

"I'm afraid so."

"Nice to meet you, sir. And you, too, pretty miss. I be called Pierre. I've seen you in the Pirate's Arms, Mr. O'Keefe. You play a mean game of darts."

Champion smiled, accepting the compliment. "Next time we're there together, I'll go a round with you."

"I'd like that," Pierre said with enthusiasm. "Darts is me favorite sport."

Within minutes they entered the Grand Case district. The Belle Princess Hotel was an oasis of light, and it was clear that something important was happening inside. Cars were jammed into the parking lot, and a stream of taxicabs crawled toward the main entrance.

"I had no idea that this was such an event,"

Season said as Pierre guided the taxi at a snail's pace toward the entrance.

"Jake invites most of the island, plus a number of business associates who live in the U. S. and Canada."

A man in a double-breasted red jacket opened the taxi door and helped Season from the vehicle.

"Welcome, miss. Go right inside, please. Good evening, sir." The man tipped his jaunty hat before turning to the next cab.

"This way, gypsy lady." Champion's hand cupped Season's elbow, guiding her toward the double doors. Colorful signs pointed the way to "Master Jake's Costume Ball," and a din of noise pulled Season like a magnet to the back of the hotel where a huge ballroom was rapidly filling with costumed guests.

A tuxedoed man held out his hand, and Champion slipped his invitation into it, then leaned forward and whispered in the man's ear. The man nodded, and lifted a microphone to his lips.

"Miss Season Templar, the gypsy lady, escorted tonight by the infamous pirate, Champion O'Keefe," he announced in dulcet tones.

A hush soothed the ballroom, smiles and waving hands greeted them, then the din overtook the room again.

Season and Champion descended the steps to the main room, melting into the crush of guests. Pierre was right, Season thought as her gaze encompassed the frilly lace and satin of Victorian gowns and Elizabethan fashions. Pompadour wigs of angel's-wing white hid contemporary hairstyles, and beauty marks donned many a pale cheek.

"Will you look at you?" Jake emerged from a cluster of guests, looking dashing in his scarlet knee britches, white stockings and blue satin waistcoat. "I can't believe you *actually* came in costume this year, Champion!"

Champion lifted a disdainful brow. "I *always* come in costume."

"Bah!" Jake laughed, then glanced at Season. "He usually dresses in a three-piece suit. I think you're having a good effect on him, Season." He gave her an appreciative smile. "You look lovely and . . . wild! Like a dark-haired, green-eyed tigress!"

Before Season could respond, Champion tapped his cutlass and adopted his growling pirate's voice.

"See this weapon, Jake?" A grin accompanied his teasing threat. "I wore it to ward off any would-be suitors of Miss Templar's."

Jake held up his hands, joining in the game. "Don't worry, Champion. I have my own tigress to defend." He turned slightly and grasped the arm of a tall Marie Antoinette. "Allow me to introduce my date for the evening. Champion, you know Leslie. Leslie Rainger, this is Season Templar, Champion's gypsy lady."

"Hello, nice to meet you." Large brown eyes met Season's before moving to Champion. "A pirate? How appropriate, Champion. It's so nice to see you in costume this year."

"Leslie, for a man who spends a good deal of his time in swim trunks, a three-piece suit *is* a costume," Champion rejoined.

"You have a point," Leslie said with a smile. "Have you located the bar yet? No?" She pointed to the right. "It's over there, and there's a long, lovely table of food, too."

"Food?" Champion captured Season's hand. "One of my favorite things. See you two later."

"Nice to meet you, Leslie." Season waved to the woman and Jake, before allowing Champion to gently pull her in the direction of the banquet table.

"Leslie is lovely," Season said as she surveyed the variety of food. "Are she and Jake serious?"

"Hard to tell," Champion answered, handing her a plate. "They've been dating, off and on, for two or three years. Oh, look! Our favorite food . . . shrimp!"

Season laughed. "Surely we can find something we like." She took small portions of prime rib, bean salad and fried papaya, then followed Champion to a vacant table.

They ate in silence, which gave Season a chance to admire the decorations and the lilting, merry music provided by a band of steel drum players. One song caught her attention, and she concentrated on it for several moments before recognizing it.

"Champion, they're playing 'Ave Maria.' Listen." She held up a hand, smiling when he smiled.

"Sounds different on steel drums, doesn't it?"

"Yes, it took me a minute to recognize it. It sounded vaguely familiar. . . ." She laughed and shook her head. "Only in the Caribbean."

"Would you like to dance?"

She nodded, pushing aside her plate. "I'd love to."

Dancing with him seemed the most natural thing in the world, Season thought as she fell easily into step. She laughed when Champion paused to reposition his cutlass, moving it around to his side so that it wouldn't bump her. The steel drums released a sultry, tropic song, and Champion's arms stole around her, pulled her close, and he rubbed his cheek against her hair. Season looked past his shoulder at the colorfully attired couples and the multihued streamers that fell from the ceiling. She thought of *The Touchstone* anchored near the Pirate's Arms tavern, waiting for her and Champion to return.

"Champion, I want a dance with you before the evening's over," a stunning brunette called as she glided past in the arms of a nobleman.

"Good evening, Mimi. Sorry, but my dance card is filled tonight," Champion answered, his arms tightening around Season.

Season looked up into his rugged face. "Champion, if you'd like to dance with—"

"I don't like," he interrupted with a grin. "What I *do* like is holding you like this."

Resting her cheek against his shoulder, Season wondered if he had any idea how he affected her. Nestled in the safe harbor of his embrace, Season surrendered to his magnetic appeal. From the minute she had laid eyes on him, she had been pulled to this moment in time. She'd dreamed of being held by him, feeling the play of his muscles beneath her hands, the soft warmth of his breath at her temple. She was oddly content just to move with him to the floating music, even though part of her yearned for the privacy of *The Touchstone*.

Melody after melody was played, and Champion never suggested that they "sit this one out." He, too, seemed perfectly happy to dance the night away. However, with each new song tension built. It was as if someone had placed a key in her back, giving it a turn now and then. Anticipation coiled inside her, winding her up to a fever pitch. Her heart fluttered, her palms perspired, and the vast room seemed to diminish before her eyes, making her feel claustrophobic.

"I've had about all of this I can stand," Champion

murmured, breaking into her microscopic world. "Let's find Jake and thank him for the evening, then make our getaway." He inched from her, his gaze seeking hers. "Unless you'd rather stay . . ."

"No." Her rapid answer was followed by a nervous laugh. "I mean, I could use some fresh air."

"Fresh air?" Champion teased. "That's not exactly what I'm craving, but . . ." He shrugged, draping his arm about her shoulders. "Whatever you say, gypsy lady."

"What *did* you have in mind?" Season asked, laughter lacing her voice.

"Oh, a little pillage here . . ." Champion dipped his head, his lips brushing the side of her neck. "A little pillage there . . ." He kissed her temple. "A few stolen kisses." His mouth whispered across hers.

"Spoken like a true pirate." She caught sight of Jake and lifted her hand to draw his attention. "There's our host."

"Jake!" Champion whirled to face him. "We were looking for you. It's been a great party and—"

"You're not leaving!" Jake fixed a scowl on his face. "It's not even midnight yet!"

"Yes, but we—"

"I insist on having just one dance with Season," Jake interrupted, easing himself between Champion and Season. "Then you can be on your merry way. Season?"

Without waiting for an answer, Jake slipped an arm around Season's waist, and she found herself being firmly escorted toward the dancers again. She glanced over her shoulder to catch Champion's frowning demeanor before Jake drew her into his arms.

"Champion's never been one to share," Jake said with a smile. "He has a strong possessive streak."

"He's only kidding."

"I wonder. . . ." A secretive smile raced across Jake's face. "He isn't quite himself tonight. First he shows up in costume—breaking with his own tradition—and then he monopolizes your time as if he's scared another man might turn your head. The last time he acted like this was with . . ." His voice died and a look of discomfort flitted in his eyes.

"Trish," Season finished for him.

"Yes, but he didn't know his own mind then."

An uneasiness settled in her, and Season searched for a different topic. She didn't want to rehash the past. Not tonight. Tonight was too special. "Where's Leslie?"

"She's consoling Champion." Jake's gaze wandered over Season's shoulder. "Women!" He shook his head and a laugh tumbled from him. "The sight of you and Champion lost to everyone except each other made her envious and she's been cool toward me all evening."

"Champion said that you two have dated for some time."

"Yes. Maybe for too long."

"Do you love her?"

He seemed surprised at her question, his eyes widening slightly. "Love her?" An ironic smile curved his mouth. "No, gypsy lady. We can't all be as lucky as you and Champion."

"Me and Champion?" Season stiffened, stepping back from Jake's loose embrace. Why did Jake include Champion in that statement? She loved Champion, it was true, but she had resigned herself to a limited emotion from him.

"Don't look so surprised!" Jake laughed in the face of her confusion. "You are two of the fortunate ones, so be grateful."

Flustered, Season disengaged herself from Jake. "Thanks for the dance, Jake, and for the party. It was lovely." A sigh of relief escaped her when she saw Champion bearing down on them. She linked her arm in Champion's and offered up a smile. "Jake's had his dance, and I'm ready for that fresh air."

"Are you two leaving so soon?" Leslie asked, taking her place beside Jake.

"Yes." Champion extended his hand toward Jake. "Thanks for the invitation. I'll be in touch soon about . . . that business venture."

Jake winked. "Right. Good night, all."

"Did Jake put his foot in his mouth? You look a little upset," Champion said as he maneuvered himself and Season toward the exit.

"No, of course not." Season shook off her momentary uneasiness. No doubt it had been easy for Jake to read the devotion on her face, but he had been imagining things if he had thought he'd seen the same emotion on Champion's. Wasn't that right? Season glanced sideways at Champion as they made their way across the expanse of coffee-colored carpet toward the hotel entrance.

Watch out! her inner voice warned. It was one thing to fantasize, and quite another to believe those fantasies. She should know that. Hadn't she imagined how wonderful life would be when Darren was well and himself again? Hadn't she dreamed of children, anniversaries, family picnics? And those imaginings had only added to her pain when reality had finally stepped onstage. Believing in make-believe was for children. No doubt Champion liked her—was even fond of her—but he was a man firmly rooted in the real world. While others engaged in fantasy about him, he scoffed at such foolishness. He knew who he was and what he wanted. "Free spirits . . . thumbing our noses at convention." His remembered description floated into her mind, unwanted. Convention. That was love, marriage, children. That wasn't what Champion O'Keefe wanted.

Emerging from the hotel, she felt sheets of rain splash her face, supplying an additional, cold reminder of reality. The cooling tropical breeze earlier this evening had been only a calling card for an angry squall.

Champion bundled her into a waiting taxi, then shook raindrops from his hair. "What's the word on this storm?" he asked the cabbie.

"Blew up quick, sir," the cabbie answered as he steered the vehicle away from the hotel. "The weather reports say it's nothing serious. It should be over by morning. They've issued small-craft warnings, though."

"Looks like we're stuck here until morning," Champion said, his voice lowering as he leaned closer to Season.

"Were you planning to sail somewhere this evening?" Season asked, joining his teasing repartee.

He laughed and pulled off his eye patch. "No. I just thought that you might decide to sail for Sea Lily tonight, instead of in the morning."

"Well, Mother Nature seems to have taken care of that possibility."

"Yes, she's a good old soul, isn't she?"

Season inched closer, nestling against his side and turning her cheek into his damp shoulder. Darkness whipped past the windows, and fat raindrops splattered against the glass. She took the eye patch from Champion's fingers and smiled.

"I think I'll keep this as a souvenir."

"A souvenir of what?"

"Of you."

"That has an air of finality about it."

She closed her eyes, lapsing into a melancholy silence.

Lightning zigzagged across the sky, casting white light into *The Touchstone*'s cabin. Season moved her shoulders, feeling her blouse stick damply to her skin. She sensed Champion standing behind her and a shiver raced up her spine. His hands closed around her shoulders.

"I hope you haven't caught another cold."

"Me, too." The ship rocked slightly, and Season reached out to grasp the back of a chair to steady herself.

"If you'd like, we can go to a hotel. It's kind of bumpy in here. You might get seasick."

"No." She took a deep breath, trying to erase the quivering huskiness in her voice. "A hotel room would seem so cold and impersonal. I feel right at home here. I won't get seasick."

His hands slid down her arms. "You need to get out of these wet things." He pushed the hair at the nape of her neck to one side and kissed her there. "Relax. Go into the bathroom and undress. You'll find a toweling robe in there. I'll make some hot cocoa."

"Hot cocoa?" Season turned her head to capture his hazeled gaze. "What happened to the direct approach? You're sounding like your father all of a sudden."

"I know you're having second thoughts about this." He sighed, shrugging his shoulders. "I know you're nervous and—"

"And did you know that I want you as much as

you want me? I've spent too many nights holding a cup of hot cocoa. Tonight I want to hold you."

He smiled before his lips touched hers. "I could take a few lessons from you on the direct approach."

"Maybe I shouldn't have—"

"Nonsense," he drawled with a touch of impatience. He wrapped his arms around her, pulling her back against him.

Season lifted an arm, her fingers sliding into his thick hair, while her body responded to the press of his. Beneath her the deck shifted, but Champion's arms held her fast. Lightning flashed again, throwing the room into momentary brightness. In that moment, Season opened her eyes to see the hunger in Champion's.

"I'm glad it's raining," he whispered. "It reminds me of that day on the beach. You don't still feel guilty about Darren, do you?"

Season shut her eyes to the explosion of images his question spawned, and she shook her head. "Please, let's not talk about that now. Not now."

"Whatever you say, gypsy lady." His hands moved down her waist, gliding along her stomach to her thighs.

Season tipped back her head, her eyes still closed. Champion's hands roamed freely over her, moving up to cup her breasts. His thumbs gently stroked her nipples, setting off another violent tremble in her. Heat spread from her stomach to her extremities. She reached backward, her hands finding the rock hardness of the back of Champion's thighs.

"I want you to be pleased," she murmured, almost to herself. "I want you to remember this for the rest of your life."

"I will, I will," he vowed with a savage fierceness.

"I can't recall ever wanting a woman as much as I want you, Season Templar." His voice broke along with his patience, and he spun her to face him. His mouth swooped to hers in a bruising, stirring kiss.

Wind whipped around the ship, moaning as Season moaned, sighing as Season sighed. The sea boiled around *The Touchstone*, but its fury was nothing compared to the tidal wave of emotion within Season as she strained to melt into Champion. He rained kisses on her face, neck and shoulders, as he removed one garment after the other until she stood naked before him. She pressed lingering kisses on his chest, her lips tingling from the feel of the crisp hair. She pushed the vest from his body. Her fingers closed upon the cutlass and she withdrew it slowly from its sheath.

"I don't think we'll need this anymore," she said with a smile as she dropped it to the floor.

"Or this," he whispered, whipping the bandana from his forehead. "Or these." He unbuckled the black belt, unzipped the knee britches, and within seconds, he, too, was nude. "So much for make-believe." He smiled, drawing her back into the circle of his arms again. "We don't need fantasy anymore."

"No, we don't," she agreed, lifting her face for another searing kiss.

He stepped forward, making her step backward, then leaned into her so that she fell back onto the double bed. Season stroked his smoothly muscled back, then discovered the taut muscles in his upper arms. He was a big, lean animal, moving on top of her, burying his face in her hair, tenderly massaging her full breasts. Instinct overtook her, and she arched her body into his and slid her feet along his hair-roughened legs. Vague memories told her that this would soon be over, and her caresses quickened. It never lasted long enough. She was always left near tears, unfulfilled. But if Champion enjoyed it, she'd be happy.

"Easy, love. We have the entire night. There's no rush."

She stared into his face, not believing his soothing words. He pushed the hair back from her face, then traced her cheekbones with nuzzling lips, his mustache adding a tingling contrast to the velvet texture of his mouth. He was true to his word, his movements becoming lethargic. Drugged kisses were placed from her shoulders to her jutting hipbones, down her legs, to the inside of her thighs. Season trembled, her fingers finding his head, stroking through the wavy mane.

When his mouth moved sideways, Season tensed, then quickly lost herself in eddying emotion, writhing with supreme pleasure.

"Champion . . . Champion . . ." Her voice was hoarse, pulsating along with her inner flame.

Unbidden, scenes of another bedroom, another time, rose up in her mind. It had never been like this then. Darren hadn't indulged in such intimacy. His lovemaking had been rapid, frenzied, disappointing. But Champion was sipping her slowly, like a rare wine. His hands roved along her waist and stomach, savoring every touch, every taste and every response. Like the experienced treasure hunter he was, he located long-forgotten pleasure points and a bounty of trembling desire.

Lightly pushing at his shoulders, Season eased him to his back so that her mouth could chart a sensuous journey down the length of him. Her questing fingers lingered on his taut stomach as she gloried in the feel of his tapering waist, tightly muscled hips and long, tanned legs. A flash of lightning lit the room, and Season drank in the sight of him. As the room was thrown into semidarkness again, she saw the sparkle of his teeth before he framed her head in his hands and brought her up to his hot mouth.

"You're beautiful," he murmured between kisses. "I want you so much." His tongue plundered her mouth, rubbing against hers and robbing her senses.

Legs entangled, they rolled together until Champion's weight pressed her into the mattress. Gently, he came to her, filling her slowly until she was panting for breath, her eyes wide with wonder. He set a lazy tempo, allowing her to experience and digest each delicious moment. She stroked his shoulders then dug her fingers into his supple skin when the rhythm quickened along with her pulses. Her ears began to ring as if she were submerged in a drowning sea. Rain pounded against the porthole overhead, adding a driving, frenzied music. Passion gripped her and she cried out Champion's name several times while wave after wave of mindless pleasure rolled over her.

His gruff voice filled her ears, but his words were disjointed and garbled. She was lost to everything except her own zenith of passion. She heard her name, whispered in a strained, yearning way, and then he was motionless for a heart-stopping moment. Her lashes fluttered up, nature's light illuminated his face and he trembled violently. She stared at that face above her, watching the play of emotions race across it, and it gave her infinite pleasure to experience his fulfillment.

Breathless, he relaxed, burying his face in the side of her neck. His breathing was rapid and warm against her skin. Silence enveloped the cabin, and

Season looked up to find that the rain had stopped. Wet streaks webbed the porthole glass. Season listened for the moan of the wind, but heard only the weak whisper of a breeze. It was over.

A small smile curved her mouth as she settled deeper into the mattress and wrapped her arms around her lover. To think that she had deprived herself of this for so long! She'd thought she knew about lovemaking, but she'd only known its shadow. With Darren there had been no sweeping passion, no tender moments, no earthshaking peak. He had been satisfied, but she had been left with a lonely craving for something more than swift kisses and rough caresses. She'd had nothing to compare it with until now . . . and there was no comparison. A sadness crept through her like a breeze after a spring shower.

Oh, Darren, we never knew this, did we? We always came short of this kind of rapture. I made love to you, but you never took the time to make love to me.

Champion stirred lazily, lifting his head and dropping tiny kisses across her eyelids and cheek.

"I hope you're not thinking about sleeping," he murmured close to her ear.

She smiled. "Is there something wrong with that? Now's the time to bathe in the glow of it all and remember."

"Yes, but not now. I have a few more things to tell you."

She opened her eyes. "You want to talk?"

He grinned and kissed the tip of her nose. "Not with words. We'll use words later."

His hand moved warmly along her stomach, then lower. Season moaned softly, arching instinctively toward the pleasure he offered—like a flower craving another rain shower. Within moments she was caught up in the foaming sea again. Drowning . . . drowning in the loving expertise of Champion O'Keefe. He shattered the calm after the storm, and told her many, many wondrous things.

Chapter Eight

The squall had left the sky a mottled gray. Season turned her face into the cleansing breeze, loving the way it combed through her hair. Sea Lily would soon loom on the horizon, a calm port after a storm of emotions that had left her feeling limp but satisfied. She turned sideways to where Champion was adjusting the sails. He cut a fine figure against the sky's dove-gray backdrop. His hair was damp from the sea's spray and more curly than usual. White duck trousers and a red-and-white-striped pullover made him dazzling in contrast with the gloomy weather.

Season looked back to the horizon. The sun was trying vainly to pierce through the overcast sky. Suddenly, Sea Lily sprang onto the horizon; a hazy green oasis in a white-capped desert.

"Thar she blows," Champion called over the roar of the sea. "Home port!" He pointed toward the minuscule patch of land.

She smiled, wishing it were truly her home. How lucky Champion was to lay claim to such a paradise. She started to tell him that, but decided against it. The bellying sails were making such a racket, she knew she'd have trouble outshouting them. Instead, she settled once more in her remembrances of last night and this morning when she'd discovered a wealth of pleasures in a pirate's arms. She smiled, recalling the historical novels she'd read about women kidnapped by pirates. Those stories always made her heart beat faster, but they couldn't hold a candle to reality. However, along with her treasured memories came an uneasiness she knew was natural. She and Champion had left calm waters and sailed into uncharted territory last night. It was a normal reaction to feel uneasy, unfocused . . . and yes, a little frightened.

If only she could burrow into his mind and know his thoughts! Was he pleased with the turn of events or experiencing a few misgivings?

She glanced at him, tensing when she saw that he was looking at her, his eyes holding the frankness of a lover.

"What are you thinking about?" he asked, his voice booming above the ship's noise.

She shrugged. "Three guesses."

He smiled, his eyes reading her lips. "I was thinking about dancing with you." He cleared his throat. "I remember thinking that you had the most beautiful eyes I'd ever seen, and that I'd like to see a lot more of them."

She averted her gaze from his, snapping her face away from those all too observant eyes. Darren had said something very similar to that . . . long ago. She closed her eyes as a searing pain constricted her heart. Those apparitions she'd thought she'd exorcized floated into her mind, making her wince. Go away! her mind screamed. Can't you leave me alone?

Sensing their approach to the island and Champion's hurried movements near her, she was thankful that he was kept busy with trimming the sails. She congratulated herself for effectively burying the loose ends of her past for the last few days. Yes, she'd managed to forget Darren and his similarities to Champion. They were both men who had been gravely disappointed. They both were looking for a source of strength; a calm port in a cruel sea. Darren had looked to her and had been refused. Was Champion steering in her direction now? Did he think she could ease his bitterness and make right the wrongs done to him?

Well, she couldn't.

Season opened her eyes as salty, stinging spray slapped her face. She just couldn't fight someone else's ghosts when she couldn't deal with her own. It wouldn't be fair to Champion or to her.

Some things are better left just as they are, she told herself. She had known a few hours of mindless bliss, and for that she'd always be thankful, but any further venture into these dangerous waters would be pure folly. It was time that she sailed back to her own port of call, and left Champion to his.

Besides, they were star-crossed lovers. Champion needed freedom, and she needed security. Eventually, this point of contention would sever their tenuous hold on one another. It was best that they part friends. Friends? A sad smile raced across her lips. Could they just be friends now? No. That had never been in the stars for them.

The Touchstone slipped into the lagoon, and Season straightened from her perch on the padded bench. She raised her arms above her head and stretched as her eyes took in the beauty around her. The island and everything it represented would always be a salve to her. When she was weary with the world, she would uncap her memories of the place and let them work their magic.

She started for the railing, but Champion's hand circled her upper arm. Season looked up into his face and tensed when she saw his determined expression.

"What happened to you back there? What did I say?"

"Nothing," she said on a laugh, twisting her arm in a vain effort to disengage herself.

"Don't give me that! You got that look on your face . . . the one that tells me I've struck a nerve. You're not still whipping yourself over Darren, are you?"

"And why shouldn't I?" She jerked free. "He was my husband. Don't you ever think of Trish?"

"I think about her, but I don't dwell on her. That's over. Finished."

"It must be convenient to think of your marriage in such cut-and-dried terms, but I can't do that." Season walked to the rail, holding tight to it while her insides churned. It was all unraveling. She could see Darren's face floating behind her eyes, reminding her of how quickly something beautiful could transform into something ugly. She had to get away from Champion and his island. She had to get away before her desperation, her despair, spilled forth in harsh words and misdirected feelings.

"Maybe this isn't the time to talk." Champion stood behind her. "We're both . . . well, a little unbalanced by all that's happened. I just want you to know that what *did* happen was wonderful and special."

"Yes, I'll always remember you."

"There you go getting all fatalistic again." His sigh was full of frustration. "Why are you talking in the past tense? This is happening *now.*"

Hugging close to the railing, she turned to face him. "I'll be leaving in the next day or so. I've finished the interviews and I need to get back to Baltimore."

He stared at her, his eyes narrowing slightly. "Just like that?"

"I . . . I don't know what you mean."

"Like hell you don't!"

She drew back from his angry tone. "Champion, where could we go from here? Be sensible. I came here on business, and while I . . . I enjoyed what happened between us, it's a dead-end situation. Your life is here, and mine is in Baltimore."

His eyes became glassy and cold. "Now who's being cut-and-dried?" He glanced up at the dark sky, then back into her eyes. "I wish I knew what was going on in that head of yours. What scenarios are you cooking up?" He rubbed the back of his neck in a distracted gesture. "God, if I live to be one hundred, I'll never understand women." He grasped her hands for a moment before his hands slid up her arms to her shoulders. His gaze followed their path, and an expression of regret covered his face. "Do you think I take a woman to Jake's party every year and make love to her afterward? Well, I don't."

Season swallowed the wedge of emotion in her throat. It was incredibly painful to watch his confusion. But it was impossible to make him understand her need for escape. She couldn't tell him that she loved him . . . worshiped him . . . and that she couldn't remain here without the security of convention. The very convention that he shunned. And she still had reservations about her ability to withstand treacherous emotional weather. Even now she was more than ready to turn tail and run back to Baltimore instead of facing the problems she knew lay ahead of them.

"Are you through?" she asked when he didn't take his hands from her.

"No." His eyes bored through her. "But, it looks as if you are." A mirthless smile touched his mouth. "Suddenly I feel like a fool."

"No, don't . . ." She raised a hand, her fingers gently touching his jaw.

Champion jerked his head back, his hands dropping from her. "Go on to the house. I have to tie things up here." When she didn't move, his brows met in an angry scowl. "Go on!"

His biting tone galvanized her into action, and Season quickly moved to the gangway. She glanced over her shoulder, saw his glowering expression and hurried down the ramp and toward the path and its concealing trees.

Champion stared after her until shadows engulfed her, then he closed his eyes. A few drops of rain splattered his face, but he stood stock-still while his rage spent itself. Confusion followed in its wake as the heavens opened to allow sheets of rain to wet him to the bone. Oblivious of the chilling rain, he jumped from the ship and secured her to the pier. When he was finished, he boarded again and ducked into the cabin. The sight of the bed sent renewed anguish through him and he cursed under his breath as he eased himself into a chair.

What was with her? Did she have a split person-ality? What had happened to that warm, loving woman he'd awakened with this morning? Now she was spouting gibberish about dead ends and her work in Baltimore. Absently he plucked at his wet shirt, then pulled it over his head. He tossed it onto the floor and stared at the wet puddle of material, but he wasn't seeing it. He was seeing *her*.

His fingertips tingled as he recalled her satiny soft skin. My God! She was beautiful! A wild, wanting thing in his arms, straining to get closer to him, to slide her dewy skin against his. There had been heaven in her touch, magic in her kiss, forever in her eyes. Where had all that gone?

"Don't do this to me, Season." He closed his eyes, resting his aching head in his hands.

Damn her for making him doubt her feelings! Didn't she know . . . didn't she understand he couldn't handle this kind of uncertainty? He'd sworn to himself that he wouldn't be taken for a ride again by a beautiful woman. He'd been certain that Sea-son was incapable of such trickery, but now he was riddled with doubt.

And she was leaving.

He rebelled at that thought, his head coming up, his eyes focusing on that bed again. Maybe it would be easier to let her go . . . go back to her beloved Baltimore, but he couldn't let her do that! Not now! Not when he'd be haunted by her for years to come, perhaps forever. It had been so long since he'd felt true *passion* for something or someone. He couldn't let that slip through his fingers. At the very least, he deserved to know how she felt about him. It was difficult to believe that she took all of this casually. She just wasn't that type of woman. Of course, he'd never been an expert on women. Trish had fooled him. Season could do the same.

No, no, no! He straightened, glaring at the bed as if it were the cause of his pain. He wasn't the shell-shocked veteran he'd been when Trish had entered his life. He knew what he wanted now. He wanted Season. Again, and again, and again. Down deep, he knew he'd never get his fill of her. He'd be forever thirsting for her special kind of loving.

Was this how his father had felt about Lily? Champion shook his head sadly. No wonder his father had experienced such grief, such desperation. All these years, he'd thought Morley O'Keefe was a sentimental fool for pining for a woman who had deserted him, but now he understood his father's anguish. Morley's anguish was now his own.

The squeak of rubber-soled shoes overhead tore Champion from his inner turmoil. Morley bounded down the three steps and into the cabin, his hair plastered to his head, his shirt and slacks wet from the rain. He wiped a hand over his face and threw Champion a quizzical look.

"What's going on? I thought you might be having trouble tying her down."

"No. No trouble." Champion leaned back in the chair, feeling tired and empty.

"So what are you doing down here? Afraid the rain might melt you?"

"I was just thinking. I needed to be alone for a while."

Morley crossed to the bed and sat on it. For an instant something recoiled in Champion, as if Morley had draped himself on a sacred shrine. He smiled at himself. He was a fool. A lovesick fool. A flash of anger seared him. He'd never forgive her for reducing him to such a sorry state!

"She's leaving, she says."

One corner of Champion's mouth twitched at Morley's subtle accusation. No need to name *her*. The old man had uncannily jumped to the correct conclusion. Morley shifted irritably, and Champion wished he could explain what had happened, but he was as much in the dark as his father.

"Are you going to talk or just sit there with that woebegone look on your ugly face?"

Champion lifted one shoulder in a quick, half-hearted shrug. "There's nothing to say. I don't know what's got into her."

"*You've* gotten into her, you stupid sea turtle!" Morley pointed a gnarled finger at him.

"Dad, I'm not going to discuss—"

"I'm not asking you to discuss . . . personal things. I'm just trying to pound something into that thick skull of yours. She's a woman, and she's confused. They get that way after . . . after sharing such things with a man. They start awonderin' what happens next, and they get all out to sea over it. She's given you something special, and now she's waiting for you to return the gift."

"I did, damn it!" Champion struggled to regain his composure, knowing Morley wasn't the one he wanted to yell at. "She wasn't there alone last night. I was there, too!"

Morley chuckled, running a hand through his wet mane of hair. "You got a lot to learn, son. *A lot to learn.*" He screwed up one eye, looking for all the world like a wily fox. "You accuse me of dragging my feet where Mrs. Lowenstein is concerned. Well, at least *I* know something about the heart of a woman."

"The heart of a woman?" Champion looked into his father's eyes, hope springing in him. "Tell me."

Morley grinned, pushing himself from the bed. "Okay. Over a couple of brews, I think." He opened the portable refrigerator and withdrew a couple of cans. He popped them open and handed one to Champion, before settling himself on the bed again. Raising his can, he gave a wink. "To women. God love them all!"

Champion honored the toast with relish, drawing deeply at the can. The beer was cold and hard. He ran a hand over his mustache, then leaned forward, his elbows propped on his knees.

"The heart of a woman," Morley began, his voice raspy as it always was when he launched into a long tale. "Aye, it's a puzzle, and one solved only by the right man. I'm not saying all women are alike," he added quickly. "Oh, no! There's always a few that throw you curves. But for the most part they're all the same, especially when they get all tangled up with men." He lifted his can, as if toasting an absent party. "That girl, she's just sailing in circles. She needs you to show her the way. I'm sure you think you're as easy to read as an open book, but you're not, son. She doesn't know you well enough yet to guess at your real feelings."

"I told her," Champion interrupted. "I told her she was special."

"Special?" Morley scoffed at this. "That's the kind of word a man uses when he's hedging."

"Dad, I can't tell her that I love her." Champion stared at the can in his hands.

"Why not?"

Champion rolled his shoulders as his muscles tightened there. "I don't know my own mind yet. Things have happened so fast and . . . well, I jumped into one marriage. I don't want to make that same mistake. I must be sure this time."

"Now examine her point of view," Morley said encouragingly. "One thing a woman hates is to take a man seriously, and not be taken seriously herself. That's what she's running from, Champ. She's afraid. You know, she was married before, too, and I don't think it was a satisfying union."

"No, it wasn't. It was ugly, and she was an innocent, but she feels guilty about the whole thing."

"I was afraid of that." Morley took another swig of the beer. "Looks like you two might be in the same boat. You're not going to let her go, are you?"

"I don't seem to have a choice." The beer tasted flat now, and Champion set it aside with a frown. "She says she has work to do. She's finished here."

"Well, if she wants to use her work as an excuse, let her!" He stood, tossing the empty can into a trash receptacle. "I'm going back to the house, and you'd best shake a leg, too. Mrs. Lowenstein's expecting you for the midday meal."

"How are you and Mrs. Lowenstein progressing? Still sharing moonlight strolls?"

Morley frowned good-naturedly. "This might come as a surprise to you, son, but me and Mrs. Lowenstein are quite happy with our . . . arrangement." He chuckled when Champion scoffed. "I know you find that hard to understand, but it's true. We've both had our chance at the great loves of our lives, and we're not looking for that any longer. We've found what we're looking for— companionship." His brown eyes took on a distant gleam. "There's all kinds of love, Champ. There's the kind that rolls over you like crashing waves, and the kind that ripples through you like a gentle stream. I couldn't hold up to those waves at my age. I'm content with what Mrs. Lowenstein offers. Aye, she's a great lady." His eyes snapped to attention. "And she has a temper. Don't summon it by being late for her meal."

Champion smiled, touched by his father's description of this gentle kind of loving. It sounded so simple and uncomplicated.

"I'll be along in a minute." The gloom was already settling around him again, and the growl of the thunder seemed to emanate from him.

Morley bounded up the steps, his shoes squeaking against the deck above. Champion rose slowly from the chair and went to the bed. He straightened the spread, his fingers trembling as he recalled a delicious slice of the night before. She'd made him feel whole again. Like a man ought to feel, but rarely did. How could she think about her work. . . .

"Her work?" He stood erect as if shot by an invisible arrow; a shaft of light piercing through the gloom. A smile broke on his face, sparkling in his eyes as he snapped his fingers. "Her work!"

He whirled and headed for the upper deck, a renewed bounce in his step. Outside it was dismal gray, but inside he felt a warming glow.

If there had been any graceful way to excuse herself from this gathering on the veranda, Season would have grasped it, but Morley had insisted that she join him and Champion for spice tea and rum cake. Lunch had been enough of an ordeal, and she didn't care to endure the siesta. Especially since Champion was in such a jolly good mood.

She had thought she'd hurt him this morning, though she hadn't intended to, but he seemed to have made a remarkable recovery, dashing her feeble hopes that he would beg her to stay. It was a bitter pill to swallow, but one for which she was grateful. She finally knew that Champion's feelings for her didn't run as deeply as her feelings for him. She'd agonized about her ineffectiveness when he'd asked her to explain her sudden desire to leave Sea Lily. She'd wanted to reveal her innermost feelings to him, but something had held her back. Thank goodness! He would have reacted just the way she'd feared if she'd told him that she was desperately in love with him and that she wanted nothing short of a total commitment. Convention. Well, he was free of that threat. She could leave him to his precious island!

Season resisted Belle's tempting sponge cake, but accepted the cup of hot tea. It was unusually chilly weather, what with the overcast sky and the promise of more rain in the wind. She stared into the cinnamon-colored brew as if it were a crystal ball and saw a scene from last night when the pirate had made love to the gypsy. She lifted the cup to her lips, quickly swallowing the memory.

Chancing a look at Champion, she frowned. Why did he have to look so luscious in those tan slacks and chocolate-brown shirt? Was she doomed to remember how happy he seemed following her announcement that she would be leaving within a day or two? How was that going to give her solace on lonely nights? Anger burned within her and she finished her tea, setting the cup in the saucer with a distinct clatter.

"Oh, I forgot to tell you!" Morley came to life, levering himself to a sitting position in the swaying hammock. "The *Pirate's Pleasure* crew sent a message while you were gone. They said that all is well. Is that good news, Champ?"

"Yes, it's good news. Very good news." Champion smiled and leaned back against the waist-high wall that enclosed the veranda.

Good news. Very good news, Season's mind mocked. How nice that everything was falling so neatly into place for him while she writhed in misery!

"What does it mean?" Morley asked, swinging to and fro in the hammock like some wizened child.

"It means adventure, Dad!" Champion's eyes sparkled. "It means that I'll be leaving in the next day or so for the Dominican Republic."

"A sunken ship?"

"Yes, Dad." Champion clapped his hands, then rubbed them together with relish.

Season felt as if a gold nugget were being held in front of her nose, but she resisted its lure. Let him sail to the Dominican Republic. She didn't care. The Dominican Republic?

"I thought the *Pirate's Pleasure* was off the Bahamas." As soon as she spoke the words, she cursed herself for giving in to her budding curiosity.

"It is," Champion agreed. "But the sunken ship is off the coast of Santo Domingo."

Season shook her head. "I don't understand. . . ." She looked at Morley, who was chuckling softly.

"He's playing tricks, he is," Morley explained with a grin. "He's throwing up a smoke screen."

"Right." Champion crossed his arms on his chest. "By the time the squatters figure out that they're on a fool's errand in the Bahamas, I'll have staked my claim a few miles off the coast of Santo Domingo. A couple of my crewmen are at the Santo Domingo wreck right now waiting for me to join them. Once I'm certain we're on to something, I'll send for the

Pirate's Pleasure." A burst of laughter bounded from him.

"Which wreck is it, Champion?" Morley asked.

"The *Marina del Rey*."

"I thought that was a posh community in southern California," Season said, a slur in her tone.

"It is," Champion agreed. "But it's also a sunken ship. It means King's Navy, me beauty."

"Don't call me that!" She didn't know who was more surprised by her outburst, Champion or herself. Champion slowly uncrossed his arms, shoved his hands into his pockets and stared her down.

"As I was saying," he continued. "There's no way to know at this point what the *Marina* might have been carrying. Her manifest listed only passengers and personal cargo, but she was heavily armed. She carried three cannons, which leads me to suspect she was hiding something."

"She wanted to discourage pirates, maybe?" Morley asked, his eyes growing more feverish with each passing second.

"That's what I'm hoping, Dad." Champion shrugged. "There's no telling what we might find down there. A king's ransom? Fool's gold?" He laughed again. "There's nothing like taking a chance to warm a man's blood."

"Aye, and to set the pulses to pounding," Morley added.

Something special passed between them; something Season could only guess at, since it was man to man. It was that sort of thing shared by a father and son, but she didn't feel left out. No, she felt a part of it all, and that made it all the more painful. If only she were truly one of the O'Keefes!

"Do you think you could postpone your return to Baltimore, Season?"

Season tensed, eyeing Champion with suspicion. She cautioned herself not to cry for the moon when she knew she couldn't have it. "There's no need for that."

"Oh, no?" He glanced at Morley, then back to her. "What about a once-in-a-lifetime adventure? A trip to the Dominican Republic, all expenses paid, and an exclusive story to boot? What would you say to that offer?"

What *could* she say? He was swinging that gold nugget in front of her nose, daring her to refuse it and knowing she couldn't. Oh, Alex would jump for joy. This was what he had dreamed of, wasn't it? Champion O'Keefe's cooperation? No, he hadn't dared to dream this dream. Even Alex hadn't believed for a moment that Champion would offer to take her along on a treasure hunt. This was a reporter's fantasy and an editor's utopia.

"Well, what do you say, girl?" Morley demanded. He stuck a pipe into his mouth and patted his pockets for his lighter. "Don't keep the man waiting!"

Season met Champion's gaze squarely, and cast aside her pride and all those vows she'd made to herself only hours ago. "Of course I'll go. I'd be a fool to refuse."

"A fool?" Something flickered in Champion's eyes; something Season didn't like. "Well, we can't have that. Take it from me, playing the fool isn't fun."

Ah, now we have it, Season thought. Sweet revenge. That was his game. Revenge had been in his eyes. She had botched her explanation of her conflicting emotions. She had been totally ineffective in making him understand that she was too unsteady to face the future. She had misled him, and now he was bound and determined to make her pay. Her shoulders slumped with the weight of it all. Feeling his gaze on her, she squared her shoulders again and forced herself to meet it.

"When will we be leaving?"

"Tomorrow. Is that too soon?"

"No, that's fine." She rose from the glider and set her tea service on the table beside it. "If you'll excuse me, I'll go pack now."

"You'll need rugged clothing and some swimsuits," Champion said when she started for the door.

"And you'd best take along some lotion, girl," Morley added. "That delicate skin of yours might burn. It gets as hot as blazes out at sea."

"Yes, I'll do that."

"Would you like me to send Alex a message by radio and tell him you'll be sailing with Champion?"

"Could you do that, Morley?"

"Sure."

Season glanced at Champion, finding it difficult to look at him for more than a second. "How long will this take?"

"It's hard to say," he answered. "But you can leave whenever you like. I can send you ashore to Santo Domingo."

"Good. Tell Alex I'll see him in a week or so, Morley."

"Will do, girl." Morley sighed, falling back into the hammock. "I envy you. I'd give anything to be fit enough to go with you two."

Season gave him an understanding smile before she went into the house and to her bedroom. Closing the door behind her, she stood in the center of the room, not going left, not going right. She recalled that flickering revenge in Champion's eyes and she winced from it. It *had* been revenge, hadn't it?

She sighed. If only she knew him better, she wouldn't be in such a fog! All she knew was that she'd agreed to prolong her torture. Champion and me on a slow boat to Santo Domingo, she thought with a bitter smile. That would be funny, if it weren't so cruel.

Crossing the room, she went to her closet and took some clothes from it. Rugged clothes and swimsuits. No more costumes or make-believe. The pirate and the gypsy lady belonged to another time.

Burying her face in the clothes, she cried like a child who had been told that the stars weren't really twinkling fairies, but solid masses in a cold universe.

The clouds had parted, revealing a canopy of stars. Season lifted her face to their weak light and tried not to think of tomorrow.

"I thought you'd be tucked into bed by now."

She whirled to face Champion. He strode across the veranda to her side and gazed at the ocean.

"I'm going to bed now."

His hand shot out to grasp her arm. "It's going to be uncomfortable on *The Touchstone* if we keep this up."

She sighed wearily. "I couldn't agree with you more." Lifting her chin, she met his gaze. "I think we should get a few things straight—"

"Oh, yes! Let's hear it. Out with the rules of conduct."

She flinched from his biting tone, but held her ground. "We should approach this as strictly business, Champion. You'll be working, and so will I. It's best if we keep . . . if we're not . . ."

"Lovers." He supplied the word that burned on her tongue.

"Yes."

"Don't worry. You'll have a chaperone. Sweetsip is going with us."

"Ben's going along?" Somehow this didn't sit too well with her. Part of her had looked forward to being alone with Champion.

"Yes, unless you'd like to crew for me?"

"No." She shook her head. "I couldn't do that." A thought sliced through her. "Where will everyone sleep?"

"Worried about the sleeping arrangements already?" An ironic grin captured his mouth. "You'll sleep in . . . our bed, and Sweetsip will sleep topside, unless there's nasty weather, in which case he'll bunk below in a sleeping bag. I'll use the other bed."

"What other bed?"

"The sofa lets out into a twin bed."

"Oh, I hadn't noticed."

"Do you feel safe now?"

Anger pumped through her. "It isn't a question of feeling safe. I just wanted to clear the air. This is a business trip and—"

"Spare me the redundancies, Season!" He almost growled at her, turning her toward him until she was forced to look up into his face. His fingers held her prisoner, burying into her upper arms. "You want a strictly business trip, you'll get a strictly business trip! Just tell me one thing. Why did you make love to me last night? I didn't force you into it. You asked for it, and you enjoyed it. Why do women have to attach all these ifs, ands and buts to such a simple thing as two people pleasuring one another?"

"I made love to you because I wanted to," she answered simply and honestly. "As for the rest, I suppose women are more pragmatic than men. We can't look at just the moment. We have to look beyond it."

He tipped his head to one side. "What did you see beyond?"

"Problems." She closed her eyes for a moment, seeing all that trouble again.

"Problems can be solved."

She nodded, opening her eyes to his. "And they can be destructive." The flash of anger in his eyes spurred her on. "Champion, I told you once that I wasn't ready for you. I'm still not ready. Can't you understand that?"

"And I told you once that I wouldn't push you into corners," he reminded her. "So be it. Just do me a favor." Imperceptibly, he bowed his head toward hers. "Kiss me once more. One for the road, Season. Just one. . . ." His whispered words died on the wind as his mouth covered hers, closing her in.

Season lifted her arms, her fingers pressing into his shirt to feel the warmth of his skin. She parted her lips, longing for the surge of his tongue. He didn't disappoint her. He took all of her, ravaging her mouth with sweeping, desperate strokes. A breeze raced through the veranda, and Season shivered. Champion's arms came around her, holding her fast. Her lungs burned for oxygen, but she knew she'd rather die than end this kiss. It had to go on and on.

One last kiss. Oh, Champion! Make it last forever!

He tore his mouth from hers and stepped back, his gaze raking over her as he clenched and unclenched his hands at his sides. His tone was cool when he addressed her.

"Miss Templar, we leave at sunrise. Good night." He spun on his heels and strode into the house.

Season stared after him as something died within

her. Strictly business, Miss Templar. Evidently, "me beauty" had been laid to rest.

"Rest in peace," she murmured, her voice breaking on a sob. Don't be a fool, she told herself. There'd be no peace for her. She could see beyond the moment, and the despair of it all ripped through her soul.

Chapter Nine

The rocking motion of *The Touchstone* lulled Season into a lethargic mood. She finished putting away the rest of the luncheon dishes, then left the galley area for the invitation of the double bed across the room. Since she was totally incompetent as one of the sailing crew, she'd been relegated to the galley, where it was her duty to prepare the meals and clean up afterward. It was dull work, giving her plenty of time to analyze her predicament. Too much time, in fact. She was having doubts about her earlier decision to keep Champion at a distance. It seemed stupid now.

They were two days out of Sea Lily, and Champion had said they should reach their destination sometime tomorrow. Thank heavens! While she found herself enjoying the easy camaraderie of Champion and Ben Sweetsip during the days, the nights were unbearable.

Seeing Champion across the room on the twin bed and not being able to touch him was torture. Champion didn't appear to have any problem sleeping, but Season rested fitfully, waiting for the dawns that signaled the end of her punishment. It was infuriating that Champion managed to drop off to sleep so effortlessly! Didn't he ache to have her in his bed? Did he ever gaze across at her with longing during the night?

Season scoffed at herself. She had been the one who had established the rules of conduct, and she must honor them. However, with each passing hour she found those rules more and more ridiculous. What was she striving to prove through this business approach? That she was made of iron? Why had she decided to deny herself Champion's lovemaking?

She furrowed her brow as she searched her memory. Oh, yes. Now she remembered. Something about being too weak to face her future . . . too wrapped up in her past . . . her past. A flash of anger seared her. Champion was right! She couldn't use her past as a crutch any longer. Besides, he had opened her eyes to a few things. Darren had been no angel. Darren had been as much to blame for their messy marriage as she had.

Unbidden, a scene wavered in her mind. Her honeymoon. Season closed her eyes as the memory unfolded. She and Darren had made love, and she was feeling abandoned. Darren, however, seemed satisfied and happy. Season remembered how desperate she'd felt that night. She'd wanted more . . . something more from Darren. She recalled how she'd gathered her courage, determined to confront him with her needs. . . .

"Darren? Darren, don't go to sleep! It's our last night here. Make love to me again."

"Give me a break, Season!" He rolled his eyes in disgust. "I'm not Superman!"

"I know, darling, but I . . . it happened too quickly for me and . . . oh, Darren, I want you. Please?" She traced circles on his smooth chest with her fingernails.

Darren grabbed her wrist. "Look, that's your problem, not mine. I haven't had any complaints until you. You're going to have to loosen up and quit being so frigid."

Frigid. She drew back from the word, her mind and heart rejecting it. Darren sighed and glanced at her.

"Darren, I'm not frigid." She tried to cool her simmering temper. "I just need more time. You . . . you rush through it."

"You've been reading too many mushy books, Season. This is real life. It's not supposed to last for eight hours!"

"I know that!" She checked her sharp tone and strived for a softer voice. "If you'd just caress me more and—"

"When I need lovemaking tips, I won't ask you." He glared at her, his pale face fusing with bright color. "I know more about this than you. A few weeks ago you were a virgin, and now you're trying to tell *me* about sex?" His laughter was harsh. "Grow up, Season."

"But, Darren—"

"Good night." He turned onto his side, his back to her.

Season stared at his shoulders, wanting to shake them. Gradually her anger subsided. Maybe Darren was right. He knew more about this sort of thing. She'd just have to try harder. It was probably her fault. . . .

Oh, the lies! And I believed every word!

Season opened her eyes as the memory dissolved. Disgusted with herself, she curled into the fetal position. No more believing in such drivel! She had positive proof that she wasn't frigid. Champion O'Keefe had righted that wrong. In his arms she had been anything but frigid. She had been a furnace of passion, and she hadn't held anything back.

A smile touched her mouth, then disappeared as another recollection trampled over her. Darren had never forgotten her implorings on their honeymoon. She hadn't realized how upset he'd been that night and how he'd taken her suggestions to heart. When he'd returned from the war, he'd revealed how he'd twisted her words in his mind. He had called her a "fishwife."

Oh, the humiliation! Season wrapped her arms tightly about herself as if trying to squeeze the life from the ugly memory, but it persisted. She stopped fighting, allowing her mind to take her back. . . .

"Why do you want to sleep with me?" Darren leaned on his crutches, his face inches from hers. "As I recall, you weren't too thrilled with my lovemaking. In fact, all you could do was bellyache."

"No, Darren." Season shook her head, refusing to let him have his way this time. "I didn't complain. I made a few suggestions. But that was long ago. I love you and—"

"Love me?" His upper lip lifted in disgust. "You've got to be kidding! You never loved me. I don't know why you married me, but it wasn't for love."

"How can you say that?" Tears collected in her eyes, making his face undulate before her. "I loved you then and I love you now. I want to help you through this."

"I don't need your help." He took a few steps back. "I don't want you in my bed. Have you got that?"

"I don't understand you, Darren."

"That's the first *honest* thing you've said to me since I got back from 'Nam." His smile was tinged with bitterness. "I suggest you go out and find some other man to nag. If you didn't like my performance during our honeymoon, you sure won't like it any better now. Unless, of course, gimps are more your style. Is that it?" He chuckled, then broke into raucous laughter. "That's it! You're kinky! You like to make it with gimps!" The laughter died as quickly as it had begun. "Go pester some other invalid. This one is through with you. . . ."

Season covered her ears with her hands just as she had then to keep out the vile accusations. She realized she was breathing quickly, as if she were near hysterics, and she forced herself to calm down.

It's over. It's over. Put it to rest.

She relaxed slowly, inch by inch, until she was in control again. He had hurt her deeply then, but she wouldn't let him keep hurting her. No! From this moment on, she would find the strength to bury all that pain. She wouldn't relive that period in her life anymore. Champion was right. She'd tried to reach Darren, and she had grieved when she'd realized it was hopeless. The mourning period had gone on far too long.

Season sat up, brushing aside the remaining cobwebs of her memories. Think about happy things, she told herself. Think about *now,* not then. Her gaze fell on a pile of rubber suits, and she smiled. Skin diving!

Her spirits lifted as she recalled her skin diving lessons with Champion as her instructor. He had insisted that she try it since she might want to look at the wreck when they arrived. With trepidation she'd agreed and had discovered a whole new world beneath the water's surface.

Oh, the colors! She'd never seen such beautiful fish and such intricate coral before! Instead of being frightened, she'd been enthralled, and Champion had said she was an outstanding student. Although they'd only ventured down a few feet that first time, the second time Champion had taken her about ten feet under. They'd spotted a shark in the hazy distance, but she hadn't been the least bit afraid. Champion had been beside her, and his presence had been all the armor she'd needed.

But there was so much to know about skin diving, and she was anxious to learn all of it. Getting used to the surroundings took some doing, and that aqualung was a burden. She had kept listening to her own breathing, distracted by the sound of it and the bubbles. Season had imagined that being underwater would make her feel insecure, what with all that ocean facing her. She had thought it would be like a vast desert, but it had been just the opposite. She had felt closed in with the water pressing at her from all sides. Gradually she'd adapted to the strangely claustrophobic world.

And through it all Champion had been the essence of patience. He'd gone over every piece of equipment with her, carefully explaining how to use the flippers, the mask and the oxygen tank.

Season brought her musings to an end, wondering, was skin diving really what excited her, or was it being alone with Champion in his world? The sight of his muscular body encased in skintight black rubber had sent shivers along her spine. He'd looked magnificent!

Longing quivered inside her, and she pushed herself from the bed and made her way to the upper deck. Ben was behind the wheel, and Champion was sitting at amidships. Season went to him, eyeing the equipment he was examining.

"Hi." She sat across from him on the deck. "What's this?" She touched a yellow apparatus with a hoop on one end.

"Hello. That's a divining rod."

"A divining rod? What's it used for?"

"For detecting metals—precious and otherwise." He picked up the strange-looking machine. "Actually, it's called an electromagnetic detector. It issues one signal for iron and a different signal for things such as silver, gold and bronze. It's very useful." He set the divining rod to one side and stretched out his long, tanned legs. "What are you up to?"

"Nothing." The longing made itself known again as she glanced over his darkly tanned body. He wore only faded cutoffs, displaying most of himself to her hungry eyes. Tearing her gaze from his wide chest, she looked up at the robin's-egg blue sky. The colorful sails fluttered in the breeze. "I never realized how much is involved in sailing a ship. You and Ben work yourselves to death!"

He chuckled, nodding in agreement. "There's always something to do on a ship like this."

When he started to reach for a length of hose, Season spurred herself to question him further. She wanted him to *talk* to her like he used to before she'd instated her rules of conduct.

"Champion, tell me more about the wreck," she pleaded. "What makes you think there's treasure on it?"

Her ploy worked, for he settled back, propping himself on his elbows.

"I've dived on her many times, but last summer—"

"Oh? So the *Marina* isn't a recent discovery?"

"No, nothing like that. Everyone knows she's down there, but they marked her off as a treasure ship years ago. Something kept calling me back to her, like a siren song. I started researching her logs and her manifest, and they just didn't ring true." He tipped back his head to watch the sails dance. "Why was she carrying thirty cannons when she had nothing worth fighting over? She'd made numerous stops along her way back to Spain, which didn't make any sense since she was supposedly carrying passengers from Mexico to Spain. The logbook even noted that cargo was taken aboard in Havana, but no mention of it was listed on the manifest. It just didn't sound right."

Season smiled, only partly listening to him. He looked so relaxed, stretched out on deck, his head flung back, his eyes narrowed against the sunlight. Perspiration glinted on his chest and arms, making him gleam like a piece of oiled mahogany. His hair was a rich chestnut, wavy and full. Season's fingertips tingled, aching to slip through that glorious mane. When he shifted his gaze to her, Season snapped out of her reverie.

"So you went to the wreck and found . . . what?"

"Nothing at first. I went down several times before I struck it lucky. A few of the crew were with me and we dug a narrow, deep hole along the side of the ship. The divining rod went crazy." His eyes took on a brilliant sheen. "Something's down there. Something big."

"Gold?" Season asked, feeling the touch of gold fever.

"I hope so." He shifted onto his side. "I found something else, too. A few pieces of a clock—made in Germany."

"Germany?" She shook her head, unable to grasp his implied meaning. "So?"

"So that spells smuggling, Season."

"Why?"

"Because Spain had a law that prohibited exports from other countries. German clocks on a Spanish ship?" He shook his head. "That's fishy."

"When did the *Marina del Rey* go down?"

"In August of 1725 during a hurricane. She ran into a coral reef that disemboweled her. There were no survivors. Right now there's a fever of salvaging activity at Samana Bay—around the coast from where the *Marina* is—and that's keeping divers away from our wreck. No one's the least bit interested in the *Marina*, except for me. Everyone else is busy nosing around the wrecks found at Samana."

"When we get to the wreck, will you tear into the hull?"

He arched a brow in surprise, then laughed. "Season, that ship has been down there for centuries! She's buried up to her upper deck in sand. It will take months to get down to her hull."

"Months?" Disappointment slammed into her, effectively dousing her gold fever. "Then I won't get to see the big discovery, will I?"

"Not unless you'd like to stay with us for a few more months. It could even take as long as a year."

"A year?" She frowned.

"You could come back when we're ready to break into the hull, couldn't you?"

She shrugged, the disappointment growing. "I don't know what I'll be doing then."

"Cheer up!" He smiled, as if sensing her tremendous disappointment. "I'll keep in touch and let you know of our progress. We'll have to carefully sift through each layer of sand, making sure we don't miss anything of value. Layer by layer will be painstakingly examined. It's a tedious business." He winked and lowered his tone to a conspiratorial rasp. "I think you're going to be a good-luck charm for us. The gum-wrapper hunter might find real silver this time!"

She laughed and rose to her feet. "You're never going to let me forget that, are you."

He looked up at her, his eyes glinting with gold dust. "There are some things I won't allow you to forget, and others I'm going to *force* you to forget."

The intensity of his gaze unbalanced her, making her stumble backward. She knew what he was implying: He was going to force her to forget her memories of Darren. She issued a shaky laugh, though she found nothing amusing in his prophetic statement; it was serious. A brisk breeze floated over the deck, lifting one corner of a canvas covering some of the equipment near Champion. Season wrenched her gaze from his, then gasped when she saw the glint of gun metal.

"What's that?" She pointed to the canvas.

Champion grabbed the fluttering corner and covered the weapons. "Rifles."

"What do you need rifles for?"

"For pirates."

"Pirates?" Season placed her hands at her waist and eyed him with a mixture of irritation and suspicion. "You're telling me that there are still pirates in the Caribbean? I'm not *that* gullible."

He shrugged and picked up an underwater flashlight. "There *are* pirates, Season. They spot a good-looking ship like this one, pretend to be having trouble with their own ship and when a good Samaritan invites them aboard, they board the vessel, draw their weapons, throw the passengers over the side and seize the ship. They outfit the ship so that it can't be traced and sell it."

"Champion, do you mean we might be in danger out here?" Fear tapped her spine.

"Don't worry, chicken." He gave her a reassuring smile. "These modern pirates are a cowardly lot. The sight of a rifle sends them running. I won't fall for their lame-duck routine. I'm not *that* gullible."

She returned his teasing smile. "I'm glad to hear that." She glanced at the covered rifles again.

"We also use them to scare off big fish," he added.

"Sharks?"

"Sometimes." He wagged a finger at her. "Don't start imagining things, Season. It's rare when a shark gives us more than a passing glance when we're skin diving."

"Have you ever been attacked by a shark?"

"No. I keep a respectful distance from them." He nodded toward the water. "That's their home, and we're trespassers."

"How far down is the wreck?"

He pondered her question for a moment before turning to Ben. "Sweetsip, how far down is the *Marina?*"

"About sixty feet, I'd say," Ben answered.

"Sixty feet!" Season moaned. "I'll never make it down that far."

"Keep the faith, sweet Season."

The endearment didn't go unnoticed. Longing

surfaced again and Season pivoted from Champion. She closed her eyes, trying to ward off the waves of desire.

"Are you okay, Season?"

She nodded, gathering her control enough to turn to him. "Yes, I'm fine. I'll leave you to your work." She escaped to the galley, where only her memories of Champion's sleek body could haunt her.

Later that night, Season stared at the blanket of stars overhead and smiled. She decided she liked the kind of sailing they were doing. It was so pleasant to "heave to" and let "Mick, the first mate" do all the work. Her smile grew as she thought of terminology used by Champion and Sweetsip. They had explained to her that "heaving to" meant trimming the sails at night, reducing their speed from eight to ten knots to one or two knots. "Mick, the first mate" was an apparatus attached to the rudder—a wind vane, they'd called it—which kept them into the wind.

Sweetsip had said that "Mick's" only drawback was in allowing them to drift off course, which made it necessary for Sweetsip or Champion to check on their progress every three or four hours. Other than that, Sweetsip had said with a grin, "Mick" was a fine sailor who didn't eat, drink or chase women.

Tomorrow they would begin the final leg of their journey and arrive at the Dominican Republic before noon. Gazing around her at the black night, Season couldn't hazard a guess on where they were at that moment. She knew they'd sailed past Puerto Rico and were somewhere at sea between that island and the Dominican Republic. She glanced at her watch. Ten o'clock. Soon it would be time to turn in for the night, but for now Sweetsip was strumming a guitar and singing a calypso ballad while she stretched on deck and communed with the stars.

Champion was below taking his "head" shift. When they'd boarded, Champion had produced a schedule, detailing when each person could perform their toiletries. Season had the morning shift, Ben the afternoon shift and Champion the evening shift. Any minute, Season knew, Champion would join them fresh from the shower, his hair damp, his jaw clean-shaven and the scent of lemon-lime clinging to him.

Turning her head, she stared at the vast darkness, then sat upright when she spotted a cluster of lights.

"Ben, what's that? An island?"

Sweetsip looked past her pointing finger, his song dying. "A cruise ship. She's probably headed for the same place we are."

"A cruise ship." Season eased back, lying flat on the deck again. They were most likely partying on the cruise ship, but she didn't envy them. She was enjoying this quiet evening with Ben and Champion. It would be their last, she told herself. Once they reached the wreck, she knew that this peace would dissolve and be replaced by a beehive of activity.

"How long have you known Champion?" she asked, shifting so that she could see Sweetsip, who sat a few feet from her.

"Oh, since he was twelve." Sweetsip smiled. "He's been my captain for a long time. I joined Morley's crew, and now I'm part of Champion's crew."

"Was the transition difficult from Morley to Champion?"

"Not very. Champion's more focused." Sweetsip set his guitar to one side, losing interest in his serenade. "Morley was one to stop at every island and every spot of land to investigate, but Champion sets his sails and doesn't let anything distract him from his destination." Warming to the subject, Sweetsip leaned forward a little and grinned. "The nature of our voyages changed with Champion. Morley liked to investigate cultures and customs. He liked people—found them fascinating. Morley sailed all over the world and he made friends along the way. It was nothing to happen upon an island and stay there a year with the people."

"Yes, I gathered that from my interviews with him. He was quite an adventurer."

"He was," Sweetsip agreed. "But Champion's curiosity is of a different kind. He likes history and he decided to be a treasure hunter . . . or what you'd probably call a salvor. At first I was skeptical." Sweetsip's grin grew. "But after my first salvage, I was hooked. There's nothing more exciting than to discover a lost ship and its treasure. It's like going back into time."

"It must be thrilling." Season tried to imagine the burning excitement of uncovering gold and silver, but she knew it was fruitless. One had to experience that kind of feeling to know it.

"Champion's single-minded," Sweetsip continued, but this time his voice was softer, as if he were talking to himself. "That's good, but it can be bad. Like when he got it into his head he was going to marry Trishy. No one could talk him out of it, not even Morley." He shrugged his narrow shoulders. "But he was just as single-minded when he decided to be rid of her. Once he knew she was a cheat, he bounced her right out of his life. He's not the kind of man who takes kindly to women who use him for their own gratification without any thought to his."

Digesting this, Season told herself she should guide Ben to a less personal topic, but she couldn't bring herself to do it. She *wanted* to hear about Champion. She was shamefully relieved when Ben continued his narrative.

"But that woman almost broke his spirit." A sad expression covered Sweetsip's craggy face. "She took his love, then tossed it right back into his face. Made a sham out of that marriage. I guess there's nothing in this world worse than watching a dream unravel."

"A dream?" Season asked.

"Yes." Sweetsip's eyes shifted to her. "Champion's dream of a home and a family."

"Well, maybe it was for the best. His work keeps him on the move so much that a family might tie him down."

Sweetsip shook his head. "A family doesn't tie a man down, it gives him security. There's nothing better than a light in the window just for you. Besides, Champion wouldn't be so wrapped up in his work if he had something else to occupy his time."

That's true, Season thought. Hadn't she jumped into her work when her life with Darren had become unbearable? It had been her refuge.

She gave Champion a rather guilty smile a moment later when he bounded to the upper deck looking shipshape in cutoffs and a white T-shirt. She knew he'd adopted the clothes at bedtime for her benefit. Champion O'Keefe, Season was quite sure, would otherwise sleep in the buff.

"Hello," he greeted them before sitting near Season. "What are you two whispering about up here?"

"Trish and you," Sweetsip answered without hesitation.

Season ducked her head, wishing she could float away on the breeze.

"Trish? What's all this curiosity about Trish?" There was a note of irritation in his voice. "Season, I'm talking to you."

She lifted her gaze and frowned. "I'm not curious about Trish. We were just . . . just talking about a lot of things and she popped up in the conversation."

"Well, allow me to set the record straight once and for all," he countered with a grave tone. "Trish was a mismatch, totally. She couldn't stand sailing because she always got seasick. She liked parties and rubbing elbows with the right people, and that made me sick. While I enjoyed my . . . nights with her, I rarely enjoyed the days. It didn't take long before I began dreading the nights, too, and—"

"Champion!" Season said, glancing at Sweetsip, who was grinning ear to ear. "This isn't the time . . . I mean, let's just drop the subject. I'm not that interested."

"Oh, I think you're dying of curiosity."

"I'm not!" She glared at him before she caught the twinkle in his eyes and realized he was baiting her.

"Okay." He shrugged and his gaze moved to Sweetsip for a moment before finding her eyes again. "What would you like to talk about?"

"I don't know." She shifted to her back again, trying to regain the peacefulness she'd felt only minutes ago. "Tell me about the Dominican Republic. Is it pretty?"

"Very lovely," Champion said. "It's got sandy white beaches, friendly natives and grass huts. Santo Domingo has a wild nightlife, and it's become quite a tourist attraction."

"It's fairly mild, other than Santo Domingo," Sweetsip added. "Unspoiled, for the most part."

"That sounds nice." Season stretched lazily. "We saw a cruise ship while you were below."

"It's probably headed for Santo Domingo." Champion yawned and reclined on his stomach beside her, leaving only a foot of space between them. "Sing us a song, Sweetsip, before we hit the sack."

"My pleasure." Sweetsip retrieved the guitar and launched into a soft ballad.

The sea rocked *The Touchstone* like a baby's cradle and Sweetsip's sweet voice added a calypso lullaby. Sleepiness edged into Season, and she closed her eyes, ready for it to wash over her.

The song ended and Season smiled.

"That was lovely, Ben. It's so wonderful just to drift out here. So peaceful." She stifled a yawn, lifting her hand to cover her mouth.

"Do you like the sailing life, Season?" Sweetsip asked as he stowed his guitar in a canvas sleeve.

"I adore it!" She smiled and struggled to her feet. "And I'm bushed. I'll bid you gentlemen good night." With a jaunty salute, she turned and started for the cabin, but Champion's hand curved around her ankle to bring her up short. She looked down at him and her heart flip-flopped. The tangy scent of his after shave wafted over her as his hand slipped up her leg to settle on her calf.

"Why don't you just sleep up here with us?" he asked in a low voice that seemed to make her heartbeats quicken.

"With us?" She glanced over her shoulder at Ben, then back to Champion.

"I'm going to. It's too nice a night to spend it below. You can use my shoulder as a pillow."

His invitation was a powerful one, but she shook her head. "No, thanks. Good night, Ben!"

"Good night, Season."

Champion's hand fell away from her, and Season quickly sidestepped him, but not before she saw his frown of annoyance. What did he expect? she fumed as she bolted down the stairs to the cabin. Maybe he was immune to her, but she certainly wasn't to him! Did he really think she could curl up beside him and just go to sleep?

She dressed for bed and slipped under the cool top sheet. She could hear the murmur of the men's voices above her and their footfalls as they checked their course before settling down to sleep. Half an hour later, she heard Champion bid Sweetsip good night.

Season closed her eyes, but sleep eluded her now. She stiffened and sat up when she heard someone coming down the stairs into the cabin. Champion's wide-shouldered form loomed in the doorway.

"Season?"

"Yes?" Her answer was a breath of sound.

"I've come to get my pillow."

"Oh." Her heart sank and she realized she'd been hoping he'd come back for her . . . not his infernal pillow!

He grabbed the pillow from the couch across from her and started for the stairs again, but he paused in the doorway and turned back to face her.

"One more thing about Trish—"

"No!" Season held up her hands. "Enough is enough. I know we shouldn't have been talking about you and her behind your back. I'm sorry."

"No, I want you to hear this." He waited for a moment, and when she seemed resigned he continued. "I never really loved her. I didn't know that until recently."

She stared at him, unable to think of anything to

say in response. Finally he turned from her and climbed the stairs, his footfalls heavier than usual. Season fell back on the bed as her heart battered against her rib cage. You idiot! Why didn't you say something to him! For a few moments, she flirted with the idea of going up to him, but she quickly rejected it. Too late for that. Your timing is off by a split second.

What could she have said? And why did he want her to know that he didn't love Trish . . . had never really loved her? Why now? It had been a true confession and one she knew she would worry over for months to come.

Champion, Champion, you're making it so hard to say good-bye.

She closed her eyes and listened to the murmur of the sea and the whisper of silken sails.

Chapter Ten

$\mathcal{E}$xcitement built in Season as Champion described the wonders beneath *The Touchstone* to Ben Sweetsip. They had arrived at the *Marina del Rey* that day and met two members of the crew of *Pirate's Pleasure* who had been flown to the Dominican Republic while the *Pirate's Pleasure* had remained in the Bahamas as a decoy. The two men, Jim and Bobby, had used an inconspicuous dinghy to carry them out to the *Marina del Rey;* and when their findings had been promising, they had wired Champion to come.

Using his arms in sweeping gestures, Champion detailed the position of the sunken *Marina del Rey,* and the way the divining rod had fairly bolted from his hands when pressed to the sand burying the ship's hull. Jim and Bobby who had gone down with him, helped him described the underwater scene.

"There's gold down there, I tell you!" Champion's voice was pitched high with excitement.

"Listen to him, Sweetsip," Jim said as he unzipped his wetsuit. "We're onto something this time. I'm itching to get to the bottom of that old rig!"

Bobby, the youngest diver, laughed and slapped Sweetsip on the back. "You can retire on this one, old salt."

Season checked the zipper of her wetsuit, anxious for Champion to take her down to view the ship. He had promised to do so earlier and . . . Her hopes plummeted when Champion unzipped his own suit.

"Let's break out the rum and toast our good fortune!"

Sweetsip frowned. "Jumping the gun, aren't you, Champ?"

"Maybe a little," Champion agreed. He whirled to face Season. "Hey, sweet Season! I almost forgot you. Are you ready to pay your respects to the *Marina del Rey?*"

She nodded eagerly and went to him.

"Good, I'm ready, too." He zipped his suit. "Jim, help Season with her tank. You'd better put on an underwater jacket. It's a bit cool down there." He waited for her to check out her gear. "Ladies first. I'll be right behind you."

Season went to the ladder and stepped down into the clear water. She was immediately wrapped in a heavy, invisible cloak. A ripple sent her sideways, and she saw that Champion had entered the water near her. He moved closer, his hands grasping her shoulders. His eyes spoke to her, asking if she was okay. She nodded, and he increased the pressure on her shoulders and guided her down with him. They made a slow descent, giving Season time to adjust her breathing and get used to this huge fishbowl. Schools of fish parted around them, sending off shards of glimmering neon. Season barely noticed them. She kept her gaze glued to Champion, whose calm eyes gave her courage.

He stopped and treaded water. Season furrowed her brow and she could see his eyes smile as he motioned her to look down. A ghost lay beneath her; the ghost of the once-great *Marina del Rey*.

Buried in sand up to her masts, she looked forlorn. Her main mast was broken in half, most of it lying on the sea floor. Above her was the razor-edged coral reef that had ripped her in two centuries ago. It still cast its shadow of death over her. Her mighty cannons were covered with time's crust and lay strewn about on the sandy bottom. There was evidence of the many salvors who had visited the ship, and Season nodded when Champion pointed out the narrow, deep hole his two men had dug near her stern.

With Champion's arm around her waist, Season descended to the *Marina del Rey*'s remains. Champion guided her from stem to stern, pointing out copper fittings, crusty cannon balls, anchors and two-feet-thick timbers that had been snapped like twigs. The evidence was there for all to see. The *Marina del Rey*'s last minutes had been horrible, and her passengers had been given precious little time to evaluate their situation. The hurricane had slammed the ship into the reef, splintered it in two and sunk it into a watery grave.

Champion took her hands and made her grasp a split timber, then indicated that she should stay there. She nodded, and he swam a few feet from her. Something had snared his attention. He withdrew a fan-shaped tool from his diving belt and began waving it above the sand amidships. Sand lifted, clouding the area around him and making it difficult for Season to see him. Minutes passed while she clung to the side of the *Marina*. There was a single-mindedness about Champion, and it transmitted itself to Season. She strained her eyes to see through the fog of sand. He was on to something! She could feel it in her bones. He stopped occasionally to tug at something embedded near the ship. Finally he pushed the tool back into his belt with a measure of frustration, and held out a hand to her. Season left her post and slipped her hand into his. They started upward for *The Touchstone*.

Champion helped her up the ladder, following close on her heels. Before Season could pull off her face mask, Champion was issuing orders to Jim, Bobby and Sweetsip.

"Get the airlift ready," he said, not bothering to remove any of his gear. "I've located something down there. It might be a clump of coins or something like that."

"Don't you want to wait for the others?" Bobby asked.

"No, I want at that thing right now." He looked past Bobby to Sweetsip. "Sweetsip, while we're at this you can take the dinghy to Santo Domingo and radio the rest of the *Pirate's Pleasure* crew. Tell them to lift the smoke screen and get here . . . pronto!"

"Aye, aye, sir." Sweetsip touched the brim of his hat.

"Stop by the government offices while you're there. Tell them I'll be in soon to start on the required paperwork."

Sweetsip paused, turning back to Champion. "You're that sure, skipper?"

"I'm positive, Sweetsip. Get a move on. The sooner the *Pirate's Pleasure* gets here, the sooner we can start."

"Aye, sir." Sweetsip jogged across the deck toward the dinghy.

A sense of loss filled Season as the men went about their tasks. Determination was stamped on their faces as they lowered the dinghy, waved Ben Sweetsip off and began preparing the airlift, which would suck sand from the sea floor and reveal the *Marina*'s centuries-old secrets. Champion was lost to her now, Season thought with a pang of regret. Another lady had captured his attention.

Inching out of her wetsuit, Season told herself it was better this way. Champion was involved with the *Marina* now and wouldn't be disturbed by her departure to Baltimore. She escaped to the cabin's seclusion and finished removing the wetsuit. Still wearing her one-piece bathing suit, Season sat at the table and opened a notebook. Focusing her attention on her own work, she made lists of the things she had to do before leaving *The Touchstone*. She would stay one more day in order to get clear impressions of the men at work, then she would have one of the crew take her to Santo Domingo, where she would obtain an airline ticket to Baltimore. Alex could send a team of photographers back here to chronicle the recovery.

Deadlines! While she made furious notes of her own impressions of the *Marina* and its background, she made mental notes to put the finishing touches on her series of articles on Morley before she began the story on the wreck's recovery. Hours slipped by unnoticed as she wrote in the notebook. She had a lot of work ahead of her, but the articles would be fantastic, would move her into a different rank of reporting on the magazine.

The pencil slipped from her fingers and Season

stared into space. Somehow, she wasn't as excited as she should have been. She was closing a door in her life and opening a window. She *should* be proud of herself! Tears burned the backs of her eyes. She *should* be, but she wasn't.

"Season!"

Champion bounced down the steps then came to an abrupt halt. "Season, why did you change out of your wetsuit?"

"I . . . I didn't think I'd be going down again," she answered, closing her notebook and pushing it to one side.

"Well, get back into it. We've just about uncovered that lump I located when we were down there together. You'll want to get a look at it first, won't you?"

"Yes!"

"Get a move on. I'll wait for you." He turned and bounded back up the steps.

Within minutes Season was encased in the wetsuit again. Jim and Bobby were manning pumps and chatting with Champion, who was perched on the rail. Spotting her, Champion reached for his diving jacket and slipped into it.

"Here she is," he said with a smile. "Jim will help you with the tank again, and wear your jacket. When we get down there, you do exactly as I say and keep well out of the way. I have to keep my attention on the airlift or it might jump out of my hands." He zipped his jacket and reached for his face mask. "Bobby will go down with us. I'll go first, then you, then Bobby." He pulled on heavy gloves, fitted his mask over his eyes and nose, and placed the breathing tube in his mouth. Giving a thumb's-up signal, he sat on the rail and rolled off.

Not confident enough for that kind of maneuver,

Season used the ladder to lower herself into the lapping water. Champion waited for her a few feet below, and she went to him, thankful for his steady hands on her waist as they dropped to the wreck. Above them, Bobby swam headfirst toward the wreck's stern, the airlift hose trailing behind him.

The activity had attracted an audience. Several species of fish hovered around the wreck now, but they were small and presented no threats. The only large fish were groupers, but Champion had told her about them. They were permanent residents around wrecks and were a bother, but nothing to fear. In fact, Champion had said that they worked like an alarm system. When the groupers scattered, that meant a truly large fish was in the vicinity.

When they reached the wreck, Season obeyed Champion's silent commands and hugged the side of the ship some twenty feet from where Champion and Bobby were preparing the airlift. Fascinated, she watched the airlift suck up great gulps of sand and throw it behind Champion. Huge clouds of sand made vision hazy. Fish scattered at first, then slowly swam back to the site, curiosity getting the best of them. Season could understand the irresistible lure. Frozen to the spot, she forced herself to breathe normally even though her pulses raced.

The hose jerked in Champion's hands, but he stood firm on the sea floor, his belt weights holding him down. Bobby floated slightly behind him, well out of the path of sand at the other end of the hose.

Then terror struck, taking them all by surprise. Season saw the moray eel at almost the same moment as Champion, but it was too late. The eel slithered from a crevice in the ship, his mouth open to reveal a savage array of teeth, then it disappeared into the airlift hose. Champion's body jerked. He

whirled toward Season, one hand extended in a
warning for her to stay put. Season dug her fingers
into the slimy timber and several of her nails broke
off into the decaying wood. Champion was looking
up at the other end of the hose. From the corner of
her eye, Season could see Bobby, motionless in the
water only a few feet from her. The hose emitted a
puff of sand and then the eel shot out. It wasted no
time. Swirling in the hazy water, its mouth agape, it
shot toward Champion like a deadly arrow.

Season screamed, emitting a trail of bubbles that
momentarily blinded her. When her vision cleared,
she screamed again. The moray eel's ripping mouth
was at Champion's chest, and Champion had released the tube and was pounding furiously at his
attacker.

Hysteria exploded in Season, making her think
irrationally of that cave in Doubloon Cove . . . that
flash of silver . . . the resident eel . . . Champion
kidding about being attacked for the sake of a gum
wrapper . . .

She was being pried from her death grip on the
rotting timber. With glazed eyes, Season saw Bobby's face floating close to hers as his arms came
about her. His legs kicked, slamming into hers as he
began striving for the surface. But Season didn't
want to go. Where was Champion . . . Champion!
She struggled and tried to push away from Bobby,
but his arms tightened and made it impossible for
her even to look down to where she'd last seen
Champion.

They were ascending quickly . . . too quickly.
Season's lungs began to burn, and black-and-red
spots appeared before her eyes. Bobby was jiggling
her breathing tube and his eyes were trying to tell

her something. What? What did he want? All she wanted was Champion. . . .

An unfriendly fist pushed into her stomach and Season exhaled her pent-up breath. The black spots grew until they obliterated everything. Her last thought was that Champion was still down there . . . down there with the ghostly *Marina* and that slithering messenger of death.

Season emerged from the blackness with a bolt of awareness, certain that only a few seconds had passed. Paneled walls greeted her, then Champion's face was above hers. She reached out, her hands clutching at his shoulders. Was he real? This *had* to be a dream. It couldn't be real. . . .

"Hey! Take it easy." His voice fell upon her like a gentle rain. "Lie back there, sweetheart. Don't try to sit up just yet. Do you know where you are?"

She frowned. What a ridiculous question at a time like this! "Yes, I'm in the cabin, and I know who I am, too. Season Christine Templar, and you're Champion Sullivan O'Keefe." Did he think she had lost her mind? Had she? Was he only an apparition?

His laughter reassured her. "That's right, smart-mouth. How did you know my middle name?" He shook his head. "That's not important now. Are you okay? Any cramps?"

More stupid questions! Her fingers dug into his shoulders, anxious for reality. "How do *I* feel? How are *you*? That . . . that eel . . . it attacked you!" Tears blurred her vision and a sob climbed up her throat as the terror of it all returned, full force.

"There, there, chicken." His voice was soothing. He gathered her into his arms and pressed her face against his bare chest. "I'm all right. That old eel just ripped my wetsuit jacket. He didn't even scratch me."

"I . . . don't . . . believe . . . you," she whispered between gulping sobs.

"You don't? Well, look for yourself." He pushed her back so that she could see his chest. His skin was coppery and unblemished. "See any blood? Any scratches?"

"Oh, Champion!" Her hands fanned across his hair-roughened chest and she bent forward to press thankful kisses across his collarbone. "I thought . . . oh, God!"

"Easy, chicken." He chuckled and framed her face between his hands. "That eel was more surprised than angry. He didn't hurt me. He just scared a full year's growth out of me."

"And out of me," she added, her gaze hungrily roaming his face. "Where is everyone? Down with the *Marina?*"

"No." He pushed her back flat on the bed again. "It's evening. They've taken a much deserved shore leave."

"Evening?" She twisted around to find the porthole where shades of twilight were being drawn. "I thought . . . how long have I been out of it?"

"For a few hours. You panicked and wouldn't exhale on the way up with Bobby. If he hadn't punched you in the stomach, you might have had a bad case of the bends. Are you sure you're not cramping anywhere?"

"No, I'm fine. You mean the rest of the crew went on shore leave after you almost got killed?" It was unthinkable! Didn't they care about Champion?

He laughed and shook his head. "I didn't almost get killed. And yes, they took shore leave. There's no point in them hanging around here. They were worried about you, but you seemed to be resting comfortably with no side effects, so they went to Santo Domingo to taste the nightlife. I don't imagine they'll be back until morning, if I know my crew. In fact, I'd be willing to bet that by now Jim is flirting with the gaming tables, Bobby is flirting with a curvaceous blonde and Sweetsip is watching those two make fools of themselves and enjoying every minute of it."

The side effects he'd dismissed were converging now. She felt as limp as a rag doll and her head was beginning to ache. Season placed a hand to her forehead and closed her eyes. Champion was safe. The relief of that made her dizzy.

"What is it?"

"I'm tired and I've got a headache," she murmured.

"I'll get you some aspirin. You lie still."

When he came back to her, he administered aspirin and hot, thick clam chowder. With his help, she propped herself up in the double bed and allowed him to lavish her with tender loving care. The chowder gave her strength, and the aspirin vanquished her headache.

An hour later, she felt herself again. Watching Champion across the room as he washed the soiled dishes, she smiled. His hands and forearms were wet with suds and he was humming a tune under his breath.

I almost lost him.

The thought sent her across the cabin to him. He jumped slightly when she wrapped her arms around him and rested her cheek between his shoulder blades.

"What's this?" He chuckled as he spoke and reached for a towel to dry off his hands and arms. "You must be feeling better."

"Much better." She rubbed her cheek against his back, letting his warmth suffuse her until she felt a glowing need. He turned around in her arms and Season rained kisses on his chest.

"Season . . ." His voice was strained. His hands came up to hold her head, forcing her gaze up to his. "We have rules against this, you know."

"Blast the rules." She moved closer, flattening her body against his. "That eel almost took you from me today. Tonight I want you to be mine again." She lifted one hand to the strap of the one-piece black swimsuit she'd worn under her wetsuit, but before she could ease it down, Champion's hand stopped her. Her eyes implored him. "Champion . . . please?"

"Let me have the pleasure, sweet Season." He gently brushed aside her hand, then eased down the strap. His lips sipped her skin as he pushed down the other strap. Nibbling kisses moved from her shoulder to the curve of her neck, setting off shivers of delight. He peeled the swimsuit from her, his hands tenderly stroking her waist, then cupping her hips. He pulled her to him. His mouth took hers. Fiery passion engulfed them.

She was swept up into his arms and carried to the double bed. He placed her there, then stripped off his swim trunks before joining her. His body slid slowly against hers, creating a sizzling friction. Their love was a frenzy, whirlpooling and sucking them under, giving no time for thought or whispered words.

Their hunger for one another was a mutual force, and Season was more than ready for him when he joined with her. The world exploded into stardust, showering Season with pinpoints of burning embers. Clinging tightly to Champion, Season managed to regulate her breathing again. She smiled when she heard Champion's chuckle.

"I wouldn't win any awards for that performance," he said, his voice tinged with self-reproach.

"Don't be so hasty to judge yourself," Season said as she lovingly stroked his smooth back. "I'm not complaining."

He lifted himself from her and shifted to his side. His hand settled on her stomach as a half smile tipped up one corner of his mouth. "You go to my head, sweet Season. Like champagne bubbles." His lips grazed the peak of one breast. "I've got something to show you."

"What?"

He pushed himself from the bed and went across the room to his desk. Returning to her, he held out his hand, palm up. "Take a look at this. I have to clean it, but you can get the general idea."

She raised herself up on one elbow and plucked the gray mass from his hand. Turning it over, she examined it carefully. "What is . . ." Season's breath whistled down her throat when she caught the glimmer of green ice and crimson fire. "Champion! Are those emeralds and rubies?"

"They are." He sat on the edge of the bed, a delighted smile on his face. "It's a ring. Once it's cleaned of coral and saltwater deposits, it will knock your eyes out. That's what I was trying to get at down there."

"How in the world could you tell anything about it?" She turned the clump around, viewing it from all sides. It was caked with a gray, hard substance. "It must have looked like an ugly rock down there."

Champion shrugged. "You develop an eye for such things. Sometimes it *is* just an ugly rock. I saw a flash of green, though, and I suspected it was a jewel."

Season handed the treasure back to him. "I'd like to see it when it's cleaned."

He flashed her an enigmatic smile. "Don't worry. You will." He took the ring back to the desk, then returned to her. Stretching out on his side against her, he looped an arm around her waist and pulled her closer. "Let's break open some rum and toast this reunion."

She smiled and nodded, but a voice inside scolded her for agreeing to such a travesty. The chiding voice persisted as Champion poured rum into two cups and handed one to her. Season pulled up the sheet, tucking it under her arms. She frowned when Champion laughed at her display of modesty.

"To us, sweet Season." He tapped her cup with his, then drank deeply.

Season sipped the bountiful liquor. It didn't erase the voice from her mind, and she sighed her defeat. "Champion, I'm going to leave for Baltimore tomorrow."

"What?" The word almost exploded from him and his eyes took on a hard sheen. "What's the rush?"

She swirled the rum in her cup, stalling for a few seconds to gather her feeble reasons. "I have a deadline to meet. I've spent almost a month on Sea Lily. And I've seen enough here to get started on the salvaging story. Alex can send a team of photographers here to document the rest of the operation."

"If you stay another day or two you can meet the rest of the crew. The *Pirate's Pleasure* will be here and—"

"I'd like to," she interrupted. "But I have to get those articles on Morley wrapped up. The series starts in a couple of months. I'll be cutting it close as it is."

"Oh, I see." His expression was crestfallen. Lifting the cup, he drained its contents.

"I'll send Morley a letter when I get to Baltimore. I didn't get to say good-bye to him." She gave a short laugh. "I'm not very good at saying good-bye. . . ."

"Then don't say it."

She looked into his eyes and his gaze constricted her heart painfully. There was a flash of determination in those green-gold depths.

"Season, let's just say—until we meet again." He leaned forward and his lips brushed hers. "I don't want to say good-bye to you."

"I . . . I want to say something to you." She shook her head when he offered to refill her cup. He took it from her and set it on the floor beside the bed. "Champion, I want you to know how . . . how much you've done for me."

"You don't have to—"

"I know," she cut in firmly. "But let me. Okay?" She smiled and reached for his hand. "When I met you I was . . . well, not myself. I was confused and riddled with misplaced guilt. I wanted to get on with my life, but I couldn't seem to let go of my past. You helped me understand that what happened with Darren wasn't my fault. You're the most patient man I've ever met."

He chuckled, shaking his head. "No one's ever accused me of that before. Most people say I lack patience."

She wrapped her fingers around his hand. "You

gave me so much understanding . . . more than I deserved." She laughed softly. "Especially considering that you'd made up your mind to hate me."

"I'm not the only guilty one on that score," he accused with a grin. "You didn't like me, either . . . at first."

"That's where you're wrong." Her gaze met his and held. "I confess, Champion O'Keefe. I was infatuated with you before I saw you in that ratty old tavern. You see, I'd researched you and Morley months before I came to the Caribbean to meet you. I read between the lines of those articles written about you, and I saw a man with a gentle heart and a kind soul. I was absolutely right, too."

He averted his gaze as if he were slightly embarrassed. "I . . . I'm at a loss for words. That's not like me."

She squeezed his hand. "I'm strong now, thanks to you. You have no idea how much you've given me."

"Season, there's no need for this—"

"Please, Champion." She smiled as her other hand tenderly caressed his cheek, her thumb tracing the path of a dimple. "I want you to know. Besides my obvious difficulties with Darren, we also had a problem . . . well, with lovemaking. We weren't compatible, and Darren placed the blame on me. I took the blame, of course, since I . . ." She shrugged, searching for the right words. "I was a virgin when I married Darren."

"I understand."

She brushed the hair back from his temple, loving him for understanding. "You showed me that I *am* capable of responding to gentle, patient love. Oh, Champion, you've taught me so much about myself. I just wish I could return the favor."

"You have." He turned his head to kiss her palm. "Tenfold. I hate to tarnish that image you have of me, Season, but I'm not without flaws. If I've been patient and gentle, you're the reason. You've brought out some qualities in me that I thought were lost. It's been a give-and-take situation."

"I'm glad." She drew a deep breath before she continued. "I want us to part . . . well, on a friendly note. I must go back to Baltimore, and I want you to understand that. I have a job there that I must finish."

"Do you like Baltimore?"

She considered her answer carefully, choosing the words with caution. "I like it, but I'm not . . . rooted there. I might move someday." She lifted one shoulder in a shrug. "I've yet to find my Sea Lily. I'm still searching for it."

"Sorry to break the news, but I've got that market cornered."

"Well, I'll find a substitute someday."

"You'll always be welcome on Sea Lily, Season."

"Thank you." She lapsed into silence, telling herself that she'd never be able to return to that heavenly place. Welcome she might be, but she couldn't go through another breaking of bonds like this one. Shaking free of the melancholy seeping into her, Season released Champion's hand and settled back on the pillows. "You'll keep me posted on the salvage operation?"

"Of course." His hand caressed one sheet-covered breast. "You haven't heard the last of me yet." Sweeping aside the sheet, he fondled her breasts until the peaks were hard with desire. His mouth took one, enfolding it in a hot cavern.

Drawing a short, choppy breath, Season's body bowed toward him of its own volition. Her fingernails lightly raked across his shoulders as he nuzzled the undersides of her breasts.

"Ooo, what you do to me, Champion." Her voice sounded strange to her ears . . . husky and dark.

He smiled against her stomach, and his mustache raised goose bumps. "There are so many things I want to do to you, and so little time. Do you realize I've never made love to you anywhere except right here?"

Season laughed. "This is like a second home. This ship has been my touchstone, in a way. I've found a few truths here."

He moved to rest on top of her, his weight pinning her to the mattress as he gazed down into her face. "She's aptly named. When I'm confused, I climb aboard and let her take me away from it all. There's something about this old tub that sets my mind at ease and makes me see things clearly."

Moonlight filtered through the porthole, bathing his face in a soft hue that threw shadows under his cheekbones and made his dimples seem that much deeper. Season lifted her arms to his neck, her fingers gliding through his thick hair. She brought his mouth down to hers. Her lips parted and the tip of her tongue flicked over his. Banked fires burst into life again in a cascade of titillating sparks.

The second time around was carefully orchestrated. Champion conducted his caresses with slow precision, fine-tuning her body until she vibrated beneath him. Season gave herself up to him, languishing in his expertise. Was it possible she had known him such a short time? He loved her as if he had known her for years. His feathery fingertips located each sensitive area, nudging her toward that shattering summit of fulfillment.

"Now, Champion, now," she whispered, and her hands moved to his hips in an urgent appeal.

"Season, Season! How can I live without you?" Anguish shook his voice. His mouth melted into hers, and his tongue swept aside any response she could have made.

Hope soared within her, but that taunting voice cruelly reminded her that passion was making him say those things and she shouldn't build her future on them. He came to her, driving out that inner voice, thrusting through her doubts. She matched his smooth tempo, riding high on the belief that he *would* miss her desperately. She would not suffer alone.

He shuddered against her, but she hardly noticed. She had reached that ultimate peak and it had left her breathless. She managed a sound of regret when he separated from her. That separation seemed so final.

No regrets, she told herself. No time for regrets. You've touched the moon. Don't whine because you can't own it.

"What'll I do . . . what'll I do . . ." he whispered close to her ear, one arm still draped across her stomach as if he refused to give up all contact.

Season turned her head to look at him. "What did you say?"

He smiled sadly. "What will I do without you, sweet Season?"

Tears clouded her vision and she closed her eyes. Shifting to her side, she wrapped her arms around him, holding tightly.

"Oh, Champion. . . ." Emotion blocked her throat. There was no answer to that. She'd asked the same question over and over, knowing there was no easy way out of this. Yes, there was a price to this passion. And she had decided to pay that price. Better to have been loved by this man, than not to have been loved at all.

The moon lifted higher, making way for the sun. Season lay awake, watching the light play over Champion as he slept. The light had changed from milky-white to amber before she drifted to sleep, unwilling to face the new dawn.

Season stared at the dinghy floating alongside *The Touchstone* as if it were her mode of travel on the river Styx.

"Well, all ready?"

She winced at Champion's jovial voice and turned to him. He was walking toward her, a definite spring in his step as if he hadn't a care in the world. His smile was full of sunshine; a sharp contrast to the gloomy atmosphere that weighed upon Season.

"I'll help you down the ladder," he said as he took her suitcases from her and tossed them to Sweetsip, who was already in the dinghy. "If you left anything on Sea Lily, Morley will forward it to you."

"I think I packed everything," Season answered as anger coursed through her. He didn't seem the least bit reluctant to see her off, and she was limp with self-pity! Hating the smile on his face, she extended her hand. "Good-bye, Champion."

"Oh, no." He shook a finger at her before slipping his hand into hers. "We agreed not to say that word, remember?" He pulled her to him and bestowed a quick kiss on her lips. "Take care. I'll get in touch about the salvage."

"Yes, please do." She snatched her hand from his and started for the ladder. Descending, she felt as if she were stepping down into Hades, and Champion was giving her a happy send-off. Damn him!

She sat on the hard bench across from Sweetsip. The dinghy's engine boomed to life, and Season looked up to see Champion waving cheerfully.

"I'll talk to you soon! Tell Alex hello for us!"

She waved back, then turned away from his view as hot tears sprang to her eyes. *He doesn't even care that we've had only a month together and I'm leaving and we'll never see each other again!* She held the tears in check until Sweetsip had motored some distance from the ship and was headed for Santo Domingo, then a racking sob tore up her throat. She sensed Sweetsip's startled look, but she was beyond caring about what he might think of her . . . crying like a lost child.

"There, there, Season." His voice reached out to her before she felt him sit beside her and drape a comforting arm around her shaking shoulders. "It's not the end of the world. You'll see Champion again real soon."

She appreciated his kindness and his hopeful words, but she was past hoping. Sea Lily was a lost paradise. Morley was a fond memory. Champion was a fallen lover. Past tense . . . past tense . . . it was all over.

Chapter Eleven

*A*lex Ketchum paced his office as he read Season's resignation notice. Season watched as his expressions ranged from disbelief to regret. She shifted in the padded chair, warding off a niggling feeling that she might just be burning her bridges instead of building new ones. Alex and Marilyn meant so much to her. They had stood beside her through thick and thin. Could she manage her life without their caring support? Season sighed. There was only one way to find out . . . do it! And that's what that letter of resignation signified. She was strong enough to go it alone now. Baltimore wasn't her home. It had been Darren's home. Alex and Marilyn weren't her parents. They had been Darren's parents.

"Season, are you sure about this?" Alex waved the sheet of paper that formally severed her ties with *Treasure Trove* magazine. "You've only been back here for two months."

"I've thought it over very carefully," Season assured him. "When I returned here, I just felt different. During the past months, I've dissected my life piece by piece." She offered up a small smile. "I'm restless here now. I need a change."

"Do you have another job offer?"

"No," she admitted, dropping her gaze to her clasped hands that betrayed her inner struggle. "I've got some money saved, and I'm going to take some time off and look around. You understand that I'm only resigning from the magazine, not from you and Marilyn. I could never do that." She lifted her gaze again to his pale blue eyes. "Alex, you've done so much for me. I'm grateful, but it's time I started fresh again. As long as I stay here, I'll always be Darren's widow."

"Yes, you're right." Alex almost collapsed in the chair behind his desk. He glanced once more at the resignation before placing it to one side. "I've noticed a change in you since you returned."

"Have you? In what way?"

"You have more self-confidence. The other staffers have noticed it, too. There used to be a—how can I put it?—a shroud of self-doubt hovering around you. It's gone now." His face crinkled with his smile. "You're almost radiant these days. Did the Caribbean give you that glow?"

"Sort of." She firmly put aside flashes of memories. "These articles have made me realize that I have talent. I'd like to explore my talent and find its perimeters. I know I can do that here, dear Alex, but I'd like to try out my wings over foreign soil."

"Two weeks." Alex sighed with regret. "That doesn't give us much time, does it?"

"You can find a replacement in that time, can't you?"

Alex shook his head. "That's not what I meant. Yes, I can find a replacement, but it doesn't give me and Marilyn much time to get used to the idea that our Season won't be around every day. We've come to think of you as our daughter, not just an in-law."

Season smiled. "There's never enough time for some things. I've finished the series on Morley, and I'm about ready to wrap up the *Marina del Rey* story. I received a letter from Morley this morning. He read the first installment of the series and he liked it."

"Of course he did!" Alex chuckled. "You put him in a very becoming light. I wouldn't be surprised if those articles don't give him a new lease on life."

"He's a wonderful man." Season swallowed hard, fighting off the wave of nostalgia. "The series was so easy to write. I felt inspired."

"We're getting our first reactions to your story."

"Oh?" Season sat straighter in the chair.

"Our circulation has taken a decided jump, thanks to you."

"Has it? I'm so glad." Pride filled her, making her resignation even more difficult to face. "The *Marina del Rey* story should definitely increase readership, since it's an exclusive." She settled back in her chair with a laugh. "I can't count how many reporters have phoned me, begging for tidbits on the salvage. That's a nice payoff. A few months ago, those reporters didn't even know I existed."

"Get used to it." Alex's smile warmed her. "There's more to come for you."

Crimson pooled in her cheeks and she looked away from him for a few moments. "Alex, you're not . . . well, upset with me, are you? You do understand why I'm resigning? It's nothing personal."

"Yes, I understand." Alex ran a hand over his face as if to clear it of its sad expression. "I sort of expected it when you came back. You were stronger and more confident. I told Marilyn that you seemed to have set new goals and that those goals might not include this magazine." He picked up a pen from his desk and studied it for a few moments. "Marilyn said that she thought you might have fallen in love."

She was instantly on guard, then she relaxed. This was Alex. No need to hide her feelings from him. "Marilyn is very astute."

Alex's brows lifted. "Champion O'Keefe?"

Season nodded. "We shared something . . . very special, but that chapter in my life is finished."

"Are you so sure of that?"

She nodded again. "Yes. We were . . . ships passing in the night. The timing was perfect, the conditions were favorable and the result was positive. But we're heading in different directions now."

"Too bad. I've always had a soft spot for Champion. I wouldn't have minded one bit giving you away to him."

The conversation was drifting to choppy waters, and Season felt a queasiness in her stomach. Maybe she wasn't as strong as she'd convinced herself she was. She stood up and went to the windows that gave a view of Baltimore's colorful inner harbor. The war-weary ship the *Constellation* dominated the harbor and tourists scampered across her decks. Season's eyes played tricks on her for a few moments, transforming the ship into *The Touchstone*. In her mind's eye, she went below deck to that double bed where Champion waited. . . .

"You say you almost have the *Marina del Rey* story finished?" Alex asked, interrupting her fanciful imaginings.

"What?" She whirled from the window, blinking rapidly as she landed with a jolt back in Alex's office. "Oh, yes. I'm just waiting for the final installment from Champion." Her brows met as she frowned. "He's supposed to supply a partial list of the treasure he's uncovered, but I haven't received it yet. The salvage is just beginning, according to Morley, and will be continuing for at least a year. I suppose we can do a follow-up when the salvage is completed. But Champion wired me that he has found an array of treasure and I can include some of it in my article. The photographers have sent some pictures of a few of the things." Her eyes widened. "You *must* look at those photos, Alex! The things they've found down there . . . oh, they are beautiful!"

Alex chuckled. "I looked at the pictures yesterday, and you're right. It's amazing that crystal glasses and decanters can still be intact after all this time. And those jewels! Flawless. The head photographer called me this morning—"

"Bob Kelley?"

"Yes. He said there's a good chance they'll find a cache of gold bars down there."

"Oh, my! Champion must be jumping for joy."

"He is."

His agreement brought her up short. "You've spoken with Champion?"

"Yes." Alex pushed himself from his chair and went to the window. "I had dinner with him last night. He's brought that information, so you can finish your article in the next few days."

"Champion is in Baltimore?" Her heart pounded, and Season was certain that Alex could hear it.

"He arrived yesterday, and Marilyn invited him over for dinner." Alex sent her a sidelong glance. "He said he'd get in touch with you today or tomorrow and set up an appointment to come by and give you the information you need."

"I'm—I'm surprised he'd leave the salvage."

"He's only in for a few days, I think, then he's going right back to the operation." He glanced at Season again. "I thought he'd probably already spoken to you."

"No, he hasn't." She turned from the window and walked to the center of the office, feeling unbalanced and shaken. Champion was here, and he hadn't called. He'd phoned Alex and Marilyn, but not her. There was an important lesson in this . . . somewhere. Season closed her eyes for a moment. Was he telling her that it was fun, but it was over? Was this his way of letting her down easy? He'll call and make an appointment. That sounded cold and detached.

Strictly business, Miss Templar.

"Well, no matter." Alex shattered the tense silence. "He'll be calling you soon. He says the dollar estimates are soaring into the millions already."

"That's nice." Her reaction sounded bland, and she turned back to Alex, a forced smile on her lips. "I'll be glad to get this article finished. The sooner the better." She started for the door, throwing over her shoulder, "I've got to get back to work, Alex."

"You'll have Sunday dinner with us, as usual?"

"Of course." She smiled at him as she opened the door. "I wouldn't miss it."

Closing the door behind her, Season let the smile fall from her lips. Her feet felt leaden as she walked to her desk and sat behind it. With shaking fingers, she picked up Morley's letter and reread it. It had given her such joy earlier, but now each word seemed to rip her heart. Everything was fine on Sea Lily, he'd written. Mrs. Lowenstein sends her regards . . . she says she misses you and hopes you'll come back soon. The first article was wonderful, but he didn't recognize himself. Wasn't there a bit of blarney in it? Mrs. Lowenstein says the article is more than flattering . . . it verges on wishful thinking. What does she know? You're the journalist and you know how to get at the real truth!

Season paused, brushing aside a single tear that tickled her cheek, then she focused her eyes on the last page of the letter.

Champion was still on his mission, and would be there for the good part of a year. Morley hated to admit it, but he missed his son. Sea Lily seemed unreasonably quiet without Champion or Season to break the monotony. The days were long, the nights uneventful. Mrs. Lowenstein says it's time to have a real family on Sea Lily.

Season folded the letter. *You are such a fool!* Anger at herself rose in her, making her hands shake all the more. When she'd read that passage earlier, she had convinced herself Morley and Belle were sending her signals that she and Champion should start a family on Sea Lily. Now that idea seemed shamefully ludicrous. Obviously Morley was talking of his and Belle's becoming a family unit.

Stuffing the letter back into its envelope, Season returned it to the top drawer of her desk. She locked the drawer, telling herself that she was locking her pitiful hopes and dreams in there, too. Hadn't she just convinced Alex that it was time to spread her wings and find her own place in this world? Wasn't it time she convinced herself of that, too? Sea Lily was not her world. It never had been. It never would be.

Season glanced around the spacious room that housed the magazine reporters. *Treasure Trove* wasn't her world, either. It had been her refuge from a life that had been too painful to face. That pain was over, but how had it left her? Rootless. Blowing in the wind like a tumbleweed. When she'd made up her mind to resign, she'd flirted with the idea of settling on St. Martin. Now that idea repelled her. St. Martin. A stone's throw from Sea Lily and ready access to Champion.

Don't follow your heart, she told herself. Follow your good sense. She didn't know where the wind would blow her, but it wouldn't be to St. Martin. That was paradise lost for her. She would be more miserable there than she was in Baltimore.

"How's our ace writer today?"

Season looked up, realizing she'd been staring into space. She smiled at her fellow staffer.

"Pretty good, Jesse. Are you still writing your great American novel?"

"Yes." He sighed, a frown pinching his face. "I'm on the last chapter. The *real* test won't be to finish it, but to actually send it to a New York publisher."

"You'll do it," Season said.

"I wish I had your self-confidence." He flashed her a smile and headed for his desk across the room.

Self-confidence? She shook her head. Funny how people misread other people. Showing confidence in others was a far cry from having it yourself. Season turned to her computer terminal and called up the story on the *Marina del Rey*. She stared at the first paragraph and Champion's name seemed to leap from the screen.

He was in town. He was going to call her. Her heart thumped and her fingers trembled on the keyboard. Season frowned, forcing her heart to slow its betraying beat.

Strictly business, Miss Templar. Strictly business.

* * *

Season thought she was ready to see Champion again, until he walked through the double doors into the staff room after lunch.

The world seemed to tip on its axis, throwing everything helter-skelter. Champion stood at the entrance for a few moments, a commanding figure dressed in a blue blazer, white open-necked shirt and dark trousers. He swept his chestnut-colored hair from his forehead and glanced around the room, his hazel eyes stopping on Season. He smiled and started toward her.

Heart pounding, Season rose unsteadily to her feet and extended a clammy hand to him.

"I thought you were going to call first," she said, then wanted to kick herself for blurting out an accusation.

He shook her hand, his gaze traveling from her sandaled feet to her cap of ebony hair. "I decided to come by and make an appointment in person. Is it an inconvenience?"

"No, not at all." She gestured toward the chair near her desk. "Take a seat." She reseated herself, feeling awkward and uncertain. "When would it be convenient for you to give me the list of salvaged merchandise?"

"My, my! Aren't we formal!" His eyes teased her, and his lips curved into a winning smile.

Good Lord! I do sound like some stuffed-shirt insurance salesman, Season thought, not blaming Champion in the least for his gentle rebuff. After all, she'd made love to this man. He was hardly a stranger, and he was worthy of much more than accusations or stilted dialogue.

"So this is your world," he said, looking around at the maze of desks and computers.

"It will be for another two weeks," she said. "I've resigned."

"Resigned?" He lifted his brows in surprise. "Just like that?"

"It was a difficult decision," she admitted. "But I need a change of scenery. I told you that I was ready to start fresh. I think it's a sign that I'm on the road to recovery."

He unbuttoned his blazer, letting it fall loose. "I'd say you've completely recovered."

"Not completely. I'm still tattered around the edges."

"Not from what I can see."

She averted her gaze from his. Oh, if he only knew how she was unraveling at this very moment! The sight of him was shredding her cool façade. Sweet memories invaded her, battling for a stronghold.

"By the way, Morley and Belle send their love. Dad is anxiously awaiting the next installment on his colorful character." Champion grinned and shook a finger at her. "You've spoiled him, Season. He thinks he's a superstar now!"

Season laughed as visions of that sweet man flashed through her mind. Dear Morley. He gave something special to the world. He broke the chains of mediocrity, daring the meek to battle their own inferiority complexes. He was Don Quixote incarnate.

"Listen, if you have time now, I've brought the list of riches we've uncovered." He withdrew a folded sheet of paper from his inner pocket. "Of course, this is only the tip of the iceberg."

"Yes, I understand that." Season took the paper from him and unfolded it. Her eyes widened when she began to read the contents. "Good heavens! I never dreamed . . ." She shook her head and cleared her voice of its note of incredulity. "Jewels, coins, pottery, nautical tools, china, silver . . ." She looked at Champion. "This is staggering!"

"It sure is. What's more staggering is the mountain of paperwork involved." He hooked his elbow over the back of the chair, adopting a casual air. "Now comes the government intervention. What a headache! However, when it's all sorted out I expect to be paid handsomely." He grinned, his eyes sparkling with devilry. "My competitors are green with envy and kicking themselves for having dismissed the *Marina del Rey* so quickly."

"I imagine they are," Season agreed. She studied the list for a few moments before sensing his keen regard. Looking up, her gaze collided with his, clinging for dear life.

"You're looking well, Season," he said with a hint of a smile. "You haven't lost any of your tan, yet."

"No, even though I haven't been outdoors much. I've been slaving away here, trying to get the articles finished before I leave."

"Your photographers have taken mountains of pictures. Have you seen any of them?"

"Yes." She opened one of her file drawers and withdrew a large envelope. "Here, take a look."

He studied the photographs while Season studied him. He had a darker tan, evidence of his hours in the sun aboard *The Touchstone.* His hair was slightly longer, curling at the tips where it was a lighter shade of brown. He smiled at one photograph, and his dimples made long creases in his cheeks. Season pulled her gaze from his attractive face and wasn't surprised to find that she wasn't the only female in the room giving him the once-over. Sally, the receptionist, was hovering near the coffee machine along with Flo and Marcie, two of the staffers. All three women ripped their gazes from Champion when they saw that Season had noticed their avid interest.

Yes, ladies, he is a looker, she thought with an inner smirk. Take a good, long look. This sailor is only here for a few days' shore leave.

Champion returned the envelope to her. "Nice. Very nice. Will you use all of them?"

"Heavens, no!" She laughed as she filed the envelope again. "We'll only use ten to fifteen. If you'd like to have the others, I can arrange that."

"Yes, please do. I have my own photographer on board, but we need lots of photographs for documentation."

"Consider it done." Season closed the drawer. "How long will you be in Baltimore?"

"A couple of days, I suppose. It all depends."

"On what?"

"I have a stack of messages for you," he said, pointedly ignoring her question. "Personal messages. Why don't we have dinner tonight?"

"Dinner? Tonight?" She winced inwardly at the sound of her squeaking voice. "I don't know . . . I have things to do and—"

"You've got to eat, don't you?"

"Well, yes . . ."

"Good." He stood and buttoned his blazer. "I'll pick you up at seven." He waved as he started to leave her desk. "Don't worry. I know where you live. Don't forget about those photos, okay?"

"I . . . okay." She watched him stride toward the double doors and push his way through them. Slowly, she registered her own appalling lack of willpower. Dinner at seven. How had *that* happened? She returned her gaze to the list before her, but her mind wouldn't focus on it. Dinner at seven. She smiled, more at herself than to herself. So much for the steel-hearted, strictly business Miss Templar! And good riddance! She couldn't regret making a date with Champion. The evening would probably be difficult, and would probably leave her sad; but she didn't care. She would see Champion any time, any way she could.

She made a valiant attempt at focusing her resources on her work, but she gave up that lost cause a few hours later. With a sigh of defeat, she locked her desk and picked up her purse.

"Calling it a day?"

She turned to see Alex standing in the doorway of his office.

"Yes. I'm having dinner with Champion tonight."

"Oh? That's good." He smiled and winked at her. "I saw him in the office earlier today."

"Yes, he dropped off that list. It's quite impressive."

"Have fun tonight. And that's an order. I'm still your boss, you know."

"Yes, I know." She smiled as he went back into his office. Alex was barking up the wrong tree. If he thought this dinner was going to be some kind of romantic interlude, he was dead wrong, Season thought with a touch of grimness as she left the office building.

She drove her compact car to her apartment, located only half a mile from the office. Most mornings she walked to work, but the day had been overcast. Now the sky was clear. Evidently, the rain clouds had passed over Baltimore. Or had Champion brought the sun with him?

In her apartment, she frowned at the disarray. Cardboard boxes littered the floor and the furniture.

She'd begun packing two days ago, and had found she'd accumulated quite a few odds and ends over the years. Some of the boxes contained items she intended to donate to Goodwill. No sense in carting them with her. If she was going to start fresh, then so be it!

And there was no sense in trying to tidy the apartment for Champion. Moving was a messy business, and he would surely understand that. Besides, she was far past trying to impress him. If he wasn't impressed now, he never would be. A spic-and-span apartment wouldn't sway him one way or the other.

She stripped off her clothes and drew herself a bubble bath. Sliding down into the warm water with its softly popping bubbles, she closed her eyes and tried to rid herself of the fluttery feeling that had been part of her since Champion had walked back into her life. Walked back? She shook her head. She had never really allowed him to walk out of her life. The memory of him was going to be hard to shake.

Lord, he'd looked good today! She inched lower into the water, letting it lap under her chin. Of course, he would be hard pressed to look bad, she thought with a grim smile. He had said that he thought she was fully recovered. He was right, in a way. She had recovered from Darren, but not from Champion.

It was a different sort of recovery process. While Darren had done her no good, Champion had been nothing but good for her. How lovely it would be if she could just let go and never think of him again, except with the fondest of memories. No pain. No rejection. No desperation. That's the way a *mature* woman would handle the situation.

She just wasn't *that* mature. Or, perhaps, she wasn't *that* dispassionate. It was hard to let go of something so wonderful. And it was even more difficult to imagine herself thinking of him in a dispassionate way. Would she ever be able to think of him without feeling the crushing weight of regret?

Time heals all wounds, she told herself as she stepped from the bathtub. She dried herself with a fluffy towel, then selected a coral-pink dress for the evening. It was an eye-catcher, she thought, as she modeled in front of her mirror. The scalloped hem drew attention to her slender legs, and the color was a good one for her, especially with her leftover tan. She hot-rolled her hair, giving the ebony mass more bounce, then applied her makeup. She chided herself for spending so much time before the mirror. Everything had to be just right. The right shade of lipstick, the right amount of mascara, the right hue of eye shadow.

Season stood back from the mirror with a self-mocking smile. "So, you're not trying to impress him, huh?" she asked her reflection. Her emerald eyes sparkled with the humor of it all. "Sure, Season, sure."

She stepped into a pair of ivory pumps and dumped the contents of her everyday purse into a matching leather clutch. She found herself looking forward to the evening. Perhaps this would add the finishing touches on a storybook romance. Not the traditional happy ending, but a *satisfactory* one, she told herself. They would behave like two worldly adults. They would have dinner, share a few laughs and a few memories, then bid each other a fond *adieu*.

Then he'll go back to Sea Lily, and I'll cry my eyes out.

The doorbell chimed, and Season jumped as if she'd been shot. She glanced around the bedroom before grabbing her purse. The doorbell chimed again, but she paused in the threshold of her bedroom and looked back over her shoulder as she realized what she'd just done.

She had glanced around the room, making sure everything was in order and that the bed was made up. Why? A frown settled on her face. She knew the answer: She was preparing the trap, just in case.

"Oh, Season!" she muttered as she forced herself toward the front door. "Quit fooling yourself!"

She threw open the door, then stepped back as Champion's appeal slammed into her like a freight train. He adjusted the knot on his striped tie as he walked into the apartment and looked around. Season stood rooted to the spot. His dark suit was nothing out of the ordinary, she told herself, but the way he filled it *was* extraordinary. His shoulders seemed so wide, so strong. And he seemed so much taller now that he'd invaded her domain.

"Did I hear you talking to someone before you opened the door?" he asked, turning back to her and giving her a bemused look.

"What? Oh, no." She laughed softly, pulling herself together enough to close the door. "I was . . . just talking to myself."

His brows lowered. "That sounds serious, Season."

She shrugged. "It's a habit I've fallen into lately." She swung an arm to indicate the clutter. "Sorry about the mess."

"You really are moving, aren't you?"

"Yes, I really am."

"Where to?"

"I don't know yet." She glanced down at her hands, clutching her purse as if it contained all her worldly goods. "Shall we go or would you like a drink first? I have some vodka, wine and there might be some—"

"No, thanks. I never drink on an empty stomach. Let's go eat, then I'll take you up on a glass of wine."

"Okay." She switched off the lights and opened the door. "Where are we going?"

"Alex suggested a place called the Bayfront. Do you know it?"

"Yes, it overlooks Harborplace."

"Sounds nice." He strolled down the hall with her toward the bank of elevators. "By the way," he whispered, bending down close to her ear, "you look fantastic."

She smiled and felt a blush cover her face. It struck her as strange that this was only her second date with him. Her second date, and she was in love with him.

It seemed she never did anything in a conventional way. But of course, she was in love with an unconventional man. And was he in love with her? Was he close to it? Was there any hope?

"You've got a nice city here, Season," Champion said as they stepped into the elevator. "I can't imagine why you'd want to leave it."

Season watched the elevator doors close. There's no hope, she thought dismally. No hope.

Chapter Twelve

Season stared at her half-eaten sirloin steak and her stomach turned over. She pushed the plate aside, calling it quits. How was she expected to enjoy a meal when her stomach was tied in knots? This was supposed to be a relaxing evening of fond *adieus,* but it was sheer torture.

"I have some good news," Champion said, finishing his steak with gusto. "Are you ready?"

"Yes." She tried to sound interested.

"Dad has taken a giant step. He told Belle that he—I'm quoting now—'fancies her.' How about that? She didn't slap him, so Dad feels like Don Juan."

"Will I get invited to the wedding?"

"Wedding?" Champion shook his head. "There won't be one."

"Don't be so sure," Season cautioned.

"No, I'm certain, because I've been given the

word by Dad himself. He isn't interested in marriage, and neither is Belle. They have an agreement. Companionship is the name of the game. They've had their respective marriages, and once around that arena is more than enough."

"Oh, I see." She plucked at the linen napkin. She *did* understand Champion's less-than-subtle hint about never marrying again, but she was confused by this news of Morley and Belle. Morley had written that he and Belle thought it was time for a family on Sea Lily. Hadn't he been speaking about himself and Belle?

"Didn't you like your steak?"

"Hmmm?" She turned startled eyes on him. "My steak? Oh, yes, it was wonderful. I'm . . . watching my weight."

He scowled at her. "What utter nonsense! Eat!"

"I'm not hungry!" She collected herself, striving for a calm tone of voice. "I had a big lunch," she lied.

"Okay." He grinned and settled back in his chair. "Then dessert is out of the question."

"Yes, but you go ahead and have something."

"No, I've stuffed myself."

"Have you had any other close encounters of the moray eel kind?" she asked.

"None. That was a once-in-a-lifetime occurrence."

"You hope," she teased.

"It was. When I told the rest of the crew about it, they didn't believe me. It's a good thing I have you and Bobby as witnesses."

"I'm surprised you left the site."

"I had to give you that list," he reminded her.

"You could have mailed it."

"I could have, but I didn't want to."

She gave him a sharp look. He seemed to be testing her endurance. It was almost as if he were baiting her, trying to spark her anger. But why? For what purpose?

"Have you ever talked to Marilyn and Alex about the problems you had with Darren?"

"No, and I don't want to." Her throat was suddenly dry and she drained her water glass. "Darren was their son. I don't want to talk out of school about him. They loved him. It would serve no purpose for me to tell them about all the ugly scenes we had together."

"I see your point. They suspect that it wasn't a bed of roses, though?"

"Yes, they know it wasn't that. They paid for his sessions with a psychiatrist. They knew he had problems."

"They are two outstanding people. You're lucky you had them for in-laws."

"I know." She crossed her arms on the table. "They could have pointed the finger at me. It would have been the easy thing to do, but they didn't. They stood by me." She lowered her gaze, not wanting him to read the sadness in her eyes. "I'll miss them."

"And they will, undoubtedly, miss you," he added softly. "You haven't a new home in mind?"

"No."

"I'm already homesick for Sea Lily. I'm going there when I leave here. I want to spend a few days at home before I join the crew again."

"I don't blame you. If Sea Lily were my home, I'd never want to leave it." She pulled her lower lip between her teeth, suddenly feeling as if she'd said too much. She raised her gaze and found him smiling at her; a smile that made her heart beat faster.

"You really like Sea Lily, don't you?"

"Yes." She bit back any further response.

"I'm glad."

"Why?" she asked quickly.

"Why?" He shrugged. "Because I like it, too."

"Oh." Season looked around the crowded restaurant/club. His answer was unfulfilling, like the evening.

"Would you like to dance?"

She whipped her head around, realizing that she'd been watching the couples dancing in the center of the room. "No."

He frowned at her abrupt answer. "Didn't you wear your dancing shoes?"

She wiggled her toes inside her pumps, then grasped the excuse he'd offered. "As a matter of fact, I didn't. These shoes are killing me."

His brows met in a frown, as if he didn't quite believe her.

"No, really," she assured him. "They're new, and they're pinching my feet. I couldn't possibly dance." She looked away from him, not trusting those probing hazel eyes. Just drop it, she silently begged him. She didn't want to dance with him. She didn't want the close contact that would remind her of . . . oh, so many things . . . so many moments. It was torture enough just to sit with him and chitchat. Dancing would send her over the edge of her endurance.

"In that case, maybe we'd better go back to your apartment so you can kick off those shoes and relax. We can have that wine you promised."

"I . . . my apartment?" She looked at him, feeling helpless. What a choice! This restaurant or her apartment.

"Come on." He stood and helped her from her chair. "What year is the wine?"

"What year?" She bit her lower lip, hating herself

for parroting him like some numbskull. "This year, I think."

He laughed heartily. "Oh, well, this has been a good year."

They left the restaurant and drove to her apartment in his rented car. Season's nerves were stretched to the breaking point when they arrived, and Champion began nosing around her living room while she poured wine into two glasses. She stared at the glasses, wishing she hadn't packed her wine goblets. Tea glasses and new wine. How unromantic!

"Here you go," she said, handing him one of the glasses. "Real class, hmmm?" She shook her head. "I do have decent wineglasses, but they're in one of those boxes and—"

"Enough said," he interrupted. "I understand." He tasted the wine, grimaced and held the glass up to the light. "This year must not have been a good one for wine." He tasted it again, struck a thoughtful pose and added, "Limp-bodied, a rancid bouquet and poor coloring. Winos will love this."

Season laughed, falling into a chair and kicking off her shoes. "Oh, nothing has gone right tonight. Why should the wine be any different?"

Champion settled on the couch, one arm stretched across its back. He studied her for a few moments. "Speak for yourself, Season. I'm enjoying myself." He ducked his head to capture her gaze. "What is it? Are you feeling blue about leaving Baltimore?"

"No." She shook her head adamantly. "I'm glad to be leaving, and I'm not blue." She straightened in her chair, determined to lift herself from the doldrums. "Tell me about the *Marina del Rey*. Do you really think she might have gold bars in her belly?"

"There's a possibility of that, but we won't know for certain for a few more months." He unbuttoned his jacket and relaxed, crossing one leg over the other. "I wish I could have brought one of those glasses to show you." He glanced at the one in his hand. "They're much prettier than this."

Season slapped him playfully on the knee. "I didn't expect company."

"I'm kidding." He rested the glass on his knee. "The *Marina*'s glasses are covered with a gray substance—saltwater deposits—but when we clean them, they sparkle like new. Not a blemish or a crack or a chip. It's as if they were made yesterday."

"Remarkable."

"Yes, very." He leaned his head back to stare at the ceiling. "And there's all sorts of jewels and tools and . . . well, you read the list. We're finding things every day."

"Are you tied up with red tape?" she asked.

"Yes." He sighed and moved his stare from the ceiling to her. "Jake is sorting out all that now. Oh! He sent you a message. He said that you are definitely on his guest list for next year's ball."

Season dropped her gaze to her glass. "That's nice, but I doubt if I'll be able to attend." Memories of that evening when the pirate had danced with the gypsy lady surrounded her. She sipped the bitter wine. Everything seemed so colorless in contrast to the weeks she'd spent in the Caribbean. So bland. So tasteless. Sensing Champion's steady gaze, she pulled herself from her depression. "Is that the personal message you wanted to convey?"

"Personal message?" he asked.

"Yes, at the office today you said you had some personal messages for me."

"Oh, yes. That was one of them." He downed the rest of the wine. "One thing you can say for this stuff, it has quite a kick. Is there more?"

"Yes, it's in the kitchen," she said, starting to rise from the chair.

"No, stay put. I'll get it myself."

She obeyed, falling back into the chair. She see-sawed back and forth, first wishing he'd leave, then hoping he'd stay. This talk of Sea Lily was getting to her. She was homesick, which was utterly ridiculous since Sea Lily was not her home. The fact that she had never been homesick for Baltimore had hastened her decision to leave the city for greener pastures. But the grass was greenest on that island in the sea. Its sea breezes had healed her wounded spirits. Its warm waters had washed away her fears. Its balmy weather had cleansed her of her past. She had found peace there. Where could she go for peace now? Where but Sea Lily?

"Do you want some more?"

She looked up at the bottle Champion extended and shook her head. "I'm still trying to choke down the first glass, thank you."

"Which enemy sent this to you?"

She laughed. "No one. I bought it."

Champion gave her a dubious glance. "And I thought you had taste."

"Not in wine," she admitted.

"How about in men?"

A tingling warning raced up her spine as she eyed him warily. "Considering my first choice in husbands, I guess my taste in men is about as good as my taste in wine."

"Unless you've improved your skills," Champion added.

"Well, we can always hope," Season said recklessly. How dare he sit there and spout such drivel! Suddenly she was angry with him. Champion wasn't empty inside. He was very perceptive. He must know that his questions were driving her up the wall. Season straightened in the chair and finished off her wine. "Champion, why did you arrange this evening? What's your true motive? You've delivered your personal messages, which you could have delivered at the office today, so now what do you want?"

"Finally," he said, with a touch of awe. "Finally you're acting like Season Christine Templar, instead of some distant stranger." He drank deeply from his glass, then refilled it.

"If I'm acting strange, it's in reaction to you," Season said, defending herself, all the while wondering if his stomach were made of cast iron. How could he drink that stuff? "You barge back into my life, throw your weight around—"

"Have I been throwing my weight around?" he asked, his eyes wide with innocence.

"Yes, you have! You didn't ask me to dinner, you ordered me to dinner. Then you invite yourself over here, make fun of my hospitality and—"

"Objection," he interrupted again. "I find no fault with your hospitality. Only with your choice in wine."

"Oh, pooh!" Season stood, anger coursing through her like a raging river. "Take the wine and leave."

He looked up at her, not moving a muscle in obedience. "Now I find fault with your hospitality."

She glared down at him, but the craziness of it all got the best of her, and she was laughing before she could stop herself. She collapsed into the chair again and reached for her wineglass. "What do you want, you idiot?" she begged, laughter lacing her words.

He sloshed wine into her glass. "They say that liquor gives you courage, but I don't believe it." He seemed to be talking to himself. "Look at this." He held out his hands. "I'm shaking like a leaf."

She stared at his hands. He was right. He was trembling. "What is it? What's wrong?" Concern replaced her anger. Was he not telling her something? Was Morley ill? Belle? "Champion, is someone sick or—"

"No, no." He laughed and gulped more wine. "Nothing tragic, chicken." He paused, tipping his head to one side. "Chicken. I call you that, but you're one of the bravest people I've ever known."

"Brave?" She fell back in the chair. "Me?"

"Yes, you," he assured her. "To go through what you've been through and come out of it with a loving nature and a sense of humor. . . ." He shook his head in awe. "That, my dear, is bravery."

She started to speak, but then thought better of it. He seemed to be struggling with something, and she told herself to give him time to voice it. Whatever it was, was important to him. She was sure of that.

"I wasn't brave," he said finally, his voice dipping to a hoarse whisper. "When I came back from 'Nam and found myself in a hopeless marriage, I bottled up all my humiliation, my disappointment, my anger, and let it lie in me until it was as rancid as . . ." He lifted his glass. "As this wine."

Season smiled but didn't interrupt. His outpouring was a form of therapy that she felt he needed.

"I told myself that I didn't need anyone else in my life. I had Dad and my island. That was enough. If I wanted a woman, I'd take one for the night." He shook his head and a grim smile touched his mouth. "I made room for everything in my life except the love of a woman. I was too . . . too chicken to accept that. Too afraid that I'd get hurt again." He looked at her, meeting her gaze levelly. "But where's the glory without the chance?"

Season smiled, remembering a snatch of conversation one evening. "Taking a chance. It warms the blood and sets the pulses to pounding."

Champion grinned, recognizing the words. "Aye, matey, it does that." He took another drink of the wine, then set his glass on the coffee table. "I'll find no courage in this brew." His gaze lifted to hers. "I'll find courage only in your eyes, sweet Season."

She swallowed the wedge of emotion his words had placed in her throat. Her insides began to melt, and she clasped her hands together tightly to keep herself from catapulting into his lap.

"I've got something to show you." He reached into his jacket pocket and withdrew his handkerchief. Unfolding it, he held it out to her. "Remember this?"

Her eyes widened when she saw the jeweled ring resting in the center of the white fabric. It sparkled under the lights, throwing off bits of green and red. "Is that the ring you found?"

"Yes. I've had it cleaned. What do you think?"

"It's gorgeous!" Her hand hovered over it. "May I?"

"Of course."

She lifted it from its bed and held it up to the light. It was gold—a rich, glowing gold. Its sweeping design incorporated two rubies and two emeralds. The jewels weren't large, but of the finest cut.

"See if it fits," Champion urged as he tucked his handkerchief back into his pocket.

"Oh, I shouldn't," Season protested.

"Here." He grasped her hand and pushed the ring onto the third finger of her left hand. "See? Perfect fit. You're a size six, aren't you?"

"Yes." She held her hand up, admiring the view. "How did you know that?"

"I'm good at guessing sizes."

She smiled. "It's strange that it fits so perfectly."

"Well, it ought to," Champion said with a chuckle. "I had it sized for you. It was a size eight before."

"What?" she asked with a bewildered little laugh. "You had it sized for me?" When he nodded, she shook her head and pulled the ring from her finger. "No, Champion. I can't take it." She held it out to him.

"You have to."

"No, I don't have to do anything. Here, take it back."

"No way," he stated firmly. "I had to go through considerable red tape to get that little bauble, not to mention paying an appalling sum for it. I won't let you throw it back in my face."

"Champion, be reasonable," Season pleaded. "I can't accept this. Please, take it back."

"I've got news for you," he said, leaning forward to add emphasis. "You'll have to accept it, if you plan to marry me. That's your engagement ring, whether you like it or not."

The ring fell from her nerveless fingers and she stared numbly as Champion retrieved it.

"Now, is that any way to treat a gift of love?" He sighed expansively and pushed it back onto her finger. "I'm surprised at you, Season."

She withdrew her hand from his loose grasp. "Is this a joke?"

He started to say something, but then seemed to think better of it. Slowly, he shook his head. "No joke, Miss Templar." He rose to his feet and began pacing the room, stopping from time to time to peer into a box. "No, this is no laughing matter. It's been . . . wait a minute now . . . it's been exactly sixty-six days since you left me." He flashed her a pointed glare. "Yes, I've been counting. In those sixty-six days, I've had maybe two good nights of sleep. The days? Well, they've been almost as bad as the nights. *The Touchstone* used to be my refuge from my problems, now it's my prison. Everywhere I look I'm reminded of you. The upper deck, where you reclined that lovely body of yours on that warm summer evening when Sweetsip sang us a love song. The galley, where you cooked up some wonderful meals. The 'head,' where you took long showers and came out looking pink and shiny. That damned bed!" He ran a hand through his hair, mussing it. "I hate that bed now. I can't bear to sleep in it."

"Champion, I—"

"Don't interrupt me!" He held up a hand in warning. "This isn't easy, don't make it any harder."

She nodded, unable to speak anyway. Her heart was in her throat. Or was it on her sleeve?

"And I can't bear the thought of returning to Sea Lily without you being there." He kicked at a box. "And to think I used to call it 'No Woman's Land.' Ha! Now, *that's* a joke, Season." His eyes darkened to an olive-green. He strode to her chair and came down on one knee. "Listen to me, Season. I won't take 'no' for an answer. I'll pursue you to the ends of the earth, I swear it!" His voice had taken on a passioned urgency. "I'm a treasure hunter, after all, and you are one jewel I will not give up."

"Oh, Champion. I can't believe you're saying these things to me." She looked down at her hands, held by his.

"There's so much I want to say to you, Season," he confessed. "The main thing is that I love you."

She examined the ring on her finger. "Champion, are you sure this is what you want? I know you value your freedom."

"Freedom?" He laughed. "What good is freedom when you're chained by your own misery? Break the chains, Season. Say you'll marry me and give me back my freedom."

"Champion, Champion." She framed his face in her hands. "Of course I'll marry you. I just want you to be sure. . . ."

"I've never been so positive of anything in my life," he vowed. "We were meant to be, Season. Don't you feel that? We were meant to raise our children on the island we both love. For once, Sea Lily will have a family in residence."

She smiled. "Have you been talking to Morley about us?"

"I might have mentioned it," he said with a grin. "Season, he knew that I loved you before I did. He loves you, too, you know."

She slid from the chair into his arms and rested her cheek against his chest. "Oh, I want to go back there with you. I want that more than anything else in the world."

"Are you sure you've come to terms with your feelings about Darren?"

She nodded, rubbing her cheek against his crisp shirt. "Positive. You helped me sort out my past and place the blame where it belonged." She lifted her face to his. "I'm all well. Can't you see that?"

"Yes," he said with a smile. "Now that you mention it, I can."

She strained upward to meet his descending mouth. His kiss was like a crashing wave, drowning her in its power. She parted her lips in an open invitation. His tongue touched hers, tasted hers, teased hers. He pulled her into the curve of his body, molding her to him. She was breathless when the kiss ended, but she wanted more. She wanted so much more.

"Season, listen to me," he urged gently. "I talked with Alex and Marilyn about us yesterday."

"You—you did?" She drew a deep breath, grappling with her soaring emotions. "Why?"

"I wanted to feel them out on the subject. I know how devoted they are to you." He smoothed back her hair lovingly, tenderly. "Alex said you put up with more than most women would in the same circumstances. In fact, he said that he and Marilyn were surprised when you didn't divorce Darren after he returned from 'Nam and started making your life miserable."

"He said that?" She slipped her arms around Champion's waist. "I guess they knew more about what was going on than I thought."

"They were both thrilled when I told them I was going to ask you to marry me." He smiled and brushed his lips across her forehead. "They want you to be happy, sweetheart. They know you deserve it."

"I want to be happy, too." She hugged him closer. "I *am* happy, now."

"So am I, but I'll be happier when you're out of that dress."

"Champion, how unromantic!"

"It's the wine," he said with a grin as his hands located the zipper at her back. "It's bringing out the animal in me."

The zipper slid down her back and his hands warmed her skin. Season pushed the jacket from his shoulders and helped him shrug out of it.

"Let's get married soon," she said as she began tugging at the knot in his tie.

"How soon?"

"Tomorrow. We can drive to Virginia where there isn't a waiting period for marriages." She smiled when he gave her a startled look. "We can tie the knot"—the knot in his tie unraveled and she pulled it from him—"and then we can get started on that family."

"You don't waste any time, do you?"

She unbuttoned his shirt with determination. "We've wasted enough time, don't you think?"

"I'm in complete agreement." He stood and pulled her to her feet. "Which way is the bedroom?"

"This way, sailor," she said, taking his hand and leading him across the room. She stopped in the threshold, her eyes taking in the orderly expanse before her.

"What's so funny?" Champion asked when she started laughing.

Season gestured at the room. "You'll notice that this is the only clean room in the apartment?" She wound her arms around his neck and stood on tiptoe to kiss him. "I'm ashamed to admit it, but I cleaned it up . . . just in case."

He chuckled, his dimples leaping into his lean cheeks. "I love it! And I love you." He kissed her, then disengaged himself from her clinging arms. He went to the bed, swept the spread from it and tossed it to the floor. "Come on, sweetheart. Let's mess up this room."

"Now you're talking!"

He wrapped her in a tight embrace and they fell onto the bed together. Laughing, they removed each other's clothing, throwing each article in a different direction. When the last of their clothing had been tossed unceremoniously aside, Champion moved on top of her and his eyes took on an intensity, as if he were etching each of her features into his mind.

"We're going to have a fine time, Season," he whispered. "The best time of our lives."

"Oh, yes! Yes!" Love overwhelmed her, making her unable to convey verbally to him what she was feeling. But words weren't necessary. Her hands told him, her lips told him, her entire body told him how important he was to her.

And his body answered, in turn.

A deep satisfaction embraced her, making her realize that she'd been holding back until she was certain of his love. The chains were broken, and she was free now to give all of herself to him. Their joy spilled over, drenching them in a mindless deluge of passion.

Champion held her tightly to him, even when the storm had diminished to a shower of contentment.

"Oh, Champion, it will feel so good to go home again," she whispered against the damp hair at his temple.

"Yes. Our home." He smiled, turning his face to kiss the curve of her neck.

"I thought it was useless to dream about returning there someday. Especially after you gave me such an indifferent farewell."

He lifted his head to meet her eyes. "I didn't say good-bye, sweet Season. Remember? I had no intention even then of letting you go. I just had to work up the courage to ask you to marry me."

"Why did you need courage for that?"

"Because I was terrified you wouldn't want me."

She laughed softly. "Champion, I think I've always wanted you. Even when I didn't know your name. I *knew* you existed out there . . . somewhere . . . just for me."

"It's too bad we had to marry the wrong people before we found one another."

"Is it?" she asked. "You have to know the lows before you can appreciate the highs."

He smiled as he kissed each of her fingertips. "So true. This makes the pain almost worth it." He kissed her deeply, his tongue searching for the treasures within.

When his mouth left hers, Season ran her tongue over her lips. "I can taste that wine," she said with a laugh. "It tastes so much better on you."

"Here," he whispered, touching her lips with his again. "Have another sip."

She accepted his offer as her need for him renewed itself, springing from an eternal fountain of love.

Silhouette Special Edition. Romances for the woman who expects a little more out of love.

If you enjoyed this book, and you're ready for more great romance

…*get 4 romance novels FREE when you become a Silhouette Special Edition home subscriber.*

Act now and we'll send you four exciting Silhouette Special Edition romance novels. They're our gift to introduce you to our convenient home subscription service. Every month, we'll send you six new passion-filled Special Edition books. Look them over for 15 days. If you keep them, pay just $11.70 for all six. Or return them at no charge.

We'll mail your books to you two full months *before they are available anywhere else.* Plus, with every shipment, you'll receive the Silhouette Books Newsletter absolutely free. *And with Silhouette Special Edition there are never any shipping or handling charges.*

Mail the coupon today to get your four free books—and more romance than you ever bargained for.

Silhouette Special Edition

MORE ROMANCE FOR
A SPECIAL WAY TO RELAX
$1.95 each

2 ☐ Hastings	21 ☐ Hastings	41 ☐ Halston	60 ☐ Thorne
3 ☐ Dixon	22 ☐ Howard	42 ☐ Drummond	61 ☐ Beckman
4 ☐ Vitek	23 ☐ Charles	43 ☐ Shaw	62 ☐ Bright
5 ☐ Converse	24 ☐ Dixon	44 ☐ Eden	63 ☐ Wallace
6 ☐ Douglass	25 ☐ Hardy	45 ☐ Charles	64 ☐ Converse
7 ☐ Stanford	26 ☐ Scott	46 ☐ Howard	65 ☐ Cates
8 ☐ Halston	27 ☐ Wisdom	47 ☐ Stephens	66 ☐ Mikels
9 ☐ Baxter	28 ☐ Ripy	48 ☐ Ferrell	67 ☐ Shaw
10 ☐ Thiels	29 ☐ Bergen	49 ☐ Hastings	68 ☐ Sinclair
11 ☐ Thornton	30 ☐ Stephens	50 ☐ Browning	69 ☐ Dalton
12 ☐ Sinclair	31 ☐ Baxter	51 ☐ Trent	70 ☐ Clare
13 ☐ Beckman	32 ☐ Douglass	52 ☐ Sinclair	71 ☐ Skillern
14 ☐ Keene	33 ☐ Palmer	53 ☐ Thomas	72 ☐ Belmont
15 ☐ James	35 ☐ James	54 ☐ Hohl	73 ☐ Taylor
16 ☐ Carr	36 ☐ Dailey	55 ☐ Stanford	74 ☐ Wisdom
17 ☐ John	37 ☐ Stanford	56 ☐ Wallace	75 ☐ John
18 ☐ Hamilton	38 ☐ John	57 ☐ Thornton	76 ☐ Ripy
19 ☐ Shaw	39 ☐ Milan	58 ☐ Douglass	77 ☐ Bergen
20 ☐ Musgrave	40 ☐ Converse	59 ☐ Roberts	78 ☐ Gladstone

$2.25 each

79 ☐ Hastings	82 ☐ McKenna	85 ☐ Beckman	88 ☐ Saxon
80 ☐ Douglass	83 ☐ Major	86 ☐ Halston	89 ☐ Meriwether
81 ☐ Thornton	84 ☐ Stephens	87 ☐ Dixon	90 ☐ Justin

Silhouette Special Edition

$2.25 each

91 ☐ Stanford	109 ☐ Beckman	127 ☐ Taylor	145 ☐ Wallace
92 ☐ Hamilton	110 ☐ Browning	128 ☐ Macomber	146 ☐ Thornton
93 ☐ Lacey	111 ☐ Thorne	129 ☐ Rowe	147 ☐ Dalton
94 ☐ Barrie	112 ☐ Belmont	130 ☐ Carr	148 ☐ Gordon
95 ☐ Doyle	113 ☐ Camp	131 ☐ Lee	149 ☐ Claire
96 ☐ Baxter	114 ☐ Ripy	132 ☐ Dailey	150 ☐ Dailey
97 ☐ Shaw	115 ☐ Halston	133 ☐ Douglass	151 ☐ Shaw
98 ☐ Hurley	116 ☐ Roberts	134 ☐ Ripy	152 ☐ Adams
99 ☐ Dixon	117 ☐ Converse	135 ☐ Seger	153 ☐ Sinclair
100 ☐ Roberts	118 ☐ Jackson	136 ☐ Scott	154 ☐ Malek
101 ☐ Bergen	119 ☐ Langan	137 ☐ Parker	155 ☐ Lacey
102 ☐ Wallace	120 ☐ Dixon	138 ☐ Thornton	156 ☐ Hastings
103 ☐ Taylor	121 ☐ Shaw	139 ☐ Halston	157 ☐ Taylor
104 ☐ Wallace	122 ☐ Walker	140 ☐ Sinclair	158 ☐ Charles
105 ☐ Sinclair	123 ☐ Douglass	141 ☐ Saxon	159 ☐ Camp
106 ☐ John	124 ☐ Mikels	142 ☐ Bergen	160 ☐ Wisdom
107 ☐ Ross	125 ☐ Cates	143 ☐ Bright	161 ☐ Stanford
108 ☐ Stephens	126 ☐ Wildman	144 ☐ Meriwether	162 ☐ Roberts

SILHOUETTE SPECIAL EDITION, Department SE/2
1230 Avenue of the Americas
New York, NY 10020

Please send me the books I have checked above. I am enclosing $_____
(please add 75¢ to cover postage and handling. NYS and NYC residents please add appropriate sales tax). Send check or money order—no cash or C.O.D.'s please. Allow six weeks for delivery.

NAME _____

ADDRESS _____

CITY _____ STATE/ZIP _____